TIME TO HEAL

Karen Young

CHIVERS

| British Library Cataloguing in Publication Data available |

This Large Print edition published by AudioGO Ltd, Bath, 2012.
Published by arrangement with Harlequin Enterprises II B.V./S. à r.l.

U.K. Hardcover   ISBN   978 1 4458 2737 7
U.K. Softcover   ISBN   978 1 4458 2738 4

Printed and bound in Great Britain by
MPG Books Group Limited

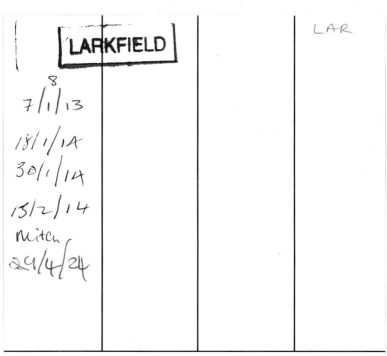

People often ask, "Of all the books you've written, which is your favorite?" I say without hesitation, *The Silence of Midnight,* which was the original title of this book. Sometimes when we authors get an idea for a book, we struggle and sweat and anguish and gnash our teeth in the actual writing, trying to make it "right." This was not one of those books. I loved the story, I loved the characters and I loved writing it. Who of us has not known families — parents — who are faced with terrible tragedy regarding their children? Maybe it's incurable illness or emotional trauma or abuse by a stranger or — God forbid — the death of a child. This book is dedicated to those parents, to their courage and the sheer guts it takes to keep on keeping on when the unthinkable happens.

CHAPTER ONE

"I think I'll get a job."

A second or two passed before Jack Mc-Adam abandoned the sports page and lifted his gaze to his wife. Her tone was soft and low in the early-morning stillness. Musical. He'd always thought of Rachel's voice as musical. It was one of the first things that had attracted him to her. Settling back, he studied her. Straight and slim, she stood with her back to him watching a fierce fight for turf between two hummingbirds just outside the kitchen window. Inside, it was quiet. Too quiet. Would he ever get used to the silence?

He swallowed black coffee and grimaced at the bitter taste. "Is it a done deed," he asked, setting the cup down gently, "or can we discuss it?"

"What is there to discuss?"

He lay the newspaper aside and stood up. "Where, Rachel?"

She shrugged, a brief lift of one shoulder. "The bank, I guess. I don't know."

He drew in a slow breath. "Which bank?"

"First State."

"Doing what?"

She turned then to look at him. There was little emotion in her voice.

"Typing, filing, clerical stuff . . ." She shrugged again. "What does it matter?"

"If it doesn't matter, why do you want to do it?"

"I can't sit around here forever, Jake. I'll go crazy if I do."

Wearily, he rubbed at the back of his neck. "Is this necessary, Rachel? Don't you have enough to do without taking on some —" he made a vague gesture "— some go-nowhere job that won't pay beans and will probably only boost us into a higher tax bracket?"

"It'll take me out of this house."

Away from the silence. Away from the reminders. Maybe she had the right idea. Maybe it would work for her. He fingered the edge of the paper. Burying himself in his job hadn't done a thing for him. Hadn't distracted his thoughts no matter how much he'd crammed into his workday. Hadn't eased the raw, desperate dread that rode him constantly. Hadn't dulled the grief that lay like a tangle of barbed wire in his gut. Hell, he couldn't blame her for wanting to escape. Reaching blindly for the paper, he accidentally knocked his cup to the floor where it shattered.

"I'll get it," Rachel said, going to the pantry to get a dustpan and brush before he could move.

"Sorry," he muttered.

Bending quickly, Rachel began to sweep the broken china into the pan. Outside, a dog began to bark excitedly. In the next house, a door slammed and a boyish voice called out a command to the dog. The next sound was the rumble and groan of a large vehicle.

The school bus.

Rachel's hands stopped. Her head bent lower, so that her blond hair fell around her cheeks. Then, working blindly, she cleared the floor of the last slivers of china and straightened, turning toward the trash can. "Don't forget to take this out," she said, her tone slightly choked. "The garbage run's today."

"I've already taken it out." Jake moved the can toward her, knowing she couldn't see. Her eyes would be filled with tears. "I put in a new liner."

"Oh. Okay."

A squeaking noise sounded from outside. Both Jake and Rachel glanced up, their faces turned to the window. The school bus again. It stopped. Timmy, the six-year-old next door, would be boarding. He yelled at Max, his big Labrador retriever, who barked a spirited farewell. The familiar sounds winged across the lawn and into the McAdams's window, heightening the tension in the kitchen. The bus changed gears and pulled slowly away. Silence descended again.

Jake moved to the countertop and poured himself another cup of coffee. He cleared his throat. "Maybe you could do some volunteer work at the courthouse. It's time for the voters' registration drive. They can always use someone to —"

"Why?"

He looked at her. "Why what?"

"Why do you think I should volunteer at the courthouse? Don't you think I have any marketable skills?"

"I didn't mean it that —"

"I have a college degree, Jake. Why shouldn't I put it to use?"

"Well, sure. I was just —"

"Not that I've ever had any encouragement along those lines," she said bitterly. "Wherever I apply, I'll probably have to start at the bottom." She made a disgusted sound. "Below the bottom."

"You're a little rusty maybe, but —"

"Thanks a lot. With that kind of encouragement from my husband, how can I fail?"

Jake slammed a hand on the table, the sound exploding like a shot in the kitchen. "What do you want from me, Rachel? Fine. Go to work! I agree, even though you drop the news out of the blue. I make a perfectly logical suggestion, but coming from me, naturally, it offends you. I sympathize when you worry about reentering the market after so many years as a housewife, and you reject that. I can't please you. So just tell me how you want me to react and I'll do it."

"I don't want to tell you anything!" she cried. "I shouldn't have to. Couldn't you just once put yourself in my place? Every day you go off to work and bury yourself in your job — Sheriff Jake McAdam, Kinard County's protector and defender. For twelve hours, you don't have to think about anything else. Well, fine. If that works for you, keep it up. Just don't try to stop me when I look for ways to cope. Okay?"

Jake slammed his cup on the counter, muttering as he reached for his jacket. There was no reasoning with Rachel lately. Especially when she was in this mood.

"And while you're at it," she said to his

back as he pulled the door open, "you might take a minute or two from your busy schedule to try to find our son!"

With the crash of the door, another kind of silence settled into the kitchen. Rachel wrapped her arms around her middle and rocked slowly back and forth as scalding tears washed down her face. Closing her eyes, she leaned forward and let the despair take her. It was a dark, familiar void. In it, she didn't have to think, to feel. All she had to do was give herself up to it, and time passed. That was the important thing. For time to pass. Survival depended on just holding herself together until the pain and despair eased to a point where they became bearable. After a while, she sniffed. Fumbling slightly, she pulled a tissue out of the pocket of her robe. She always carried a tissue now for the tears that could well up and overflow in an instant. It didn't matter where she was — in the shower, driving a car, in the checkout line at the grocery store, in the middle of the night. She must have shed enough tears to rival Florida's last hurricane since Scotty —

Anguish, quick and arrow-sharp, pierced her breast. Where was he? Where was her baby? She could not believe he was gone, vanished. One minute playing with Timmy and John-John and the next snatched up by someone, something, some —

She got to her feet, wiping furiously at her cheeks and blowing her nose. She knew what would happen if she sat here and let her thoughts run away with her like this. Too many times in the past three months she'd been too close to the edge. She couldn't tempt fate that way anymore. The shaky control she'd managed to hang on to since Scotty's disappearance was too fragile to stand much more. That was why she had decided to get out, to get away from the house, at least during the day. Everywhere she looked were reminders. Six years of precious memories were housed under this roof. The rooms echoed with bursts of laughter, childish shouts, sharp sounds of slamming doors and running feet. She honestly thought she'd die from the pain sometimes. Why couldn't Jake understand that she had to do something?

A pang, different but no less distressing, sent her hurrying to the sink. She turned on the water and began rinsing cups, spoons, scrubbing the counter where he'd splashed coffee when she'd finally pushed him too far. Why did she do that? Why did she keep on and on until he lost his temper and they began shouting at each other? Wasn't this a time when they needed each other? Shouldn't they be able to find some kind of solace in grieving together? Worse yet, why had she said that to him?

Her hands slowed, stopped. Closing her eyes, she heard the cruel words again. She hadn't seen his face because he'd been on his way out, leaving because he knew their argument would only get worse, the words more cutting, the accusations wilder, more unreasonable. She didn't know why. She didn't know how to stop. About the only thing she knew was that she needed something else to think about. She was desperate, and if she was going to survive this, then it was up to her and her alone to work it out.

She forced herself to finish up at the sink, then headed upstairs to shower and dress. As she passed the phone, it rang. It was her sister.

"Just checking to see if you'd like to meet me at Flanagan's for lunch," Suzanne said. "I've got a client appointment at one-thirty this afternoon, but we'll still have plenty of time. What do you say?" Suzanne had been running her own business for eight years. She was a beautiful ash blonde with amber eyes, unlimited energy and self-confidence, a husband who adored her and encouraged her to reach for the sky if she felt like it. On top of all that, she was the mother of three.

"I don't know, Suzy." Rachel stared into the trash can at the broken pieces of Jake's cup. "I may have something going today. I know how busy you are, and I don't want to promise and then have to cancel."

"I'm never too busy to have lunch with my baby sister. But you know that. So, what's on your agenda?" She hesitated. "Is it Scotty? Has something turned up?"

"No, no. Nothing like that. Actually, it may be nothing at all. At least, nothing as of this minute. I —"

"Wait a minute, whoa up. I think there's an answer in there somewhere, but it's so scrambled I can't make it out. Now, tell me again . . . slowly."

"I'm thinking about getting a job."

"Hallelujah! It's about time. Where?"

"I don't know. The bank, I guess."

A small silence. "Doing what, honey?"

"That's exactly what Jake said."

"Well, when somebody says they're getting a job, the next logical question is where — and the next is what."

"Right."

"So?"

"I don't know which bank, because I

haven't even applied yet. And since I haven't applied, I don't know what I'd do." Rachel sighed. "I don't even know that I can *get* a job in a bank, or anywhere else, for that matter."

"You can get a job. Lots of jobs. I think this is the best idea you've had since —"

"Since Scotty disappeared?" Rachel said softly.

"Yes, honey. You need to do something to keep from dwelling on it." Suzanne paused. "But math was never your best subject, was it?"

"It was my worst."

"Then why in the world do you want a job in a bank?"

Rachel shrugged. "Can you suggest anything else?"

"How about the hospital? Don't you know Ron Campbell, the administrator?"

"Yes."

"Don't you do a lot of volunteer work there?"

"Well, I used to before . . . Yes, I did."

"Then Ron would probably be able to find something. He'd probably be tickled to death at the opportunity to get a person with your brains and obvious talent to work full-time. Don't waste a minute," she advised. "Get dressed and get over there

16

before you change your mind."

Rachel rested her forehead against the wall. If she had a fraction of Suzanne's energy and self-confidence, she wouldn't have to build a fire under herself just to apply for a job doing grunt work. With Suzy's attitude, she would never have found herself in this position in the first place. She would have been managing house, children, career and husband as well as life's curveballs easily. Instead, Rachel thought, here she was, almost forty years old, trying to find some kind of sense, some meaning, in the way she'd lived all those years.

"Rachel?"

"I'm here."

"What brought this on?"

"Why? Is it so strange for me to start to take charge of my life for a change?"

"What does Jake say?" Suzanne asked after a moment.

"Nothing. Nothing useful, at any rate. He told me to do it if I thought it would make me happy." She gave a short, bitter laugh. "Just the kind of reply he would make to a child when choosing treats at a candy store."

"He does want to see you happy again, Rachel," Suzanne said quietly.

"Then he should find Scotty."

17

■ ■ ■ ■

Entering the double doors of the Kinard County sheriff's department, Jake acknowledged the greetings of his staff without slowing his stride, heading directly to his own office in the rear. The familiar Monday-morning sounds swirled around him without penetrating. Somebody slammed a file drawer. Frank Cordoba, his chief of detectives, raised his voice to a caller on the phone, then crashed the receiver down. A deep-toned exchange began between Frank and another deputy then ended in a burst of shared laughter. Groans came from both as Mavis, the radio dispatcher, passed on a message.

"Coffee, Jake?" Mavis said as he reached his office door.

"Yeah, thanks." He took the mug.

"You've got company."

He paused with one hand on the doorknob and drew in a slow breath. "Who is it?"

"Chief Gonzales."

Great. Just the man to make his day, J.B. Gonzales, the town's police chief. Tidewater's finest wanted his job. Gonzales had already filed to run against Jake in November and was playing up problems from every possible angle to keep his name in the news. Since most of the territory in the county was out of Gonzales's jurisdiction, he spent a lot of time directing the citizens' attention to the drug traffic coming into Tidewater, rather than to problems within the city limits.

"He's brought Mr. Crenshaw with him."

Jake frowned. Joe Crenshaw was the principal of Tidewater High School. The incidence of kids using drugs was down dramatically. What was Joe's beef?

"Are they in my office?"

Mavis nodded, making a face.

At her look, he gave Mavis his first genuine smile since he'd rolled out of bed that day. She grinned in return and punched him playfully on the shoulder. "Go get 'em, boss."

The smile lingered in his gray eyes as he opened the door. Gonzales, whose dark eyes and jet-black hair proclaimed his Cuban roots, was waiting. Beside him, looking slightly uncomfortable, his fair skin flushed, was Joe Crenshaw.

"Morning, gentlemen."

Gonzales returned the greeting with a politician's suave charm, not quite meeting Jake's eyes. Crenshaw nodded and rose with his hand outstretched. "I hope this isn't an inconvenient time, Jake. I know it's early, but —"

"The sheriff's door is always open, even early on a Monday morning," Gonzales said. "Isn't that right, Jake?"

"Right, J.B." Jake took off his jacket and hung it on a battered metal pole. Then, heading for his desk, he began turning back the cuffs of his shirt. He always wore a suit jacket, but it invariably came off the minute he got to his office. Mavis teased him about it. How could he maintain a spit-and-polish image if he conducted business in his shirtsleeves?

Image had never meant much to him. Results were what mattered. In his campaign for sheriff twelve years ago, he had promised to clean up a gambling and prostitution racket operating outside the city limits. He'd managed it, even though it had taken three years. In doing so, he had alienated a lot of people. And it never stopped. There were countless incidents since then when he'd been personally responsible for thwarting a criminal scheme. Or a criminal, for that matter. Forgetting the two men in his office, he stared at his hands. Was that the missing link? Was Scotty's kidnapper a man with a grudge? But who? Which one?

How on earth was he going to find his son?

"We've got a problem in the high school, Jake."

Blinking, Jake stared at Gonzales, then turned to Joe Crenshaw. "What kind of problem, Joe?"

Crenshaw shifted, crossing one knee over the other. "Well, I don't know if it means anything yet, Jake, but in one of the lockers in the gym, we found a couple of bags of marijuana."

"It was new stuff, high quality," Gonzales put in.

"Whose locker?"

"That's just it. It was an unassigned locker."

Gonzales spoke up. "We got an anonymous tip. A kid called 911, obviously disguising his voice."

"The problem is," Crenshaw said with obvious concern, "that there is probably more where that came from. I'd hate to see new users cultivated just when we've had such a good result in reducing usage at THS."

"That's why we're here, Jake." Gonzales stood up. He moved quickly to the door, motioning Jake into his seat as he began to rise. Jake was a good six inches taller, and the chief never stood directly beside him if he had any choice. "If it's homegrown, you need to flush out the creeps who're cultivating it. Locate the fields, destroy them. Arrest the growers."

"What makes you think it's grown in Kinard County?"

"Something the kid said when he called in." Gonzales reached into his pocket and pulled out a tape. "Here, I brought it with me. Listen to it, have your guys study it. Maybe you can come up with something."

"Thanks," Jake said dryly, knowing that if anything of substance had been on the tape, Gonzales would have already acted on it.

"Naturally my men will cooperate if it turns out to be something within my jurisdiction."

"Naturally."

"I'll hold off making this public," Gonzales said, pausing with his hand on the door. "For the moment."

"Yeah, J.B. I appreciate that."

As the two men filed through the door, Joe Crenshaw paused then turned back. "Have you heard anything new on the disappearance of your son, Jake?"

"No, nothing." He set his jaw.

"I'm sorry. I still can't believe it happened right here in Tidewater."

"Yeah."

"If there's anything —"

22

"Thanks, Joe."

"Tell Rachel that Marge said she's in her prayers."

"I will. Thanks again."

When the door closed, Jake was still for a minute. Only his fingers moved, massaging the bridge of his nose. One of the hardest things he had to endure was the well-meaning sympathy of others. He knew it was crazy, but it made his failure to uncover a clue in Scotty's disappearance even worse. Here he was, charged with the protection of the people of Kinard County, and he'd failed in the most elementary way. Did they wonder if he could do his job, having failed to safeguard his own flesh and blood?

Was that what Rachel was thinking? That he'd failed her because he hadn't been able to find Scotty? Was that why she had closed him out? Was that why they lived like strangers in the same house?

His fingers stilled and he stared at the phone. He'd left mad. Maybe he should call. . . .

As his hand hovered over the receiver, his intercom buzzed.

"Yeah, Mavis. Who is it?"

"You've got another visitor, Jake. He's —"

"Can somebody else handle it, Mavis? I can't get a thing done around here if I spend the day talking." He thumped the unopened mail stacked in his in basket. Lined up neatly beside his phone were half a dozen pink phone messages. "I haven't even had time to return my calls. If anything was important, it's probably too late."

"Nothing was a matter of life and death, Jake. You know I always handle those calls."

He chuckled in spite of himself. "Okay, Mavis. For a minute there, I got carried away thinking I was indispensable around here or something."

"About this visitor, Jake . . ."

"Okay, who is it?"

"A kid. His name is Michael. He —"

"Mavis, I'm up to my armpits in here. Get Jacky. She's the juvenile officer."

"He insists on seeing you."

"Well, who's in charge out there! Tell him —"

"Jake, I think you ought to see this kid."

He slammed the receiver on its cradle and closed his eyes. When Mavis was that determined, there was little point in arguing. He drummed his fingers on his desk. Actually, on a regular day when Mavis was that determined, he *wouldn't* argue with her, because she usually had a good reason for making a stand. As the thought formed, his door clicked and opened slowly. Jake waited

24

expectantly. When no one appeared, he called out, "Come on in."

Finally, the door swung fully open to reveal a tall, skinny, scruffy-looking kid wearing a cap bearing the logo of the Miami Dolphins. He quickly gazed around the room, then looked shyly at Jake.

"Hello, sir."

"Hello . . . Michael, is it?"

Michael nodded, shifting the strap of a worn denim knapsack so that its weight rested on the floor. Despite the warm May weather, Michael wore a denim jacket that was nearly as worn as his knapsack. Looking closer, Jake could see that his jeans, too, were threadbare, as though they'd seen a lot of miles and countless washings. His orange T-shirt looked new, though. Across the front was a huge ocean wave and the words "Pensacola Beach, Florida."

A runaway. First thing they did was spend their precious resources on an overpriced T-shirt. Jake ran an experienced eye over him, stopping at his feet. He'd have been better off buying new shoes. His were battered beyond recognition. And big. The kid must wear a size twelve. *If he ever grows into those feet and hands,* Jake thought, *he'll be my size.*

"Have a seat, Michael," Jake said.

25

Michael eyed the chair for a moment or two, then shifted his knapsack and sat, awkwardly bending his long legs to fit the straight contours of the chair. He pushed at the bill of his cap and looked into Jake's eyes. For the first time, Jake noticed their clear, bright color. They were gray. He was a good-looking kid. Looked you right in the eye. Jake liked that. So many kids today didn't. Of course, a lot of the kids he talked to these days were already criminals. Many of them — some no older than Michael — had already killed.

Jake leaned back in his chair. "How old are you, Michael?"

"Fourteen, sir."

"Fourteen. You live around here?"

"No, uh . . . not —"

"Where do you live?"

"I used to live in Des Moines, Iowa."

"Des Moines, Iowa," Jake repeated slowly. "You're a long way from home, aren't you?"

"I don't live there anymore."

Jake drew a deep breath. A runaway — he knew it. "Do your folks know where you are, Michael?"

"I haven't got any. At least, none in Iowa."

"Haven't got any folks? What about your mother? Your father?"

"My mother was killed in an accident a

26

long time ago. I lived with my grandmother, and she just died."

"I'm sorry."

"I'm on my own now."

"You don't say."

"I can do it. I've already been on the road six weeks and I made it all the way down here."

Where, Jake thought grimly, was the kid's father? Here was a boy who ought to have someone taking care of him while he grieved for his dead grandmother.

"Why are you here, Michael?" he asked, recalling that the boy had insisted on seeing him.

Michael's eyes met Jake's. Jake wondered at the look. There was a world of wisdom in those eyes. What had he seen since he'd been on his own? What had he survived? Jake hoped suddenly, painfully, that the boy hadn't suffered things that would never leave him. He wouldn't be the first fourteen-year-old who got a sordid education on the streets in six short weeks.

"I've heard a lot about Florida," Michael said hesitantly, as though the words didn't quite express his thoughts.

"Florida," Jake asked, "or someplace special in Florida? Did someone in your family live here?"

"Not in Tidewater, no." Then, with a frown, he added quickly, "At least, I don't think so. But my mother lived in Miami. Mama Dee told me that much."

"Mama Dee is your grandmother?"

He nodded. "Margaret D'Angelo."

D'Angelo. Somewhere in the back of his mind, the name rang a bell. But he couldn't place it. The DEA came to mind. He'd been in Miami then, but still . . . He shook his head.

"So . . ." Jake studied him closely. "You're from Des Moines, Iowa, and your name is Michael D'Angelo."

"No, sir." Michael, who'd finally relaxed a bit in his chair, sat up straight again, as though bracing for something. "I mean, I am from Des Moines and my name is Michael, but not D'Angelo."

Jake was getting impatient. Questioning the kid was like chasing a bubble. But he didn't think it was a deliberate tactic on Michael's part. He just seemed to find it difficult to say whatever it was he had to say. Jake glanced at his watch. He had a full day's work — and more — in front of him. He'd have Mavis call Jacky Kendall in and maybe Juvenile would be able to work something out. They'd know how to begin trying to locate the boy's father. That is, if

Michael knew his name.

"What's your name, Michael? We'll see what we can do about locating your father."

"McAdam, sir. Same as yours."

"What?"

"Yes, sir. Michael McAdam. And I think you're my father."

CHAPTER TWO

For a few seconds Jake simply stared. Through the door, which Michael had not quite pushed shut, came the sounds of office routine: a ringing phone, raised voices, footsteps, a sharp clatter as somebody dropped something. None of it made any impression on Jake. It was simply background accompaniment as he took in Michael's words.

"How could I be your father, Michael? I don't know you. I've never seen you before in my life."

"I know that, sir." He shook his head and suddenly looked as young as his years. "I never knew anything about any of this until Mama Dee died. There was this chest in her bedroom and it had a bunch of old stuff in it. One thing was a metal box with my birth certificate."

As he spoke, he leaned down and ripped at a zipper in the knapsack. To Jake, the harsh sound was like the scrape of nails on a blackboard. He tried to collect himself as Michael rummaged through the articles in the opened pouch. There was no order in the way he had packed his belongings, Jake thought vaguely. Rachel would never allow Scotty to pack like that. She would —

He pushed aside the thought of his wife and son almost as soon as it flashed into his mind. He got to his feet like a man who'd been kicked in the stomach. Michael had located whatever it was he was looking for and now he, too, stood.

"Here it is." He held out a paper, expecting Jake to take it.

Jake did so, but did not look at it immediately. His gaze was fixed on the boy. Had he noticed Michael's gray eyes because they were a mirror image of his own? No! What was he thinking? It was crazy! Impossible! He was married to Rachel and had been for eighteen years. To have a fourteen-year-old son, he would have had to have sex with another woman, what, fifteen years ago!

"Look at it, sir. I don't know for sure, but I think it's the real thing."

Jake stared blankly at Michael's earnest expression before slowly dropping his gaze to focus on the document the boy had given him. Name, birth weight, time, place of birth. The facts swam together before his eyes. It was all there. Parents. Mother: Anne-Marie D'Angelo. Father: Michael Jacob McAdam.

Anne-Marie D'Angelo. Could it be?

Jake's hand shook, making the document waver slightly as both Jake and Michael studied it. With his heart thudding, Jake suddenly sat down on the edge of his desk.

Anne-Marie. He remembered her now, although if he'd been pressed to recall her last name, he never would have been able to. It had been in Miami, a DEA undercover assignment. She had been involved in a major case. A DEA contact. He had been the one to recruit her.

"You say your mother died in an accident. What kind of accident?" he demanded suddenly.

"A trucking accident, I think. I don't know any more. It happened when I was about five years old," Michael explained, his eyes trained on Jake's. "I don't remember much about her. Mama Dee hardly ever talked about her. To be honest, I don't think they got along."

"Did you live with her until she died?"

"No, I've always lived with Mama Dee."

The hand holding the birth certificate curled into a fist, wrinkling the document.

Just another unwanted kid shunted off by his mother to a more responsible grandparent. "Why didn't someone contact me before now!"

"I didn't know about you, sir. Whenever I asked about my dad, Mama Dee always said you were some kind of lawman in Miami and that you'd probably been shot down on the street, considering the way things are there. She said my mom had always had bad taste in men and that it was just as well she had raised me herself."

What kind of upbringing was that? Mama Dee sounded deeply resentful and more than a little bitter. It seemed she'd had good reason.

"How did you locate me?"

"There was a letter." Michael went down on one knee and began rummaging again through the items in the knapsack on the floor. Jake stared at the dark head bent to the task. Scotty had Rachel's blond coloring and except for his gray eyes looked like her people. This boy, Michael, was like Jake — the same dusky skin, same nose, same high cheekbones and a firm, square chin. Even those rangy, long limbs with their promise of above-average height proclaimed his paternity. No wonder Mavis had been insistent that he see this kid.

"Here it is." Michael straightened up, holding a single folded paper. There was no envelope. "It tells everything. Your name, the town you live in, where you work, stuff like that. She didn't give me your address, I guess because she didn't think I ought to just walk up and ring your doorbell one day." He handed the letter to Jake.

"I think Mama Dee wrote it after she got sick and knew she wouldn't ever get well."

Jake stared blindly at the letter, but so many emotions coursed through him that he couldn't read it. Not yet. He cleared his throat. "Was she sick long?"

"Not really. Only six months."

"What was it?"

"She had a heart attack. I found her when I got home from school. When she got out of the hospital, they got the hospice people to watch over her during the day. I wanted to stay with her but Mama Dee had a fit. She said I shouldn't miss school that much. But she was going down, I could tell. Then one night she told me she was too tired to watch TV." He looked up at Jake. "We always ate and watched TV at night. So I helped her to bed, and when I went to check on her a little later, she, uh, she was . . . She . . ."

Jake pushed away from the desk. He

sensed Michael was holding himself together by sheer willpower. Reaching out, he squeezed the boy's shoulder and felt the shudder that ran through his body. Michael ducked his head quickly and sucked in his breath.

"I'm sorry, Michael." *More sorry than you know.* Jake's features were grim as he thought of the hardships the boy had been forced to endure alone.

Michael drew another breath, fighting for control. "It's okay," he mumbled. Unconsciously, Jake began kneading the bony shoulder with his hands. He felt Michael begin to tremble, and moved closer. His own throat was thick with emotion. Then, with a rough sound, he pulled the boy into his arms. Michael's arms went tightly around Jake's waist. After a moment, he realized the boy was crying, a deep, silent outpouring of grief that racked his lanky body. Inside, Jake felt the boy's pain and loss as though it were his own. What difficult choices Michael must have faced to wind up here today. His arms tightened, and a feeling, something new and deep and warm, was born.

With a strangled sob, the rest of the boy's control fled, and he gave in to the wonderful, healing luxury of tears. After a while,

Michael pulled back from Jake and self-consciously wiped his wet cheeks. Jake handed him his handkerchief.

"S-sorry," Michael mumbled, blowing his nose.

Jake smiled, looking briefly over Michael's head to a picture of Scotty and Rachel on his credenza. "It's okay to cry when you lose someone you love."

"I never have before."

Which meant he hadn't cried over his mother's death. There'd been precious few people to love in this boy's life. Fate had certainly dealt Michael more than his share of bad luck. Suddenly Jake felt every single one of his forty-two years. What on earth was he going to do about this?

With a quick knock, Mavis stuck her head around the door. "Excuse me, Jake, but there's a call from Rick Streeter in Miami. Do you want to take it?"

Streeter was a DEA connection from the old days and had phoned Jake a couple of weeks before to alert him to some suspicious activity in a nearby county. The entire coastline along the Gulf of Mexico was notoriously convenient for illicit drug activity, but because it encompassed thousands of miles, it was virtually impossible to police it all. He'd had these calls from Streeter before, and most of the time nothing came of them. Still, he couldn't afford to disregard even the most remote possibility that Kinard County might be involved, especially with new drugs turning up at the high school.

"Yeah, I'll take it," he told Mavis. Then he gently pushed Michael toward her. "Take Michael to the Coke machine and get him something to drink, will you, Mavis? You can bring him back in here as soon as I get off the phone with Streeter."

"Sure thing, boss." Mavis gave Michael a friendly look. "How about it, Mike?"

Michael's smile was shy but genuine. "Okay, sure. Thanks."

Jake stretched to reach over his desk. "And take this up to Dan, Mavis. It's a tape of a 911 call sent to us from our friends at City Hall. Have Dan listen to it and see if there's anything we can use on it. A possible new source has surfaced at THS."

"I'll tell him." Mavis took the tape, motioning Michael ahead of her, and together they left Jake's office.

His call from Streeter was brief. To his relief, nothing had materialized from the suspicious activity a couple of weeks before. They exchanged a few words, made a bet on the next major-league baseball game,

37

then Jake leaned back in his chair.

"Rick, do you remember a woman a few years back named Anne-Marie D'Angelo?"

"Give me a hint, man. When, where and which phase of my life are we talking here?"

"DEA, about fifteen years ago. Miami."

"Fifteen years, huh? You were here then, weren't you?"

"Yeah. Can you recall anything?"

"Hmm . . . Anne-Marie D'Angelo." His chair creaked as he leaned back. "D'Angelo. D'Angelo. National Trucking. Dispatcher, right?"

"I think so. You remember anything else?"

"It's coming, it's coming. Tall, curvaceous brunette. Dynamite, as I recall."

His head bent, Jake massaged the bridge of his nose. "I mean, do you remember anything about her personally?"

"Her looks and the company she worked for aren't personal?"

"What else?"

"Smart, she was. And cool as a cucumber under pressure, if I recall. Yeah, yeah, the Colombian Connection. I'm getting total recall now, man. We nailed Jaco Ramirez. Got him hauling the goods. Sweet Anne-Marie had to get out of town fast." He paused a minute. "Hey, wait a minute, Jake. That case isn't likely to fade away on you.

38

You almost bought the farm when we charged that warehouse."

"Yeah." Absently Jake rubbed the ridged scar below his collarbone.

"So, what's going on? Has Anne-Marie turned up in Tidewater?" He chuckled. "No offense, man, but I don't think Tidewater has enough action to keep that lady entertained." He paused again. "Wait, wait, something else. Leon Morrison. Yeah, Leon Morrison. She was really hung up on Leon, you remember that?"

"I remember."

"I could never see why. He was one mean dude."

Yeah. One mean dude. Rick launched into an anecdote featuring Leon Morrison and ending with his apprehension a few years back, but Jake barely heard. By then Anne-Marie had already died. Apparently Leon was even worse than he'd known. Jake thanked Rick and replaced the receiver softly. Mama Dee was right. Anne-Marie had bad taste in men.

So what did that make him?

He groaned, closing his eyes. It was all coming back now. It had been a bad time for him and Rachel. One night they'd had the granddaddy of all arguments. The subject, as usual, had been his job. Rachel hated it. DEA undercover work did not conform to her idea of what was a suitable career for a family man. She was a basket case whenever he was on assignment. She was scared for him, she said. And with good reason, as it turned out. She had told him she was going home to Tidewater to do some thinking. And that she wasn't sure she would ever be back.

Jake turned in his chair and looked out the window. They had had other problems then, too. Rachel had wanted a baby more than anything in the world. So much that Jake had begun to wonder whether having a baby wasn't more important to Rachel than he was. He had begun to wonder if she hadn't married him just for that purpose. For some reason, whenever she did manage to conceive, inevitably she miscarried. The effect on their sex life had been devastating. The effect on Jake's ego had been devastating.

That was how the thing with Anne-Marie D'Angelo had happened.

For two weeks he'd waited for Rachel to come home. Finally, one night he'd called her and demanded that she come back. They'd argued fiercely but settled nothing. Hanging up, he'd slammed out of their apartment and gone straight to a bar. Anne-

Marie had been there, quietly getting drunk because Leon Morrison had just run out on her. It was a familiar scenario. Both feeling rejected, they'd drunk too much. Then they'd spent the night together consoling each other. The funny thing was, he'd known it was a mistake almost before they'd gone to bed.

None of which excused his behavior. Jake stood up and went to the window, staring out at the row of palms gracing the front of the building. A child had resulted from that impulsive, dishonorable episode. He raked a hand through his hair. Now there was a price to be paid. He would have to take Michael into his home. With the boy's grandmother gone, there was no other option.

He watched a young mother cross the street holding on to the hand of a small boy. The scene wrenched at his heart and he thought of Michael's face as he'd held out his birth certificate. His eyes had been dark with uncertainty. He'd looked so earnest, braced for outright rejection. Scared, too. Jake felt something twist inside him. He didn't want any other option, he realized suddenly. Scotty had been taken from him, but now, for some reason, he'd been offered this chance to rescue and care for his firstborn son, and he wanted it. He hoped it wouldn't be more than Rachel could bear.

Turning from the window, he picked up the phone to call her. He wasn't certain she'd been serious about applying for a job. If she was still at home, Michael could wait here while he went to her. He couldn't just spring this on her without first trying to explain. He punched out the number and waited. After several rings, he knew she wasn't there. He could try her cell, but he didn't want to risk interrupting her if she was speaking to someone at the bank. He'd have to wait, keep Michael here with him. Settling in his chair, he decided it was probably best. Maybe by the end of the day he would've come up with some way to break the news to Rachel without destroying his marriage.

Standing before the closed door of Ron Campbell's office, Rachel fluffed the ends of her hair and moistened her lips. She was being interviewed for a job, not marching to the guillotine, she reminded herself. Ron's secretary had given her a curious look when she'd asked to see him. Any other time, as president of the hospital auxiliary, Rachel would have been assured of her welcome by the administrator. As the man responsible for the management of the hospital, he was well aware of the dollar value of service performed by volunteers. Deeply appreciative, as well.

But she wasn't here in her capacity as a volunteer. She was here to get a job, a real job. A job where she would earn a paycheck. A job she hoped would keep her thoughts fixed on something — anything — besides Scotty.

Her fingers clenched and unclenched on the strap of her bag. She wondered if she looked right. Glancing down the hall at the double glass doors separating the business offices from the rest of the hospital, she gave herself another keen inspection. Straight cinnamon-colored linen skirt, cream silk blouse, midheel cinnamon pumps and no jewelry except for her watch and small pearl-and-gold earrings. She'd dressed in the outfit Suzy suggested, and Suzy ought to know, she reassured herself.

She was acting like a teenager on a first date. With an impatient toss of her tawny hair, she pushed the door open.

"Rachel!" Ron Campbell stood, his face lighting up. "This is a pleasure. Come in, come in." He started around his desk toward her.

"Hello, Ron." Rachel closed the door softly behind her, putting her hand in his outstretched palm.

"How are you, Rachel? You haven't been by in so long that we wondered if you'd forgotten about us."

"No, it's just —" Her smile collapsed.

His face sobered suddenly. "Of course. I'm so sorry. It's unbelievable that something like that can happen right here in Tidewater."

"Yes, it is."

He smiled at her again. "Here, sit down. Can I get you anything? Coffee? A soft drink?"

"No, nothing, thanks." She sat down, holding tight to her bag.

Ron didn't go to his chair. Instead, he leaned against his desk, crossing his legs at the ankles. Gray argyle socks, she noted, just right with his loafers and his horn-rimmed glasses.

"How's Jake?"

"Fine." She cleared her throat. "He's fine." Jake and Ron had never particularly liked each other. Rachel suspected it was because they were so different. Jake was so straightforward and up-front, a what-you-see-is-what-you-get sort of man. He was direct and uncompromising, excellent qualities for a lawman.

Ron, on the other hand, with his ready

smile and feel for people, seemed to have more patience in . . . The word *manipulation* came to mind, but she rejected it quickly. It seemed unfair to Ron, and she liked him. He was an adept politician, more so than Jake. It was an asset in his dealings with the board and the physicians on staff and in managing the employees of the hospital. She knew he could be tough when the situation called for it, and that was why she knew getting a job wouldn't be the piece of cake Suzy thought it would be.

"What can I do for you, Rachel?"

She laughed uncertainly. "This is turning out to be every bit as difficult as I imagined."

He frowned slightly while still smiling. "What is?"

She drew in a breath. "I'm here for a job, Ron."

He didn't say anything for a moment or two. Then he moved away from the desk and went around to his chair. Strangely enough, it made Rachel feel more comfortable. She relaxed slightly.

"What did you have in mind?"

"I wish I knew. I don't feel particularly qualified for anything, Ron, but I've spent years volunteering here. I'm familiar with all the services and facilities of the hospital.

I even know most of the employees. I've decided to go to work, and I'd like it to be here." She laughed nervously. "I'm trying the banks next."

"Is that blackmail?"

"No! I don't have enough to offer for that."

"Suppose you let me be the judge."

There was something in his expression that she couldn't quite decipher. He was eyeing her thoughtfully while fingering a gold pen, tapping it on one end and then reversing it. Over and over.

"Can you type?"

"Actually, yes, I can. And I'm familiar with the public health database you use here at the hospital, too. I guess I should have mentioned that, but I thought you'd suggest something like public relations or patient liaison — or manning the information desk."

"Glorified candy striper, you mean."

"Well, it seemed logical."

"I think you'd be bored in two weeks. Besides, it would be a waste. Don't you have a degree?"

"I have a BA in psychology."

Ron looked interested. "How would you like to work in Emergency?"

"I'm willing to work anywhere. What

would I do?"

"The clerical duties would be no challenge, but there's more to it than that. I should warn you that Emergency is not like a doctor's office. We get a lot of accidents, drug overdoses, indigents and the like. But with your training, you should be good at handling scared, sick people. And occasionally," he added, "freaked-out ones."

For the first time since Scotty disappeared, Rachel felt a stirring of interest in something other than her loss, her pain. She'd grasped at the idea of a job for one reason only, to distract herself. What if she should actually like it, actually do something?

"Well, would you like to think about it?" Ron asked.

"I don't need to think about it, Ron. I'll take it."

Michael hoped he wouldn't throw up. He was so nervous about what would happen in the next few minutes that he felt sick. He'd already thrown up lunch, but he hadn't told anybody. It had been a Big Mac, too. He hadn't been able to afford a Big Mac in so long that he used to dream about them when he was hitching down to Florida. His dad had sent one of the deputies out to get lunch. That was nice. Having his lunch bought by his dad. And that was how he thought of Jake, even if he wasn't sure Jake quite believed he was who he said he was.

Michael climbed into the front seat of the squad car, fumbling to buckle his seat belt while Jake buckled his. He hunched forward a little, his fingers clutching the strap of his knapsack. He couldn't quite relax enough to lean back. This was it. They were going home. At least, Jake's home. He closed his eyes for a second or two. Everything hung on whether or not they believed him. If they didn't, he didn't know what he was going to do.

He felt the thrust of power as the car pulled out of the spot marked Sheriff. Any other time he would have flipped out at the chance to ride in a squad car. He fixed his gaze on the dash. He'd always wondered about the radio equipment in police cars, the radar stuff used to nab speeders, the lights and the siren. If he got to stay, he would ask his dad to show him how it all worked. *If* he got to stay.

He glanced at Jake. His dad seemed okay, but Michael sensed he wasn't a man who showed everything on his face. Like when he'd responded to Michael's question about the picture of the lady and little boy on his desk. The boy was his son. Scotty. Michael didn't think he'd ever forget the look on Jake's face when he'd said Scotty's name. Blank, sort of. As if he would never smile again. He understood why. It was too bad about the kidnapping. It must be awful to wonder whether Scotty was okay or . . . not okay. He drifted off into a dream where he was instrumental in finding Scotty and bringing him safely home. For a few moments, he basked in the fantasy of having Jake and Rachel lavishing smiles and goodwill on him, delighted by his part in restoring their son to them.

"There's the high school," Jake said. The sound of his voice startled Michael. He looked at the low, sprawling white stucco walls. Everything seemed so white around here. So bright.

"It's already the end of May — you missed most of this term." Jake stopped for a red light and looked at Michael. "Let's see, fourteen. . . . Are you in eighth or ninth grade?"

"I'm in the ninth. I started school early because my birthday's in October."

"Then you're almost fifteen."

"Yes, sir."

Jake nodded toward the white building. "Rachel does some substituting at the high school, now and then."

Rachel. Michael repeated the name a couple of times in his head. He liked the sound. It was . . . soft, sort of. He hoped she would be a nice person, like her name. She was pretty, too. Especially her hair. It was exactly the color of corn silk. He ought to know because he'd seen a lot of corn in Iowa. As they turned into a residential area, he scanned the clipped green lawns, his eyes troubled as he thought of Rachel. He could just imagine how she was going to feel when Jake introduced him. His stomach churned at the thought, and he held his knapsack tight against his middle. Sometimes that helped when his stomach got this way.

Jake slowed and turned into a street divided by palm trees in the middle. Two boys wheeled by on ten-speeds and waved. His dad waved back. They were probably getting close. He forced himself to think of his brother. He was filled with a sort of wonderment mixed with sadness. All these years he'd had a little brother and he hadn't even known it. He refused to think he would never get to know Scotty. Miracles did happen sometimes. Just look at him today. Where he was. Who he was with.

He stared absently at the houses as they passed, preoccupied with his thoughts. He used to imagine being part of a real family, having brothers and sisters, living in a neighborhood like this. He'd never dreamed it might really happen. His eyes started to get wet and blurry. He looked down, fixing his gaze on his hands. His knuckles were white as they gripped the strap of his knapsack. He'd better go easy dreaming that kind of stuff, because it still might not happen.

"Here we are." Jake braked suddenly and turned into a long driveway. The whole side of the yard was covered with bushes loaded with bright pink flowers. At the edge of the house there was a wood fence, which separated the front from the back.

"Do you have a dog?" Michael asked, thinking a fenced yard would be a good place for a dog. He could hear one barking.

Jake got out of the car. "No, but our next-door neighbors have a Labrador retriever. That's him making all that racket now." Straightening, he waited until Michael had gotten out of the car. "Don't worry, he's friendly. He just senses a stranger in his territory. He'll soon get to know you."

Michael slammed the car door and hefted his knapsack onto one shoulder, then came around the front of the car where his dad waited. He wasn't worried about making friends with the dog next door. He liked animals and they liked him. What worried him was making friends with the lady who was married to Jake.

"Michael —"

He looked into his dad's face.

"Look, son . . ." Jake put a hand on Michael's shoulder. "I haven't had a chance to talk to my wife yet. I think it would be a good idea to give me a few minutes with her before I introduce you. Do you understand?"

Michael nodded. "Sure. Do you want me to walk around the block or something?"

Jake smiled. "No. No, I don't think that's necessary." He pointed somewhere beyond Michael's shoulder. "There's a gate in the fence. Go through it along the side of the house, then follow the brick walk and you'll come to the patio and pool in the backyard. There are chairs and a table. Just make yourself at home while I . . ." He stopped, rubbing the back of his neck. "This will be hard for Rachel, Michael. It may take a while before she —"

"I understand, sir."

For the space of a few heartbeats, Jake simply stared at him. Michael waited a moment more and then turned, locating the gate. He took a step.

"Michael —"

He faced Jake. "Sir?"
"I don't think I told you . . ."
Michael waited, his heart thumping.
"I'm glad you're here."

CHAPTER THREE

Jake walked slowly along the brick path that led to his front door. Fifteen years ago he'd bought this house for Rachel, and he still loved it. It was a popular style in Florida — low, sprawling stucco painted a soft coral with red tile shingles, a style reminiscent of the Spanish explorers whose influence was seen the length and breadth of the state. Originally, there were only three bedrooms and no den, but as he and Rachel prospered, he'd added a big family room on the back and put in a pool. A couple of years later, he'd added a roomy master bedroom with a lavish bathroom, complete with a sunken tub, which Rachel loved to use. His fingers clenched on his keys. Slowly, a little unsteadily, he put his key in the lock and, giving a little shove, pushed the door open.

Something smelled good. It took him back for a minute. For weeks he'd been coming home to no dinner, or at best something thrown together with little regard for his or Rachel's taste, something that took little effort and less imagination.

"Rachel, I'm home."

Rachel came in from the direction of the kitchen, wiping her hands on a towel. "Hi, you're a little early, aren't you?"

"Yeah, a little." He tossed the jacket he was carrying on the seat of a chair in the foyer. Rachel used to greet him with a kiss when he came in at night, but that along with lots of other little demonstrations of affection had stopped with Scotty's disappearance. "Something smells good."

"Roast beef. It's been a while since we had it." She hesitated and, looking at her, Jake narrowed his eyes, wondering. Then he realized that she was smiling. Almost. She hadn't really smiled in a long time, but this was close.

"How about a drink before dinner?" she suggested.

"Sounds good."

When she turned to the family room, he followed. "I'll fix it," he told her.

"Okay. I'll have some wine."

He looked at her. Rachel hardly ever drank anything, not even wine. "Are we celebrating something?"

She did smile then, a quick, soft curve of

her lips. It was gone almost instantly. "We are."

He had the whiskey in his hand, ready to pour. He stopped, looking at her. "What is it, sweetheart?"

She shook her head, gesturing to the bottle and his glass. "No, fix your drink first." She reached up and got a wineglass. "Don't forget mine."

He splashed a good double shot into his glass and then, working the cork free on a bottle of chardonnay, poured some for Rachel. She took it as he lifted his own.

"Here's to —" he looked at her questioningly "— what?"

With her glass poised, she said, "I got a job today."

He didn't move. "Well, that's great, honey. Congratulations."

"Thanks." She leaned forward and clinked her glass gently against his. "Wish me luck."

"You bet." With his eyes locked on hers, Jake sipped his drink.

"It was a lot easier than I expected. You can't imagine how nervous I was."

He cleared his throat. "Which bank?"

She set her glass aside. "Neither. I went to the hospital instead. Suzy called as I was trying to decide. She reminded me of the years of volunteer work I've done at the hospital and suggested Ron Campbell would probably think that counted for real experience." Rachel smiled. "He did. I'm working in the emergency room starting Thursday." With a lift of one shoulder, she made a little face. "That's because their payroll is set up for the first and fifteenth of the month, and Thursday is the first. I would have started tomorrow morning — or even fifteen minutes after I got the job — but I guess I can use the time to polish up my typing and check my clothes to see if I've got the kind of things you wear to an office."

She hadn't spoken so many words with so much zest in ages. "What are your hours?"

"Just regular office hours. I told Ron I didn't think I'd like the midnight hours and, of course, the evening shift — three to eleven, you know — means we'd hardly see each other."

"And would that have mattered?"

She looked at him, then turned away, taking her wine with her. "Yes, it would have mattered, Jake. I feel that I turned a corner somehow today. I don't know if getting out of the house and into a job or if testing myself in some capacity other than as an extension of Sheriff Jake McAdam will change anything, but for the first time since . . . it happened, I feel hopeful. I'm going to do this. My mind's made up. I hope you understand. If you don't . . ."

Jake looked down at the whiskey in his hand. He didn't want to hear the end of that statement. He'd waited weeks — months — for Rachel to decide she wanted to keep on living, and now it had happened. She had color in her cheeks, hope in her heart. Both would be wiped out when she heard what he had to tell her. Why today? Why not six months ago? Or six months in the future? He drew in a deep breath.

"Rachel, we need to talk."

"Oh, Jake, don't ruin this for me! Why can't you understand that —"

"It isn't about your job, Rachel."

She looked at him. "Then what is it?"

"Come on, let's sit over here." He walked to the couch and stood waiting. After a moment, Rachel moved toward him. With her eyes on him, she sat down slowly.

"Something happened today, Rachel." He turned his head and stared out the window he'd planned so carefully. It overlooked the patio and lawn to the pool beyond. The whole backyard area could be seen from the family room. There was no sign of Michael. He was keeping out of sight. Jake wasn't sure how he knew, but he did. His heart

58

twisted at the emotions that must be eating at Michael as he waited. He moved to the windows.

With his back to her, he asked quietly, "Do you remember the time in Miami when you left me?"

"What?"

"It was over fifteen years ago."

"Yes, I remember. Of course, I remember. How could I forget?" Frowning, Rachel studied the rigid line of his shoulders. "Jake, what —"

"I was working a case, a big one. Ramirez, the Colombian Connection, Rick called it."

"All I remember is you almost got killed."

He turned then and looked at her. "I was never sure about something, Rachel. If I hadn't been shot, would you have come back to me?"

She stood and went to the bar. The stem of the wineglass almost shattered as she set it down. "Why are you bringing all that up now, Jake? It was a hundred years ago. I did come back, so what else is there to say?"

She hadn't answered his question, and both of them knew it.

"I didn't force you to leave the DEA. You decided it without a word to me." Her mouth thinned. "Par for the course. In those days you made all the decisions."

"Deciding to stay married was a big decision, and you made that one."

"That was a difficult time for me," she said quietly. "When you announced you were leaving the DEA, I thought of it as a second chance for us, for our marriage. Whether I loved you was never in question. I did. I do. That lifestyle was one I never felt I'd chosen. I think that was a major part of the problem."

He took a deep breath, wondering if his next words would mark the end of their marriage once and for all. Being forced to accept choices she hated had almost driven her away once.

"I had a visitor today. A boy."

The color drained from her face. Reaching for support, she put her hand on the bar. "Scotty," she whispered. "You've heard something about Scotty."

"No. Rachel —" He went to her, pulled her against him, groaning as he felt the shudders that racked her body. He rubbed her back and shoulders as if he could stroke away her tremors. "It's not Scotty. This doesn't have anything to do with Scotty. Sweetheart, don't . . ."

She pulled away. "I'm all right." She put a hand to her throat. Her mouth wasn't quite steady as she said, "What is it you're trying

60

to tell me, Jake?"

"The boy who came today . . ." He stopped, rubbing the back of his neck, not meeting her eyes. "I . . . That time when you left, I went to a bar. There was a woman there. I knew her. She was a DEA contact on the Ramirez case. We had a few drinks, too many drinks."

He dared a quick glance at Rachel's face. It was a frozen mask. Her hand was still at her throat, unmoving. As still as death.

"We went to her apartment."

"I don't want to hear any more."

Her tone almost undid him. "I have to, Rachel. We spent the night together." He sent her a pleading look. "It was just that one time. I knew it was a mistake. It didn't mean anything. It . . . She . . . I didn't even remember her at first when —"

"When what? What!"

"The boy who came to my office today, Rachel. His name is Michael. He's almost fifteen years old."

She stared at him, uncomprehending. "What are you saying?"

"Rachel, he's my son."

The enormity of it was almost too much for Rachel to take in. Suddenly the bar was not enough to support her. On trembling legs, she moved to the couch and sat down again, sinking deep into the cushions. She wished for a crazy moment that she could sink all the way to China.

"I'm sorry, Rachel," Jake said quietly.

She stared at her hands. "How can you be sure?"

He sat down on the couch, not too close, before answering. "I'm sure. There's a letter from his grandmother, some other documentation and a birth certificate. It's —"

Rachel burst into tears. Finally, when she could speak, Rachel asked coldly, "Where's the moth— the woman?"

"Anne-Marie D'Angelo is her name. She —"

"Who cares about her name? Where is she?"

"She's dead. She died when he was five."

"Then his grandmother. Where is she?"

"She died two months ago. He's alone, Rachel. It took him six weeks to find me."

She bent over suddenly and put her face in her hands. "I don't care! You can't just come in here and tell me this, make this sordid confession and expect me to . . ." She stopped and raised her head to look at him. "What *do* you expect me to do, Jake?"

"He doesn't have anybody, Rachel."

Her eyes teemed with emotion. "What do you expect from me? Answer me!"

"He's my son."

She wrapped her arms around herself, rocking in anguish. Jake put out his hand, moving closer.

"Don't touch me!"

"He's waiting outside, Rachel."

"He can wait until doomsday!"

Jake was silent for a minute. "You're tired and shocked. I don't blame you. I'm —"

"Don't blame me!" She gave him an incredulous look.

"I'm sorry," Jake went on firmly. "Would you like to go to the bedroom? You can meet Michael when you're a little calmer."

She stood up. "I'm never going to be calm about your extramarital affairs or your 'son,' " she said through gritted teeth.

He took another step, bringing them nose to nose. Catching her by the arm, he said softly, "Don't ever take that tone about Michael again."

She stared at him wordlessly, her eyes bright with unshed tears. He let her go.

"Now. I'm not going to leave my son outside like a homeless person. Not when we have three thousand square feet in this house and two extra bedrooms." He headed toward the French doors that opened onto the patio.

"We only have one extra bedroom," Rachel said.

He stopped. "How is that, Rachel?"

"Because that's how it will be when you move into one of them."

Jake was dead silent for an awful moment. "You're saying I'm not welcome in our bedroom?"

"That's exactly what I'm saying." For a minute, she thought he would do something violent. He looked that fierce.

"Are you sure?"

Some of her rage abated. "I'll never forgive you for this, Jake."

A bleak, almost tortured look was in his eyes. And then it was gone. He straightened. "So be it, Rachel."

Michael sat on the grass with his back against a tree trunk well away from the broad expanse of glass that he guessed was the family room. He was lost in wonder at the scene before him. He'd seen places like this in movies, naturally, but never in person. A patio with flowers and furniture and a swing. A lawn that looked too green to be real. He'd actually bent down to see if it was artificial turf, the stuff they used on football fields. But, no. It was real as rain. Best of all was the pool, of course. A real, live pool. Big, too. One thing he excelled at was swimming. He'd never had the time to devote to practice so he could be on the swim team in Iowa, but the coach had once asked him. He couldn't wait to try out that diving board. Man, it was something! Jeez, he'd landed in heaven.

He glanced uneasily at the French doors leading into the house and wondered if he'd be invited in or if Jake would have to take him to the office to sleep somewhere until he could figure out what to do with him. He didn't think he'd like to sleep in jail, even as a guest. He'd seen the jail. One of Jake's deputies had given him a tour, making a big production out of it.

He pulled his knapsack tight against his belly and fought off the images of the home he'd left. Mama Dee kept everything neat and clean, but the place was rented and the faucets leaked, there was never enough hot water for a long shower, the heater needed better venting and made the place smell like heating oil most of the winter. His eyes fell on twin air-conditioning units situated in a little wooden ell that matched the fencing. He bet Jake never had any trouble like that. His dad never had any duns from the utility company, either, he bet, where they threatened to shut off the electricity. And Scotty and Miss Rachel — as he'd decided to call

Jake's wife — probably never shopped for groceries with food stamps, either. Resting his head against the rough bark of the tree, he squinted through the pink flowers of the tree to blue sky and sunshine. And dreamed. . . .

Jake opened the French door and stepped soundlessly onto the patio. Michael was propped against the base of a squatty palm. Moving closer, he realized the boy was sleeping. Something twisted inside him as he gazed upon the youthful features. He hadn't thought to ask Michael where he'd spent last night, but he knew it couldn't have been a hotel. More likely on the beach, sheltered by some stranger's pier. It had rained, Jake recalled suddenly. Not a soft spring shower, but a torrential downpour. Common enough in Florida, but hardly what Michael was used to in Iowa. Fortunately, it was May. The temperature hardly ever dipped below sixty-five at night. He drew in a deep breath, thankful for small mercies.

He bent and gently squeezed the boy's shoulder. "Wake up, son."

Michael blinked sleepily, staring with momentary confusion into his father's eyes. Jake saw the instant he recalled where he was, who Jake was. He made a move to scramble to his feet, darting a quick look beyond Jake toward the patio doors.

"Is it okay?" he asked anxiously.

"Yeah, it's okay. Come on inside. You've got to be hungry. It's been a long time since we had those burgers."

"Yes, sir." Michael slung the strap of his knapsack onto his shoulder and fell into step beside Jake.

Setting his jaw, Jake opened the door and ushered the boy inside. The room was empty, he noted grimly. So this was the way Rachel meant to play it. For the boy's sake, he'd hoped she would put aside her emotions, at least for tonight. None of this was Michael's fault.

"Here, let's just drop that knapsack on the floor by the door," he said, removing the strap from Michael's shoulder before the boy could respond. "We'll get you settled soon, but first you'll probably want to look around, sort of get the feel of the house. The main bathroom's just down that hall. The kitchen's straight through there. See, just beyond the breakfast nook."

Michael nodded, following Jake's eye. "Yes, sir."

"I'll just check on dinner." Jake started toward the double doors leading to the kitchen, but something about Michael stopped him. "What is it, Mike?"

Standing still, Michael was taking everything in. "This is sure a nice place."

"Yeah, I like it, too," Jake said softly, looking around. The house had a spacious, welcoming look to it. Rachel had a special touch. Several windows, draped with green hanging plants, let in ample light. The furniture was deep and comfortable, invitingly strewn with extra pillows. One whole wall was shelved, artfully displaying books and mementos of their eighteen-year marriage. Their latest acquisition was a large entertainment center with a large-screen TV and sound system. Rachel was a music lover.

He gestured toward the new wing. "That's the master bedroom," he told Michael. "It was added not too long ago. My wife —" He broke off as Rachel suddenly appeared. Meeting her eyes, Jake felt a rush of emotions — surprise, gratitude, relief, anxiety — so many emotions, he couldn't begin to identify them. She stood there, her expression unreadable.

Putting a protective hand on Michael's shoulder, he cleared his throat. "Michael, come meet my wife . . . Rachel." Holding her gaze, he nudged the boy forward slightly. "Rachel, this is my son . . . Michael."

"Hello, Michael." To save her life, Rachel couldn't smile. She wanted to, she tried to, but it just wouldn't come.

"Hello, ma'am."

He was so like Jake. Why did he have to look so much like Jake?

She realized she'd been standing and staring too long when Jake said, "Why don't we all sit down for a minute."

"Yes, fine." She watched as Jake guided Michael around a table to a love seat and gently urged him down. He waited while Rachel sat down opposite them on the sofa. Seeing them side by side facing her, their expressions almost identical — wary, waiting, as though she were a black widow spider — she felt suddenly desolate. The space separating them might as well have been the Gulf of Mexico.

"I was just showing Michael around," Jake said.

Michael looked at her. "This place is really nice," he said earnestly.

"Thank you," she murmured. He looked scared. Seeing fear in those eyes — so like Jake's! — she felt a pang of something. Sympathy? Pain?

"I was telling him we'd get him all settled, but first maybe we could have something to eat."

"Yes." As Rachel started to rise, Michael scrambled to his feet. "Where are you from, Michael?"

"Iowa. Des Moines, Iowa. Have you ever been there?"

"No, I've never been to Iowa."

"It's pretty flat, like Florida in a way, but not so green." His gaze went to the windows. "I've never seen so much green." He laughed suddenly, softly, and Rachel's heart caught. It sounded so much like Jake's chuckle. "I even touched your lawn to see if it was real."

She flicked a glance at Jake and found him watching Michael with an expression that scared her. He looked bemused, completely absorbed. And loving. There was no other word for it. Michael had been in Jake's life less than a day, and Jake was ready to make a place for him in his heart. *Oh, but what about Scotty!* her heart cried.

"I thought it might be like at the Superdome or the Astrodome," Michael was explaining. "You know, artificial."

Rachel nodded. "Yes, I know."

"I promised Michael something to eat, Rachel." Jake spoke quietly, without force. He was leaving it up to her.

Rachel's mind went blank. She'd prepared something, hadn't she? Oh, yes, roast beef.

70

Although it had seemed like forever since she'd felt like preparing a complete meal, tonight she'd wanted something special, not because of her new job, but because it was time she shook off the terrible lethargy that had claimed her since Scotty . . . Her eyes raked over Michael and bitterness welled up in her throat. It wasn't fair. It just wasn't fair.

Looking up, she caught Jake's eye. He was silently watching her. Waiting. She turned away, feeling bleak and very frightened. Pulling herself together, she turned and went into the kitchen.

Chapter Four

Jake stood in the doorway watching Rachel do the few last-minute things required to put their meal on the table. Standing just behind him, Michael watched, too.

"Do you need any help?" Jake asked. "We can carry something."

Rachel lined a bread basket with a linen napkin and began transferring warm rolls from a pan. Looking up, she gestured to three glasses filled with iced tea. "The tea, I guess. And the salt and pepper."

"Right." Jake reached for the glasses. "Mike, you take the salt and pepper. I've got these."

Leaving them, Rachel carried the basket to the table and scooted a couple of dishes around to make everything fit. Candles and fresh flowers adorned the center of the table. She'd picked them up at the market on the way home, along with the most substantial grocery order she'd had in months. Now she whisked the candles away, dropping them in the drawer of the antique sideboard that stood under the window in the dining room, and closed it with a sharp snap. Her celebratory mood was gone.

Michael's eyes widened at the attractive table. He looked like a child watching his first magic show, Rachel thought, stubbornly holding on to her resentment. Wordlessly he handed the salt and pepper shakers to her. And after a slight hesitation, she took them and placed them on the table.

"Take a seat, Mike," Jake said, still wearing that half-smiling, bemused expression.

Rachel spoke curtly. "Did you wash up?"

Michael flushed, looking quickly at his hands.

"Uh-oh, my fault, Mike." Jake, in the act of sitting, stopped. "Everything smells so good, we forgot our manners. Remember me pointing out the bathroom through that door?" Jake gestured with his chin. "Yeah, that's the one."

"I'll just be a minute," Michael murmured, scraping the polished surface of the parquet floor as he shoved his chair back. "Uh, sorry," he mumbled, shooting Rachel a quick look.

"No problem," Jake said quietly. "We'll wait."

With the sound of the bathroom door closing, silence descended. Rachel busied herself shaking out her napkin, fiddling with the place mat, rearranging the silver alongside her plate. All her satisfaction in landing a job was forgotten, a ripple on the surface of her mind washed away by the tidal wave of Michael's appearance. How was she going to bear being around him, seeing him, being reminded of Jake's . . .

"I'm going to take him to school tomorrow and get him enrolled," Jake said.

Rachel lifted her glass and put it down again, refusing to look at him. "What's the point? School will be out in a month anyway."

"I know, but he needs to get to know the kids. I'm going to talk to the guidance counselor about summer school. He's been on the road six weeks. He'll need to catch up."

"In two months? Good luck."

"What does that mean?"

"Just look at him, Jake." She kept her voice low. "He doesn't exactly strike me as a model student. He doesn't know —" She shook her head, deciding not to go into all the things Michael obviously didn't know. "I'm no expert, but from the way he acts, it's going to take more than a couple of months. I don't think his . . . family placed a lot of importance on school or, for that matter, on other things that we take for granted."

"How can you tell after only forty-five minutes with him?" Jake demanded.

"How can you tell otherwise after only one day with him?"

Jake clenched his hands. He dropped his head and stared at his plate for a long moment, then pulled in a deep, slow breath. "Why don't we finish this later, Rachel?"

"Fine."

From the vicinity of the bathroom came the sound of a door opening, then footsteps. Reaching the dining room, Michael hesitated. Jake looked up.

"Hey, all set?" Jake sent him a reassuring smile. "Okay, I don't know about you, but we're starved. Let's eat."

For Rachel, only one other day had ever been worse: the day Scotty disappeared. By the time bedtime rolled around, she was hanging on to her fragile composure by a thread. She seethed with emotions too intense to identify. Every time she looked at Michael she felt as if her body was charged with explosives about to shatter her into a million pieces. Every time she looked at Jake she felt such an overwhelming rage it almost scared her.

Almost.

They hadn't talked yet. There really hadn't been an opportunity. Michael's presence at the dinner table prevented her from doing what she longed to do: annihilate Jake with words, spew out her sense of betrayal, her bitterness. But not jealousy. No, indeed not. She comforted herself that she wasn't jealous because he'd turned to some conscienceless woman all those years ago. She couldn't be jealous if she didn't love him. And she didn't love Jake anymore. Focusing on that thought, she discovered, brought a numbing sense of calm.

The French doors opened suddenly. Jake and Michael came in looking relaxed and totally at ease with each other. They had been outside a good thirty minutes. After she'd waved aside their offer to help with the dishes, they'd escaped — there was no other word for it — to the garage and boat shed. Scotty had loved to spend time with Jake there. Man stuff, he'd informed his mother with endearing male superiority. The boat was out there, Jake's power tools, his fishing tackle, his archery equipment, the spiffy new bow rigged with some kind of apparatus that made it possible for even a six-year-old to cock and shoot. Jake had been teaching him. Pain caught in her throat.

Pulling the door closed behind them, they were halfway across the den before catching sight of Rachel. Jake's expression became guarded, Michael's wary. From outdoors wafted the scent of sweet olive. She'd planted the shrub there so her family could enjoy its unique fragrance.

Her family.

Jake and me and Scotty! Not this scruffy, needy adolescent.

"We've been in the boat shed looking at the *Pelican,*" Jake told her, reaching around Michael to flip off the light switch for the shed.

"So I assumed." Rachel swallowed hard. Scotty had named the boat for his favorite bird. She and Jake had laughed, unable to figure out why he had chosen such an awkward, unattractive bird when he could have chosen the exotic flamingo. Or white crane. Or even the small egret that inhabited every spot in Florida that held water. But *Pelican* it was, and because Scotty had named it, the *Pelican* belonged to Scotty. Jake had no right . . .

"It's a real beauty," Michael said, bright eyed with excitement. And happiness. A blind person could see the joy in the boy's

77

face, Rachel thought.

"We'll take it out soon," Jake promised, taking pleasure in Michael's enthusiasm.

"That'll be great!"

Jake smiled. "Yeah, it will."

"You won't have to worry about me, either," Michael said.

"Worry? How's that, Mike?"

"I mean, I can swim and all. I don't know much about fishing, but at least I won't drown."

Jake laughed and clapped him gently on the shoulder. "To tell the truth, I assumed you could swim, Mike. And as for learning to fish, there's nothing to it. A couple of times out and you'll be pulling 'em in so fast we won't have enough room in the freezer. Trust me."

Trust me. Rachel turned and headed toward the hall, unwilling for them to see her face, to know her thoughts. How could Jake even speak those words in front of her? And to Michael, the very embodiment of his own betrayal!

"Rachel?"

"I'm going to check the linens in the guest room," she said stiffly. Let him figure out which room she meant. His or his brand-new son's.

■ ■ ■ ■

As though he knew where to draw the line, Jake assumed the task of showing Michael where he would sleep. He helped him make the bed with fresh linens, easing his awkwardness in unpacking his meager belongings and placing them in the drawers of the chest. Pausing in the hall, Rachel heard them, Jake's tone deep and calm, Michael's hesitant at times, then responding like a puppy to kindness. When she heard Jake send him to the bathroom to shower, she drew in a tense breath. Finally bedtime. Now she and Jake could have it out.

Leaving Michael's bedroom, Jake caught her eye. He stopped, and for a few long seconds they studied each other by the soft glow of the night-light on the wall. With the insight learned in eighteen years of marriage, both knew they'd reached a crossroads. The certainty thrummed in the air around them. What they did, what they said tonight might sever the fabric of their relationship beyond repair. Neither of them was prepared for the heartbreak that seemed to have come to them. First Scotty, now Michael. Eyes clinging, searching, they stood motionless as if moving would set in motion something both feared. After a while, they heard Michael turn off the shower. Then, still without speaking, they turned to head for the den.

The telephone rang just as Jake was fixing himself a drink. Jake picked it up, and from the tone of his voice and his terse replies, Rachel knew it was business. She got off the sofa irritably, only half-aware of his conversation. Surely he wouldn't be called out tonight of all nights!

At the French doors, she stopped. Considering what they had to talk about, it would probably be best to do it out on the patio. She glanced at Jake, who lifted a hand to signal he'd be a minute.

He covered the phone and spoke in a low tone. "Check on Michael, will you? I think he's got everything he needs, but —" He removed his palm and spoke suddenly into the mouthpiece. "This is not in the city's jurisdiction, Frank. Tell Gonzales —"

He glared at the palm tree on the patio while listening to Frank Cordoba. "Okay, okay. Then tell Gonzales's man that he can check with us tomorrow, and *if* I think it's legitimate, and *if* it's city stuff and *if* they have the paperwork, we'll cooperate. You got that?" He dropped his eyes to his feet, listening. "All right, all right. Put Milt on."

Rachel walked out. There was no telling how long Jake would be. Reluctantly, she stopped at the door of the room where Michael was, her hand raised, ready to knock. The door was ajar, but the only light in the room came from the fluorescent tube on the aquarium that was built into the bookcase. She blinked a little in surprise. Fresh from the shower, wearing only a towel and a rapt expression, Michael was standing in front of the aquarium watching the fish. As she watched, he hitched the towel up with one hand and reached for a can of fish food.

He was gangly and adolescent and slim as a reed. Still, he was so like Jake. He had the same stance, one hip thrown slightly forward, his feet cocked at almost ninety degrees. Even the slope of his shoulders was familiar. How many times had she seen Jake tip his head just that way to study something that particularly interested him? Moving closer, she could see the tiny brown birthmark on his shoulder that was identical to the one she'd kissed a thousand times on Jake.

Finally sensing her presence, Michael glanced around. "Oh, hey, Miss Rachel. I didn't see you there."

"Probably because you didn't turn the light on."

He shrugged sheepishly. "I had it on, but the fish were so neat that I wanted to look at them in the dark. You know, with only the light of the aquarium."

"Do you like goldfish?"

"I guess so. I mean, I never had any." He turned his eyes back to the tank. "But, yeah, I do like them. I was just watching them sort of cruising around, their fins waving so slow and easy, like they don't have a thing in the world to worry about. It's nice."

Rachel looked at the aquarium. It held nothing exotic, only common fantail goldfish, but she knew exactly what Michael meant. Just watching them made her feel peaceful and relaxed. Or it used to.

"When I'm in bed, I'll be able to hear the sound of the water bubbling like that. I like it," Michael said. He chuckled suddenly. "It sure beats a freight train."

"Freight train?"

"I was thinking about where I used to live. We were pretty close to the railroad, and when I lay in bed at night, I'd hear every train that went by until I finally fell asleep."

"It must have been . . . irritating."

He stared silently as a big spotted fantail made its way slowly across the tank. "You get used to it."

She felt a tug of emotion, the first that

wasn't resentment or anger or injury, then quickly stifled it. "Do you think you'll miss Des Moines?"

He shook his head, still watching the fish. "Nah. There's nothing there for me anymore."

He stated it without emotion, but for some reason it touched Rachel more than anything he'd revealed yet. Fourteen years, the sum total of his whole life, dismissed almost casually. Hadn't there been a single special friend? Someone at school? Something at school? Sports? A part-time job? Church? A relative, for heaven's sake. How could there be nothing a boy would regret leaving? As she pondered it, he hitched at the sagging towel again.

"Are your pajamas in the laundry?"

He glanced down and for the first time seemed aware of his near nudity. "Ah, well . . ."

Before going outside, she had heard the washing machine and assumed Jake was putting in a load of Michael's things. Laundry and pajamas and settling a boy into bed were things she handled a lot better than the sort of deep water she might wade into talking about — thinking about! — Michael's past.

"I'll just run and get them," she told him.

"Uh, Miss Rachel —"

"It shouldn't take more than fifteen minutes for them to dry." Her tone was brisk. Enough of this boy and his unfortunate upbringing. She didn't want to think about it anymore tonight.

"Miss Rachel, wait."

With her hand on the doorknob, she turned. "What is it, Michael?"

"You don't need to get the laundry. I don't have any pajamas."

"What?"

"I don't have any."

"At all?"

"No, ma'am."

She drew in a sharp breath, wanting only to get away, then recalled her original purpose in checking on him. "Jake wondered if you needed anything," she said without looking at him.

"Oh. I'm fine. Thanks, Miss Rachel."

"Well, in that case —"

"Ah . . ."

She closed her eyes then faced him again. "Yes, what is it?"

He set the fish food on the shelf. His gaze, meeting hers, was hesitant. "Is it all right to call you Miss Rachel? I thought about names and all, and Miss Rachel seemed the best thing."

Rachel stared at him, her heart beating with pain and confusion and a fierce desire to reject Jake's illegitimate son no matter how appealing he was, no matter how disadvantaged a life he'd had.

"I know it's kind of hard for you," he went on in a low tone when she didn't reply right away. "Me showing up here like this and you not even knowing I was ever born. I mean, it's different for Jake since he's my dad and all." His expression as he met her eyes held regret and apology. Then he straightened up, as though bracing for the worst. "You're probably real upset."

"It is difficult," Rachel murmured, rubbing a temple that suddenly throbbed. For a moment, she and Michael simply looked at each other, much as she and Jake had done a few minutes ago in the hall. From the fish tank came the soft gurgling sounds that both found comforting. None of this was the boy's fault. Surely she still had enough compassion left in her soul to acknowledge that.

"Call me Miss Rachel," she told him. "That will be just fine."

He smiled with relief. "Okay. I guess I'll see you in the morning."

In the den, Jake was just replacing the receiver. He looked up in the act of reaching for his drink. Seeing her expression, he downed a good half of it before answering. "What is it?"

"You'll have to go in there, Jake."

"Why? What's wrong?"

She looked away as though searching the room for patience. With a deep breath, she faced him again. "Michael is ready to go to bed, Jake. As you asked, I went in to see if he needed anything."

His brows lifted. "Yeah, so?"

"He does need something. He needs pajamas."

"Pajamas?"

"Yes, Jake," she repeated with measured patience. "As in clothing, something to cover his body. Pajamas, Jake!"

"Well . . ." He glanced toward the laundry room, then clapped his head with one hand. "Hell! I forgot to put that stuff in the dryer, didn't I?"

"There are no pajamas in the laundry, Jake. He doesn't have any."

"No kidding?"

"Go see for yourself." She made an exasperated sound. "He seemed to think it was okay."

"Hey . . ." His tone was meant to soothe. "Don't worry, I'll go get him some clothes and then I'll talk to him. He's only behav-

86

ing as he's been reared to behave, Rachel. He wants to please us — he'd probably sleep in a three-piece suit if I ask him to."

"Fine." She turned away. "I'll wait for you on the patio."

The door was slightly ajar when Jake reached Michael's room. He held an old T-shirt in one hand. With the other, he rapped softly before stepping inside. "Hey, everything okay in here?"

"Yes, sir. Everything's fine."

The glow of the aquarium bathed the room in soft light. Michael lay on the bed on his side, one arm crooked beneath his head. His only covering was a sheet draped partially over his middle. As Jake approached, he scrambled up until his shoulders rested against the headboard. He was whipcord lean, his skin winter pale, but the promise of strength and power was there, just as it had been in Jake at the same age.

Recognizing it, Jake felt sudden fierce father love. It gave him a shock. It was so quick, so . . . elemental, that he simply stood there at the bed for a moment, his errand forgotten. The boy had walked into his life less than fourteen hours ago and already he felt a kinship that could only be compared with his first moments with Scotty. Scotty had been tiny and discolored and squalling, outraged by the harsh reality of birth and the bright lights and chill of the delivery room. But just one look and Jake's chest had swelled with emotion, a reaction that went beyond pride, beyond simple joy. It had been instantaneous and profound, and he'd never thought to experience it again.

He'd been wrong.

"You, uh . . ." Jake laughed softly and pinched the skin at the bridge of his nose. "You found everything you needed in the bathroom?"

"Yes, sir. More than I needed. I had my own toothbrush and stuff, but I've been out of toothpaste for a few days."

Jake sat on the edge of the bed. "What were you using?"

Michael happily shifted over. "Oh, you know, soap or whatever else was handy. Pepsi." He gave Jake a quick look. "That works pretty good. It foams and all."

Jake could only imagine. "Here, I brought you something." He handed him the T-shirt.

Michael took it, holding it out to read the words on it. "Kinard County Sheriff's Department, 1990 Champions." He looked up eagerly. "Champions of what? Baseball? Basketball?"

Jake smiled. "Would you believe waterski-ing?"

"Waterskiing! Oh, man, I've always wanted to water-ski. Do you think I could learn?"

"Sure. First week in June, we'll take the boat out and you'll get your first lesson."

Michael stared, mute for a second or two. Then he shook his head. "I can't believe this is really happening."

"Want me to pinch you?" Jake asked, taking pleasure in the boy's uncomplicated delight.

Michael laughed softly and began carefully folding the T-shirt. "I'll wear this tomorrow."

Jake reached out and touched his shoulder. "We'll find something else tomorrow, Mike. This is to sleep in tonight."

"Huh?"

There was such complete bewilderment on his face that Jake had to hide his smile. "I guess you're not used to sleeping in pajamas back in Iowa."

"No, sir." He shrugged. "Nobody sees 'em, so what's the point?"

"That's true."

"It saves having to do laundry, and since I was the one who had to go to the laundromat, it made a lot of sense."

"You've definitely got a point there."

"But I guess things are different here, huh?"

Jake took a breath. "Well, we do have Rachel to think about. Women have certain ideas about these things."

Michael nodded, suddenly full of understanding. "I sure wouldn't want to do anything to make her mad."

"It'll take more than a little misunderstanding over wearing pajamas to make her mad, Mike."

Michael stared at the lettering on the T-shirt. When he spoke, his tone was solemn. "I know she's already mad. Who could blame her? Having a kid you never even heard of walk in and having to let him live with you." He shook his head. "It's a wonder she didn't toss me out right on my, uh, my tail."

Jake took a minute before replying. "It was a shock to her, Michael. I won't deny that. But you don't have to worry about anything now. You're my son, and wherever I am, you'll be with me."

Michael just stared at him.

"What is it, Mike?"

"Do you mean that?"

"Yes. Absolutely. You have my word on it."

Tears welled in Michael's eyes, but he refused to let them fall. Words, Jake could see, were beyond him. Seeking to ease the moment, he asked, "While you were on the road, where did you sleep, Mike?"

"Truck stops, mostly."

"I mean where specifically? Not in a motel room at a truck stop. I know you couldn't afford that."

"No, sir. Mostly in the back of trucks or sometimes at rest stops on the interstate."

He spoke offhandedly, but Jake knew the situations a fourteen-year-old faced hitchhiking twelve hundred miles. His experience in dealing with runaways filled in the blanks all too well. Something twisted in the pit of his stomach. Why was it that his children, first Scotty and now Michael, seemed fated to experience such hardship? For a moment, he felt a depth of rage that rendered him speechless.

"It's okay, Dad. I made it." Michael grinned suddenly and pulled the T-shirt over his head. "Not that I'd recommend traveling like that, you understand. A couple of times, I almost freaked. You gotta be tough."

"Oh, yeah?" Jake reached for him, succumbing to a need to touch him. He caught him around the neck, playfully locking Michael's head in the crook of his arm. With his other hand, he ruffled the boy's dark hair. "What's the matter? Don't you know

91

not to leave home without your credit card?"

"I wish!" Michael laughed, then his arms tightened around Jake's middle, and just for a few seconds they held fast to each other. When Michael settled back against the headboard, his smile faded. "Will you thank Miss Rachel for the meal and for giving me this room?"

"Yeah." Smiling faintly, Jake added, "But remember what I told you. You don't have to feel grateful. You're my son. This is your home. And that's the way it's supposed to be."

"I'll try not to bug her too much."

"I'll tell her."

After a moment, Michael crossed his arms over his chest. "It seems almost too good to be true."

"It's about time some good things came your way. Right?"

For a second, two pairs of gray eyes met and held. Then Michael said softly, fervently, "I don't want you to ever be sorry you let me stay."

Jake reached out and wrapped a hand around his son's neck, bringing the dark head close. "No matter what," he told Michael, meaning it from the bottom of his heart, "that'll never happen."

"No kidding?" The words came out

muffled, a little thick.

"It's a promise." Jake felt the slight shoulders relax before releasing him. He stood up. "Now. Lights out. You've got a big day tomorrow — school, shopping, because you need some new clothes — and you need to check out the neighborhood. I want you to feel at home here."

Michael scooted down, making himself comfortable. "Will you go with me or Miss Rachel?"

"Me, probably," Jake replied, looking at him. Smiling faintly, he watched as Michael's eyes grew heavy. Exhaustion finally overtaking him, his breathing evened out, deepened. Jake reached over and snapped off the aquarium light, plunging the room into total darkness. He wondered how long it had been since Michael had slept in a real bed with a full belly and a sense of security. Looking around, he changed his mind and turned the tank light back on. If his son woke up in the middle of the night, Jake wanted him to see something that made him happy.

From the patio Rachel watched the light go out in Michael's bedroom, then after only a second or two, come on again. With an impatient sigh, she got out of her chair and began pacing. She wanted the confrontation with Jake over with. How long did it take to give a kid a T-shirt and explain a few basic points of etiquette? Stopping before a bed of daylilies, she pulled off a few dead blooms, her movements abrupt. It would take a long time if Michael opened up to Jake the way he'd seemed willing to do with her.

She tossed a handful of withered yellow blooms into the flower bed. He was probably full of horror stories from his travels across the country. As shocked as she was at having Michael show up on her doorstep, she couldn't help but admire him for having the grit to undertake such a quest. Six weeks of searching for a father who was a total stranger living twelve hundred miles away couldn't have been easy. Nor homelessness. Fortunately for Michael, there had been a happy ending. For Scotty . . .

Her thoughts scattered with the sound of the patio door opening.

Spotting her in the shadows, Jake closed the door softly. "Michael wanted me to thank you."

"Whatever for?" she said coolly.

"For taking him in, I suppose," Jake said, wearily rubbing a hand over his face. "For giving him the first square meal he's had in six weeks. For treating him decently when you could have refused even to speak to him. He's well aware that his appearance is a shock."

"None of this is his fault."

Jake dropped down in the chair she had just vacated. "I'm happy to hear you say that."

"I'll bet you are." With a hard twist of her wrist, she snapped a flower from its stem.

For a long moment, he studied her rigid back. When he spoke, it was in a soft, almost defeated tone. "Okay, Rachel, let's get it over with."

She whirled to face him. "You'd like that, wouldn't you?" She kept her voice low, but its very softness underlined her rage and sense of betrayal. "You'd like it if we could have a simple shouting match, just say everything there is to say about what you've done and then go on as if nothing's changed. Well, you can just think again, Jake! A few questions and answers aren't going to make everything peachy. Whether you think so or not, everything *is* changed. You were unfaithful. You cheated. You —"

"It was fifteen years ago, Rachel! I've already said I was wrong. I made a mistake. We need to —"

"Carry on?" Her tone was heavy with

sarcasm.

He drew in a deep breath before lifting his eyes to hers. "I know that's not possible." He reached over and pulled another chair close. "Come over here and let's try to sort this out."

For a moment, she hesitated. Then she tossed the flower away and sat down.

"I told him I'd get him enrolled in school tomorrow."

"He needs clothes, Jake. If those rags he wore today are the best he has, then you'd better take him shopping first and then see about enrolling him in school."

"Yeah, I guess so," Jake agreed with a sigh. He looked at Rachel. "What do you think, a couple of pairs of jeans and some shirts?" Suddenly he got out of the chair. "I don't know what kind of stuff fourteen-year-olds wear nowadays! The only thing I'm sure about is sneakers. I haven't seen a kid in years wearing a real pair of shoes."

"Clothes are the least of it. It'll take more than a spiffy wardrobe to make Michael fit in."

He glanced at her. "What does that mean?"

"You saw him at the dinner table. He didn't think to wash up. He ate with his elbow propped on the table. He wouldn't have used his napkin if I hadn't said something." She stared off in the distance, her expression stony. "His manners are deplorable."

"Only because he hasn't had the advantages other kids have."

She shrugged. "Anyway, it's your problem."

"I don't see it as a problem, Rachel." Jake struggled to control his temper. "Manners can be taught. He's a good kid, he's got a good heart. And he's my son. Hell, I feel lucky that he managed to find me."

"Congratulations, then." Rachel stood up abruptly. "I'm going in. You know where the extra linens are."

Jake got reluctantly to his feet. "You're sure this is what you want?"

She looked at him. "Does it really matter?"

"Of course, it matters, Rachel! I don't want this to destroy us." The look he gave her was bleak. "We've already lost so much. We can work this out, but we both have to make the effort."

At the door, she stopped with her hand on the knob. "That's just it, Jake. I'm not sure there is anything left." She opened the door. "I'm sorry, but right now that's the way I feel."

CHAPTER FIVE

When Rachel went into the kitchen the next morning, the smell of coffee was strong, but there was no sign of Jake or Michael. Going to the cabinet, she took down a cup, glancing at the clock. Six forty-five. Jake sometimes went in to work early, but hardly ever at this hour.

Her gaze strayed toward the hall and Michael's room, where the door stood open. Taking her coffee, she headed that way. Except for a slightly rumpled look to the spread, his bed was empty. No discarded socks lay on the floor, no articles from emptied pockets littered any surface. There was no sign that anyone had spent the night there. Was he gone? Had Jake changed his mind, decided to take him someplace else? Feeling faintly anxious, she pulled the top drawer open. Inside, neatly arranged, were his meager belongings. She straightened thoughtfully. So he hadn't gone away like a bad dream with the coming of daylight.

And Scotty was still gone.

Lying alone in bed last night, one thing had suddenly become clear to Rachel. She had believed that nothing could hurt her again, that nothing could touch her emotions, because with Scotty's disappearance, her ability to feel anything had simply gone away. Wrong. So wrong.

Jake's infidelity hurt.

The fact that it had happened fifteen years ago and that they'd been having some really tough times meant nothing. All night long she'd wrestled with her tangled emotions. Underneath the anger, the betrayal, the seething need to pay him back in some way lurked the inescapable truth: she was hurt. She was crushed to discover that her mate had been unfaithful. Now all that remained was to decide what to do about it.

She turned on her heel and walked quickly to the kitchen. Opening a cabinet, she stared blindly at the array of breakfast food, telling herself that it didn't matter that Jake and Michael had left without a word to her. This was the way she wanted it. She was reaching for a box of cereal when the back door opened with a clatter and Jake and Michael came in.

They were laughing but sobered quickly

when they spotted Rachel. Both of them. She plunked the cereal box on the counter and jerked a drawer open in search of a spoon. What was she, she thought with irritation, the Wicked Witch of the West? She stalked to the refrigerator.

"Would anybody like some juice?" she asked, taking out the carton. So far, except for that one quick glance, she'd avoided looking at either of them.

"Good morning," Jake said quietly.

"Morning," she replied, focusing just beyond his shoulder. Against her will, her gaze settled on Michael, who gave her a quick, shy smile. He wore the same tattered jeans from yesterday and the same worn-out sneakers. Only his T-shirt was different. It had probably once been navy blue, but was now faded to a soft, almost gray hue, the shade of his eyes. The shade of Jake's eyes. She slammed the refrigerator door.

"We've been at the boathouse," Jake told her, "checking the *Pelican*'s battery and gas level. Mike and I might take her out today if I can manage to get away from work at a reasonable hour."

Rachel gave him a sharp look. For the past three months, Jake's workdays had stretched to twelve and fourteen hours. On top of his regular responsibilities, he'd devoted a lot

100

of time to the search for Scotty. In spite of his efforts, not a single substantial lead had surfaced. It was as though Scotty had just dropped off the face of the earth.

"If something surfaces that I should know about, they can contact me," Jake said, reading her thoughts.

"Are you still planning to shop for clothes?" she asked.

"Yeah. I thought I'd take Mike in to the office with me and then when the mall opens, we'll run over and get what he needs." The look he and Michael exchanged expressed the universal male reluctance for shopping. "After that, enrolling in a strange school will be a piece of cake, huh, Mike?"

Michael just grinned.

"What time does the mall open, Rachel?"

"Nine," she said curtly, resentful of the quick camaraderie that was developing between them without knowing quite why. As though removed from the scene and watching her own behavior, Rachel knew she was acting horrible, but she didn't seem to be able to control herself. Spending the night apart from Jake had done nothing to cool her anger or to reduce her sense of betrayal. It had only given her time to recognize her hurt.

She jerked open a lower cabinet door and

pulled out a skillet. "Does anybody want breakfast?"

When there was no answer from either Jake or Michael, she looked up. Jake glanced at his son.

"How about breakfast, Mike?"

Michael shrugged. "Well, sure. I guess so. If it's not too much trouble."

"It's no trouble," Rachel said, struggling not to bite their heads off. "Does bacon and scrambled eggs and toast suit everyone?"

"Fine."

"Yes, ma'am."

She put the cereal into the cabinet and went to the refrigerator for eggs and bacon. Without looking at Jake, she said, "It'll be ready in a few minutes. You've got time to shower and shave if you want to."

Jake hesitated, looking at Michael before nodding. "Good idea. Mike, you can make your bed and neaten up your room while I'm gone. Then we'll be all set to hit the road after we finish breakfast."

Rachel snapped open a carton of eggs. "He's already cleaned his room," she said quietly. After a moment of silence, she met Jake's gaze. "He'll be okay. He can help me here."

With Jake gone, she directed Michael to the bread to fix the toast, a task he accomplished quickly and with no awkwardness. With a sick grandmother, he had probably been forced often to make his own meals, she decided. While she microwaved the bacon and whipped eggs, her thoughts turned to Jake. He'd obviously been reluctant to leave Michael alone with her. She wondered irritably what he'd thought. That she'd say something cruel or spiteful? Surely he knew her better than to think she'd be unkind to a child. Even a child thrust into her life under these bizarre circumstances.

"Do you want me to put out some jelly?"

Startled, she turned quickly and found Michael standing just behind her. "Oh. Um, yes." She waved a hand toward the refrigerator. "There's strawberry and peach. Get them both out."

But not grape. The grape jelly was for Scotty.

Breakfast was a little more relaxed than dinner had been the night before. After Jake showered, shaved and dressed for work, he stopped at the door of the kitchen where Rachel and Michael were setting the table. They worked well together, he decided after observing them a few minutes. Unlike Scotty, Michael responded quickly and obediently to Rachel's soft directions. Even at six, Scotty had challenged her every command. It was because he sensed her reluctance to refuse him anything, as Jake had pointed out more than once. She adored Scotty, and he had blatantly exploited her love. Jake's mouth twisted wryly. That shouldn't prove a problem with Michael.

They were just finishing breakfast when the phone rang. Jake answered, and before he'd said half a dozen words, Rachel knew it was something out of the ordinary. She got to her feet and began stacking plates.

"It's an accident with injuries on the interstate," Jake said, replacing the receiver. "Maybe a fatality. The dispatcher wasn't sure. Three units are on the scene, and an ambulance is on the way." A possible fatality definitely canceled any plan to take Michael.

She dried her hands on a towel. "You'd better go, then."

Jake turned to Michael. "Mike, I'm sorry. From what the dispatcher said, this one could take a while to clear away. I don't know when —"

"Don't worry," Rachel told him. "I'll take him shopping and then, if you're still tied up, I'll go with him to school to see about enrolling."

Jake sent her a quick, grateful look. "I'll

104

wrap it up as soon as I can," he promised. For a second, he hesitated, wanting to kiss her or, failing that, just to touch her. But she'd already turned to the sink. Instead, he squeezed Mike's shoulder. "Lend a hand with these dishes, son."

"Yes, sir."

Jake grabbed his keys from the counter. With one final look at Rachel, he left.

Wishing for his own unmarked Ford, Jake got in the big police car that he'd driven home the night before. He'd taken it because he'd seen the look on Mike's face when he'd spotted it parked in front of the station. It was juiced up and loaded with every available piece of modern police paraphernalia known to man and, to Jake, unwieldy as a tank. Now, gunning the unfamiliar vehicle to a speed that would get him to the interstate as fast as possible, he wished again for his own car. He was a man who liked the familiar. He also preferred driving an unmarked vehicle. He wasn't quite sure why. To most of the criminal element of Kinard County, Jake McAdam's face was as familiar as the president's, so it didn't really make much difference.

Today the demands of his job weighed heavy on him. He hadn't wanted to leave Michael. Not so much because Mike would be disappointed, but Jake didn't want Rachel to feel he'd shifted the responsibility for Michael onto her. God, it was such a mess! He felt like a man torn. He wanted his wife, wanted the chance to put together the pieces of their life that had nearly shattered when Scotty disappeared. But he wanted Michael, too. The almost instant affinity he'd felt with the boy grew stronger by the minute.

Please don't make me have to choose.

He rounded a curve, and the accident scene was before him. In a sea of flashing red and blue lights, a jackknifed eighteen-wheeler dwarfed two midsize cars locked in a tangle of metal and glass. He counted three ambulances. On the side of the road two bodies were draped with white sheets. There were two of his own Kinard County black-and-whites and two units from the state highway patrol. Off to the side, with little apparent damage, was a run-down pickup. The driver stood slouched against the mud-splattered fender. A small child was being wheeled into one of the ambulances. Close by, a medic gently supported a dazed woman whose head was bleeding through a white bandage. When the child was in place, the woman was coaxed to lie down on a second gurney, then whisked into the ambulance.

Jake got out of his car, taking it all in. One look and his stomach was in a knot. No matter how many years he put in as a lawman, he would never be able to witness the carnage at the scene of an accident and remain detached.

Frank Cordoba walked over to him. "Morning, Jake. Hell of a wake-up call, huh?"

Jake grunted, his eyes on the two cars. "What happened?"

Frank followed his gaze, his notebook open. "Two fatalities, both female. Driver of the Toyota and one of the passengers in the BMW. See the lady they're settling in the ambulance? She was driving the BMW. They're all related. Traveling together, heading to Orlando for a few days at Disney World, according to what I could get out of her. She's pretty upset."

"Where's the driver of the rig?"

Cordoba nodded to his right. "Over on the side of the road behind his rig being sick. I hate to say it, but it looks as if the women were at fault. They were traveling together, the Toyota in the lead. They came up behind the eighteen-wheeler, then changed lanes to pass him. Doesn't appear anybody was speeding, either. Anyway, once the Toyota cleared the big rig, she pulled into the right lane in front of the truck. The BMW followed without waiting to clear the rig." He shook his head. "I don't know if she misjudged or was just careless. I couldn't get a coherent statement from her. Looks like she's in shock. The truck driver slammed on his brakes and went into a jack-knife, but it was too late. He hit the BMW, which rear-ended the Toyota. They both went out of control."

Cordoba looked up as two of the ambulances started to move out. "The EMTs patched up two more passengers. I guess they're taking them out now."

Jake glanced at the pickup. The driver was still propped against the fender. "What about him?"

"He's been drinking," Cordoba replied, "but he wasn't the cause. He was behind the big rig and slammed on his brakes when he realized it was all going to hell. He rammed into the truck, but both of them had managed to slow down enough that there wasn't much damage. We're citing him for DUI."

"Is he local?"

"Yeah. Lives out in the boonies, beyond those fishing camps at Cross Corners."

"Any priors?"

"Not for DUI, but he's an ex-con. Poaching and illegal possession of a firearm. Small-time stuff. He's mean, though. He gave the boys some lip when they didn't want to let him drive away."

"What's his name?"

"Willard Biggs."

Jake nodded. "Yeah, I remember him." Again his gaze swept the scene, lingering on the draped bodies, the twisted remains of the two cars. There was an overpowering smell of gasoline and burned rubber. The driver of the big rig appeared around the front of the truck's cab. He was pale but seemed to be steady on his feet.

"Did you get the name of the rig driver?"

"Walter Hammond."

Relegating the ex-convict to the back of his mind, Jake drew in a deep breath and started toward Hammond. "Thanks, Frank," he said. "I'll take it from here."

"How about a cold drink?"

Rachel didn't know about Michael, but she was more than ready for something cold after two hours of serious shopping.

"Will you let me buy?"

She turned quickly to look at him. "Have you got any money?"

He nodded. "My dad gave me some."

My dad. A day and a half and he spoke as familiarly as if he'd been in Jake's life forever. "No problem," she told him. "You treat this time, and next time I'll buy."

In the food court they got soft drinks, found a table and sat down opposite each other. For a while, Michael was busy drinking root beer. Then, his thirst quenched, he began toying with the straw. Obviously something was on his mind.

"Can I ask you something, Miss Rachel?"

"Sure. Ask away." She sounded offhand, but she tensed a little. Michael's questions, she knew, could pack a wallop.

"Do I have any grandparents or cousins or . . . or any relatives? From my dad's family, I mean."

"I'm afraid there's no one, Michael. Jake's parents died when he was very young. He grew up as a ward of the state, in foster homes."

He gave her a startled look. "No kidding?"

"No kidding."

A few moments passed as he considered that. "They were going to do the same thing to me after Mama Dee died, but I thought it over and decided I could probably manage okay on my own."

"Well, you've certainly done that."

"I'm lucky I knew who my dad was and

110

where he lived." He fiddled with his drink, then looked directly into her eyes. "It's funny that the same thing happened to my dad, isn't it?"

"It is odd," Rachel agreed. She'd been thinking the same thing. And more. It was a strange twist of fate, and it made the bond between Jake and Michael even stronger.

"But my dad didn't let it get him down, did he?" Michael's eyes shone with pride and admiration for Jake. "He's a real important man in this town. Respected. I could tell when I was at his office. Those people jumped whenever he said the word. If I manage as well as that, I'll do okay, won't I?"

"Without a doubt."

"Tell me some more about my dad. Please," he added, seeing her hesitate.

"Well . . ." She drew a deep breath. "Jake didn't have a lot of opportunities when he was growing up, but as you noticed, it didn't seem to hamper him. As soon as he was old enough, he broke away and managed on his own. Then he joined the army. After he got out, he went to college. He has a degree in history, of all things."

He nodded his head. "I like history, too."

"It must run in the family," she said dryly.

"I don't know about that," he said seriously, "but I bet I know why he chose it."

"Oh, really? Why?"

He closed both hands around the big plastic cup, frowning thoughtfully at his root beer. "Because when you don't have much family, you sometimes feel you don't have a . . . a place in things. You know? But understanding the people who lived in the past sort of gives you something to fasten on to." He gave her an intense look. "You've got to be related to some of those people, right? I mean, we all came from something even if we don't know who and where and why."

Oh, Lord, she didn't want to hear this. She didn't want this kid tugging at her heartstrings. She didn't want to hear adult philosophy from a boy whose thoughts should be taken up with things like passing geometry and sports and video games.

She reached blindly for the packages that lay on the bench beside her. "We'd better get back out there and finish this up, Michael. It's getting late and we still need to get to the high school."

"Yes, ma'am." He gathered up his share of the packages and fell into step beside her, hurrying a little, since she seemed to be picking up their pace. "But I don't need anything else, do I?" He thought of the stuff they'd already bought. "I've never had half this much to choose from. And everything's so expensive. I don't want to be a pain."

"You have to have new sneakers."

He gave his beat-up, no-name shoes a considering look. "Well . . ."

"You have to have new sneakers, Michael."

Michael recognized that tone and clammed up. He hadn't been around Rachel McAdam a whole day yet, but he knew better than to argue. If she wanted him to have new sneakers, then he would have new sneakers.

"Is there a special brand you prefer?" she asked briskly.

"Well, not really, I guess." He cleared his throat, trying to decide just how much of an opinion he should express. "Whatever's cheapest."

She made a sharp turn into the shoe store and he almost stumbled following her. "You can try them all on, then we'll see what fits best."

Boy, if Mama Dee could only see him now!

By Thursday, Rachel was more than ready to begin her job. At home the tension was almost unbearable. She wondered sometimes if the wall between her and Jake could ever be taken down. Michael was a constant reminder of Jake's infidelity and, for Rachel, of her loss. Her only child might be gone forever. But, she reminded herself bitterly, Jake would always have Michael to fill the void. And so resentment and anger seethed within her. Feeling it, Jake walked around like a man picking his way through a mine field.

She probably would have been more nervous about starting a career this late in her life had her problems at home been less consuming. As it was, there was little time left to work herself into a state. So, at eight o'clock she was at the hospital eager to begin.

Immediately after completing the paperwork in the personnel office, she was sent around to Helen Falco, the head nurse in the emergency room, where she received a brief familiarization of the computer and emergency-room routine. Helen showed her the desk she'd occupy, along with other essentials such as the location of the coffeepot and the employee lounge. It was only a few minutes past ten when a commotion at the entrance sent everyone into a state of alert.

Outside, instead of an ambulance, a police car shrieked to a stop and two uniformed officers jumped out. Rachel recognized both as sheriff's deputies. One was Leon White, big and burly and black, a veteran of at least ten years. She'd always liked him. The other, the driver, was Ed Sims, younger, but sharp. A good lawman, she'd heard Jake say. While White dealt with the people in the backseat, his partner hurried through the hospital's automatic entrance. "We need some help here!" Sims yelled. Then, without waiting, he turned and headed toward the vehicle at a jog.

Through the car window, Rachel could see a girl, a teenager, she thought. She was not unconscious, but there was clearly something wrong. She was weaving slightly, her gaze fixed. Beside her was a teenage boy. He was pale and subdued. At a gesture from White, he climbed out of the car and stood watching as Ed Sims dealt with the girl. There was no response when he called her name. Sims looked relieved when he spotted the trauma team headed his way. With well-rehearsed efficiency, the gurney was wheeled to the police car. The deputy pulled back to allow the medics access. When he did, the girl slowly keeled over.

Within half a minute, it seemed to Rachel, the girl was on the gurney, being rushed through the doors. Gesturing for the deputies to follow, the medics snapped out questions.

Did they suspect a drug overdose?

Did they know what she'd taken?

How long ago?

Rachel watched everything with a feeling of helplessness. She went to her small desk and sat down, mostly because she was afraid her trembling legs would buckle beneath her. It was supposed to be her job to take patient information, she reminded herself, looking at her shaking fingers. She wasn't certain she could type even if she could remember what she was supposed to ask. Someone touched her shoulder.

"I'll take this one, Rachel."

She looked up into Helen Falco's blue eyes. Only fifteen minutes before, Helen had explained what she was expected to do when a patient checked in. She glanced at the file separators where all the forms were kept. Caving in at the first emergency wasn't the way she wanted to begin her job. She was in the emergency room, for Pete's sake. What had she expected? Taking a deep breath, she pulled herself together.

"Thanks, Helen, but I think I can do it."

Helen's eyebrows lifted. "Sure?"

Rachel reached for the admissions form. "Not really, but I may as well give it a try.

Stand by, if you will. I may need help."

The girl's name was Regina Melrose. She carried no identification. What meager information they did get came from the boy who'd been picked up with her. His name, he told Rachel, was Jerry Purdy. Regina was fifteen. Address unknown. Parents unknown. She was a student at Tidewater High. Jerry, too, was fifteen years old. This from Ed Sims, who stood at the boy's side while Rachel coaxed information from him. She'd noticed Sims's surprised look when he recognized her. Her job coming so close on the heels of Michael's arrival would probably generate a lot of speculation. She'd already thought of that and dreaded it. Unlike her sisters, she had always avoided anything that drew attention to herself.

"I need a signature on this form," she told Sims. "Isn't there some way you can locate her parents? They're bound to be somewhere in this area."

"Unless she's a runaway," Helen Falco said.

Sims shook his head. "I don't think so. This one's county, I believe. According to Jerry here, she's living with a foster family, but he doesn't have a name or address."

Rachel looked at the boy. He was pale and sweating. It was obvious that he'd taken something, too, but he'd been luckier than Regina. He was still on his feet. Barely. She pitched her voice low, sensing that any show of aggression would be the wrong approach. "Jerry, do you know anybody we might contact for Regina?"

"No," he mumbled sullenly, looking at his feet.

"How long have you known her?"

He shrugged. "I don't know. Couple of years, I guess."

"And you've never met her family? Her mother? Anyone?"

He raised his eyes to hers. "She don't have nobody. And it won't do any good to call those people, because they don't care about Regina."

Rachel glanced at Ed Sims, whose look gave her no help. "You mean her foster family?" she asked Jerry.

"Yeah, I guess." He was sullen again, his quick flare of temper spent. He looked at Sims. "Can I go now?"

"Yeah, you can go," Sims said, clamping a hand on one of the boy's thin shoulders. "You can go straight to Juvenile and sober up, Jerry. Then you can spend a little time with Jacky Kendall. You remember Jacky, don't you?"

"Yeah, I remember her." Jerry tried to

shake Sims's hold on his shoulder, but the officer ignored it.

"She's gonna be disappointed in you, Jerry. Last time we busted you, you promised her that you were turning over a new leaf."

"I tried," he mumbled.

Sims swore in disgust, but Rachel sensed it was directed more at the world in general than at the boy.

"Go get in the car," he growled. "That girl could have died just now, you know that?"

As Jerry faced off with Ed Sims, his eyes were suddenly too bright. His throat worked and he swallowed once, hard, but said nothing. Then he turned, stumbling slightly, and headed for the door.

Rachel's heart twisted. "Ed . . ."

He released a sigh. "It's okay, I'm not going to hassle him anymore. At least, not today. The condition he's in, he probably won't remember it anyway. Maybe Jacky can do some good with him this time." He gave her a brief half smile. "Y'all take care of Regina. When we saw the shape she was in, we didn't waste any time hauling her over here. Not even ten o'clock and they're both wasted."

"Where did you pick them up?"

119

"The roadside park on Route 6, right out in the open." He shook his head.

The small park was just out Tidewater's city limits, barely a mile from the high school. Rachel frowned. "Where do you think they got it?"

"Tidewater High, without a doubt."

"How do you know? Did Jerry say that?"

"No, he wouldn't name anybody, but he didn't have to. We've been alerted to a new source there, except that we were told it was high-grade homegrown marijuana. Jake is going to be hot when he finds out there's other stuff, and a lot worse."

"What do you think they were taking?" Rachel asked, her head whirling with new insight into Jake's world.

"I think Regina got hold of some angel dust." Ed shrugged. "But I'm no expert."

He looked up as Leon White appeared from the vicinity of the treatment room where Regina had been taken. "Hey, Leon. What's the scoop, man?"

Leon rubbed a huge hand over his short curly hair and replaced his cap. "She'll be okay. This time."

"What was it? Did they say?"

"Angel dust." Leon took out a cigarette pack but crumpled it in disgust when he found it empty.

Wondering what she'd gotten herself into, Rachel walked with them to the door and watched them climb into their vehicle. If she hadn't misread the expression on Leon White's face, he was truly concerned about Regina. And so was Ed Sims. Both were seasoned men who dealt with this kind of thing often, and in spite of the personal toll it must take, they managed to carry on. Ron Campbell had warned her when they first talked about this job, but his words had sailed over her head. This was not going to be like serving coffee to the families of surgical patients or passing out mail to new mothers. Before her doubts had a chance to defeat her, an ambulance pulled up at the entrance.

"Heart attack!" someone yelled.

She was too busy the rest of the day to think about failure.

CHAPTER SIX

"You like that stuff a lot, don't you?" Michael wrinkled his nose watching Rachel selecting snow peas from a display of Oriental foods. It had been a little over three weeks since he'd moved in with his dad and stepmother, and he'd eaten a wider variety of food than ever before in his life. Some of it was great, but some of it wasn't too good. Like those salads she made with little sprouts and things that tasted like grass.

"I like fresh vegetables, yes." Rachel dropped two eggplants into a plastic bag. "It's never too early to start watching your cholesterol."

"Does Dad?"

Rachel tossed a bag of spinach into the cart. "He doesn't. I do."

"Oh. Okay." If she was into this cholesterol-watching business, then Jake would no doubt go along with it whether he liked it or not. It hadn't taken Michael more than a day in their house to see that his dad was crazy about Miss Rachel and that he'd do almost anything to keep her happy.

He studied her as she turned to select bananas. She wasn't happy. Even a stranger could see that. He hoped it wasn't because of him. He knew that alone was enough to cause a lot of trouble in a marriage, and he still hoped everything would work out, but he sensed there was more. It was probably their little boy, Scotty. Miss Rachel's heart was broken over that. And his dad felt awful because he hadn't found him.

He gazed beyond Rachel through the wide windows, where bright June sunshine cast a sheen over everything. He'd been asking around at school to see what he could learn about what happened to Scotty. Everybody in town knew all about it. Flyers had been put out. Television and newspapers and radio had been full of it. Volunteers had searched the whole state, just about. Still, nothing had turned up. No clues. Nothing. Michael picked up an apple and idly rubbed the smooth surface with his thumb. Wouldn't it be neat if he could somehow figure out what happened?

"Rachel McAdam! Where have you been keeping yourself?"

As she looked up, Rachel stiffened. Joan

Gonzales, wife of the city police chief and the most notorious busybody in town, was heading her way from the vicinity of the store delicatessen. "Hello, Joan," she said politely. "I've been keeping busy. How about you?"

"Oh, swamped as usual. Just swamped." Her gaze went from Rachel to Michael. As Rachel watched, the woman's eyes narrowed with undisguised interest. "I don't believe we've met." She looked at Rachel.

Rachel wasn't fooled. She saw the malice behind the saccharine smile. Joan's husband was planning to run for sheriff. For obvious reasons, the Gonzaleses would be extremely interested in knowing that an illegitimate son had suddenly appeared in Jake's heretofore exemplary life. What was she going to say? She looked into Michael's face and saw with a shock that he understood her dilemma. There was no expression on his face, but he was tense, waiting.

Waiting to be denied. Or rejected.

Her chin went up a notch. "This is Michael," she told Joan Gonzales. "Jake's son. He has been living with his mother's family in Iowa, but from now on he will be living with us here in Tidewater. Michael, this is Joan Gonzales. Her husband is the chief of police here in town." Let Joan make of that what she would, Rachel thought, feeling a compelling urge to move closer to Michael.

Michael put out his hand. "Pleased to meet you, ma'am."

"Jake's son. My, my." Joan lifted her eyebrows in malicious surprise. "I didn't know he had a son. Iowa, you say. . . ." Realizing Michael's hand was still outstretched, she took it and gave it a brief shake.

Rachel rushed into speech. "I've been meaning to give you a call, Joan. I wondered if you would be interested in taking my place on the board at the country club. I have a job now and I'm going to have to drop a few things."

"Well, I —" Joan's eyes left Michael reluctantly. "The board? At the club?"

Knowing that the woman would kill to have her place on the board, Rachel gave her a bright, false smile. "I've just started working at the hospital in the emergency room. It's fascinating, but it does take a lot of the time I used to devote to other things." She was chattering, she knew, intent on preventing the woman from prying and consequently hurting Michael.

"I never thought of you as a career person," Joan said.

"Oh, really?"

"Is it full-time?"

"Seven to three."

"Gracious! That *is* a real job." Joan shuddered. "Such early hours, too."

"Yes. But I love it." Rachel grabbed a couple of large pears. Michael held out a plastic bag and she dropped them in. "Thanks, Mike."

"How will you manage the campaign and a new career?"

"I don't think I'll have any trouble." Busy body. Rachel handed Michael a bunch of grapes to bag.

"Well, I know J.B. would have a fit if I were to do something like that right before the campaign starts." Joan lifted a sly eyebrow. "Speaking of which, how did Jake react?"

"He's very supportive."

"Uh-huh. Well, lots of luck." She looked again at Michael, her expression alive with speculation.

"I'll mention your name to the board committee at the club," Rachel put in quickly.

"Hmm? Oh, yes. Thanks, Rachel."

"We'd better run, Michael."

"Yes, ma'am."

Joan smiled with a show of perfect teeth. "Welcome to Tidewater, Michael."

"Thank you, ma'am."

Neither Michael nor Rachel moved for a moment as Joan wheeled out of the produce department.

"Her cart's empty," Michael remarked.

Rachel grimaced, then tossed back a head of cabbage she didn't remember taking. "She wasn't in this section for fruits and vegetables."

"I guessed that."

Rachel looked at him and found understanding in his eyes. She sighed. "I suppose we might as well get used to it, Michael. Jake's a public figure and the election's coming up in November. Things may get sticky."

"I can take it if you can, Miss Rachel."

"In that case, we'll both be fine."

Her voice was confident, but inside she wasn't convinced. Joan Gonzales and her malicious looks were only the beginning. When Jake began making the public appearances that were so necessary during the campaign, she wasn't certain she would be able to handle it at all.

Jake handed Rachel a glass of wine before settling himself into the patio chair beside her. Most of the evening, she'd been deep in thought. The underwater lights in the pool cast a soft blue-tinted glow over her features. The truth was, Rachel had been quiet every night since Scotty had disappeared. With Michael around to complicate things even more, Jake wasn't sure what constituted a normal evening at home. And yet this evening he'd sensed something further.

It wasn't Michael, he decided. In fact, Rachel and Michael seemed to have hit it off remarkably well, for which Jake gave heartfelt thanks. Rachel's hours at the hospital just happened to coincide with Michael's school hours. He rode in with her in the mornings and she picked him up in the afternoons. It was an arrangement she had suggested. Jake, ever alert to ways to cement the relationship between the three of them, had been elated. Ever since the boy's arrival, Jake had been holding his breath, hoping and praying that Rachel would stay long enough to learn to like him. Now he wanted more than that. He wanted Rachel to love Michael as he did.

He wished other things would work out, as well. He and Rachel still slept apart. He missed her, missed having her close in the night. Over the years, they might have had other problems in their marriage, but they'd never slept apart before. Her presence grounded him, made his love for her seem like a tangible thing. Until lately, he had been confident that Rachel felt the same. Now he wondered. Could she just turn her feelings off at will? Was that her idea of love? Had she ever really loved him?

He leaned back so that he was slightly behind her, watching her. "Something on your mind tonight?" he asked.

She was still for a second before shifting in the chair and crossing her legs. "No, not really."

"How's the job?"

"Busy, interesting, hectic."

He studied her, frowning. Two of his men, Ed Sims and Leon White, had rushed a pair of drugged kids to Emergency the very first day she'd been on the job. He hated for Rachel to be exposed to that kind of thing. "You don't have to stay with it, Rachel. You can —"

"I like it, Jake."

Jake didn't want to argue, but he couldn't just drop it there. "You always hated it when things got hectic here at home. How can you like it at work?"

"I don't know. It's just different at work. Challenging."

"You see some bad stuff in Emergency,"

he said, disapproval making him sound gruff.

"I realized that within the first hour." She scooted her chair back a little to face him. "Jake, how is it that I'm married to the sheriff in this county and yet I feel as though I've been living in a dreamworld? I read the papers. I know we have a drug problem, every place does. I know about teenage pregnancy and homelessness and alcoholism. But my grasp of these problems was so superficial. Every day I go into the hospital and see these things firsthand, I wonder where in the world have I been? Would I have been willing to stick my head in the sand and pretend everything's lovely forever?"

"Just because you weren't on speaking terms with all the crime in the county or didn't associate with the dregs of humanity doesn't mean you're a failure as a human being."

"You're missing my point," she said impatiently. "I just feel that somehow I could have been more involved, especially since I'm the wife of the sheriff."

He got up and went to the edge of the pool, his back to her. "It's because I see so much of it that I want to shield my family."

"Maybe I don't want to be shielded anymore."

Jake's heart started to beat faster. Was she going to walk out now? Is that what she'd been brooding over all evening? His next words were forced. "What do you want, Rachel?"

She stood and walked over to a bright pink bougainvillea. "I'm not sure. I'm still confused and upset over . . . things."

Holding his breath, Jake pressed a palm against the back of his neck. "Things" meant his infidelity and Michael and, maybe worst of all, his failure to find Scotty.

"Right now I'm just taking each day as it comes," Rachel murmured. "My job helps. At least I'm doing something constructive."

He relaxed a little. For one heart-stopping moment, he'd braced himself to hear her ask for a divorce. He felt like a prisoner handed an eleventh-hour reprieve. He didn't know how much longer he could go on like this! He needed something from her, just some small sign that there was still some love left in her heart for him.

The distance of the patio separated them, but he turned, wanting to pull her into his arms and show her in the most basic way how much he loved her, needed her. He was taking the first step when she looked up, meeting his eyes.

"Jake . . ."

He stopped. "What?"

"Do you . . . Have you heard . . ."

Scotty. If only he could give her the answer she craved. He was glad it was dark and she couldn't see the despair in his eyes. The failure. "No, nothing. I have feelers out everywhere, Rachel. My contacts are all alerted. His picture has been released nationwide. The —" He stopped. Excuses. Even to his own ears, it sounded like excuses.

She looked away. "It's . . . I was just hoping . . ." She crossed her arms over her middle, shaking her head. He heard her draw in a quick breath, then somehow she dredged up a weak smile. "The campaign will probably start to heat up within a month or so."

It was a second before Jake could reply. "Yeah."

"How is Liz working out?"

"Super. She's doing a fabulous job."

Thank God for Liz, his campaign manager. Rachel's oldest sister was a lawyer with a feel for politics. She'd been very active in his last successful campaign and was throwing herself into this election with even more enthusiasm. Michael's sudden appearance in his life could have spelled political disaster, but Liz was determined to make the voters love the teenager as much as Jake did. Being family was a decided advantage in a campaign manager.

"Are you ready?"

"I've neglected it, what with everything else that's happened. Unfortunately, I can't have the job if I don't campaign for it."

Rachel said nothing. With her face in shadow, he couldn't tell what she was thinking, either. He tossed the ice from his drink into the pool. "The chamber is having a kick-off rally next Saturday night. Meet the candidate. You know the kind of thing."

"Already?" She didn't bother to hide her dismay.

"We need to be there."

She snapped off a pink bloom. "I don't think so, Jake."

"Rachel —"

"No. I'm not going. I can't."

"Is it Michael?"

She stared at him. "What do you think it is? Of course, it's Michael! Everybody's talking about it, Jake. How do you think that makes me feel?"

"I know it's hard for you. I —"

"You know?" Jake heard the skepticism in her voice. "Then tell me, has anybody got up the nerve to ask you about it to your face?"

"Well —"

"I thought not." She laughed harshly. "Well, somebody asked me. Just today, as a matter of fact. And she's probably the first of many."

"Who? Who was it?"

"Would you believe Joan Gonzales? Your opponent's wife, Jake. At the supermarket yet. In front of all of Tidewater."

"I'm so sorry." Pain shot through him and he raked a hand through his hair. "What happened?"

"We were —"

"We?"

"Michael and me."

He closed his eyes, prepared for the worst.

"The woman's curiosity is exceeded only by her gall," Rachel muttered angrily.

"What did she do? Did she say anything to hurt Mike?" When she just looked at him, he saw that Rachel believed his concern had been only for Michael. The feeling that he was treading dangerous ground intensified. "Tell me," he said bleakly.

"I managed to deal with her. And you can relax. Michael seemed to take it all in stride. She demanded an introduction, of course."

"What did you do?"

"I introduced him, Jake. I told her the truth, as much as she needed to know." She turned and began fussing again with the plant. "What did you expect?"

"I'm sorry, Rachel. I know how Joan is. She must have taken delight in finally getting to you."

She glanced up at him. "What do you mean by that?"

"She's always been jealous of you."

"Whatever for?"

"Because you're well liked and respected, you have countless friends and important family connections, you're involved in a dozen things that she only wishes she could do and you're gracious and lovely and very much a lady."

She stared at him, speechless.

"Why are you looking at me like that?"

She shook her head. "Aren't you describing my sisters?"

"No! I'm describing my wife."

"I . . . I don't think of myself like that. And I never knew you did, either."

"Then I've been a fool for not saying so. You're all those things and more, Rachel." He started to touch her, longed to, but pulled back at the look in her eyes. "I hate it that I've put you in a position to take heat from people like Joan. I hope you explained to Michael that she wasn't worth losing any sleep over."

Rachel nodded.

"I know she's a pain. She'll probably blab this all over the county and enjoy doing it. J.B.'s been looking for something to use against me."

"Well, he's got it," Rachel said bitterly. "What better weapon than an illegitimate child?"

He flinched inwardly, knowing her words to be true. "The best way to scotch the rumors is for us to show a united front, Rachel." He did touch her then. He caught her arm to keep her from turning away from him. "When we're alone together, you can punish me as much as you want, but by going to the rally and giving the appearance of having accepted Michael, you make it tough for J.B. to get much mileage out of this." Unconsciously he stroked the soft skin inside her elbow with his thumb. "Won't you at least think about it?"

She refused to look at him. "All those people . . . whispering, snickering, speculating." She shuddered. "I hate it! You know I do."

It's me she hates. Jake ached with the pain of it but could see no alternative. That is, if he wanted to keep his position as sheriff.

Rachel had never been entirely comfortable in the spotlight of a politician's wife, but for his sake she'd accepted it. Only those closest to her realized how truly introverted she was. He let out a long breath. He wished he could tell her he wouldn't run this time, but he couldn't do that. In his job he had complete access to the system, and that was the surest way to locate a missing child. If he was an ordinary man in the street, those doors would be closed to him. He had to run again.

"I'll make it up to you, Rachel," he said quietly. "I don't know how, but I will."

"You can make it up to me by finding Scotty."

He clenched his jaw. "Do you think I'm not trying my best?"

"I don't know anymore."

He tightened his hand on her arm so that she was forced to look at him. "What is that supposed to mean?"

She twisted loose. "You have Michael now. It's not the same for you!"

For a second or two, he was so angry he couldn't speak. "You think my loving Michael somehow diminishes the love I have for our son?"

"No . . . not exactly." Rachel unconsciously rubbed the spot on her arm where

Jake's fingers had been, but she wouldn't look at him. "I just think having Michael in your life has helped to fill the void for you. I sometimes wonder if you have the same incentive to search for Scotty now that Michael's here."

For a moment Jake simply looked at her. When he finally spoke, his voice vibrated. "I'm going to overlook what you just said, Rachel. I know your grief has been almost unbearable. I know Scotty means more to you than anybody in the world." The thought had been with him a long time although he'd never said it. "But if you ever — I repeat, Rachel — if you ever dare insinuate that I wouldn't give my life to have Scotty back, that I'm not making every conceivable effort to try to find my boy, then you won't have to put up with me another day, because I'll walk out myself. This marriage, our relationship, everything we've ever shared will be history, Rachel."

She stared at him rebelliously, both of them caught in the taut pain of the moment. Faint sounds came from the pool. Nearby a car door closed. The neighbor's big dog woofed softly. They stood still, oblivious to everything. Then, with a choked sound, Rachel brushed past Jake and ran.

Left alone, Jake released the breath he'd

been holding and felt his rage fade with it. He'd probably screwed up beyond redemption. Closing his eyes, he pressed his fingers deep into his eye sockets. A sound escaped him, like a fatally wounded animal.

From the very beginning of their relationship, Rachel had evoked his most protective instincts. There was something about her that was so sensitive, so vulnerable, that it touched the best and deepest part of him. For eighteen years he had taken intense, masculine pleasure in caring for her, in running interference for her. To the best of his ability, he had always tried to see that life's harshest realities didn't touch his Rachel. A knife through his heart couldn't hurt him any more than Rachel's belief that he would shortchange their son.

He looked at a sky devoid of stars and whispered her name in a tortured voice. "What are we doing to each other?"

"Okay, what's the party line?" Suzanne demanded, leaning forward to take a tall glass of iced tea from Rachel. "I've been fending off the most intrusive questions, sweetie, but sooner or later we're going to have to give. So, what's it to be?"

Liz, Rachel's oldest sister, took her glass from the tray Rachel held. "Suzy's right,

Rachel. All this speculation is terrible for Jake's image. Better to hammer out a story right up front, seize the initiative before J.B.'s people can do too much damage."

Rachel smothered a sigh and sat down. "You sound like a lawyer, Liz."

"I *am* a lawyer, Rachel, and I'm also Jake's campaign manager. It's my job to get down and dirty, but better me than some stranger at the five-and-dime."

"She's right, Rach," Suzanne said. "In my job, I have my finger on the pulse of this town, too. Jake's name is up. Things could get really awkward."

Rachel picked up her sunglasses and put them on. Dark lenses were a frail barrier to the kind of grilling she was going to get from her sisters, but it was the only protection she had. They both knew her so well. Which was the reason she'd been avoiding them. She'd known they'd want details as soon as they heard about Michael. With their considerable political savvy, they had quickly realized the potential for disaster Michael's sudden appearance represented to Jake's campaign. They were sure to be full of advice for Rachel on managing the crisis.

As the youngest, she had grown up trying to fend off her sisters' well-meaning attempts to manage her life. Besides running smooth households, they each managed high-powered jobs with ease. Neither had ever been satisfied watching Rachel devote herself to a life devoid of any real career. Rachel was so different from them that she sometimes wondered if she had been born with a missing gene. They meant well, but she was struggling to run her own life now.

Suzanne cleared her throat. "Rachel?"

"Why is everybody so concerned about the effect of this on Jake's campaign?" she asked, looking from one to the other. She knew what she was going to say would shock them. "Why are both of you tiptoeing around the obvious fact of Jake's infidelity? He had an affair! What about the effect on me? What about the effect on my marriage?"

For once, neither of her sisters had a ready comeback. They stared at her, their faces mirroring their distress. Seeing their discomfiture gave Rachel an odd feeling. It wasn't often she found the grit to withstand their combined strength.

"Oh, Rachel," Suzanne murmured.

"You're going to have to let it go," Liz said.

But Rachel wasn't ready to let it go. "What if I don't feel particularly concerned about Jake's campaign and what people will say? What if I don't want to hammer out a party

141

line? What if right now I don't give a fig about Jake McAdam?"

There was a moment of shocked silence. Then Suzanne reached over and laid a hand on Rachel's knee. "You don't mean that, honey."

"I do mean it."

Liz spoke. "You're ticked off, naturally. That's understandable. But it —"

"Ticked off?" Rachel stood up abruptly. "Ticked off is how you feel when somebody cuts in the line ahead of you, Liz. Ticked off is when you get the wrong stuff on the pizza you ordered. The way I see it, when your husband has an affair that results in a real, live child, ticked off isn't quite strong enough. Do you think you'd feel ticked off if Cliff's fourteen-year-old son suddenly showed up on your doorstep?"

Cliff was Liz's husband of twenty years. "I'm sorry, Rachel. It was stupid of me —"

"It was stupid of both of us," Suzanne broke in quickly. "We shouldn't have mentioned this at all until you brought it up yourself, Rach, if and when you decided to. You're right, of course. If Liz or I discovered that Cliff or Alan had been unfaithful, no matter what the circumstances, we'd both be out for blood."

Rachel bent her head and pressed on the

bridge of her sunglasses with her forefinger. "I know the whole town is buzzing over this. I know Jake's campaign is jeopardized because of it. I know I ought to be thinking about what to say in public, but frankly, as things stand now, what the public thinks is pretty low on my list. My life has been turned upside down. The voters of Tidewater will just have to wait to hear the sordid details!"

If she'd suddenly stripped in a public place, her sisters wouldn't have been more surprised at her outburst, she realized. Liz, with the most at stake as Jake's campaign manager, frowned then busied herself pouring more iced tea. Suzanne anxiously patted the chair Rachel had just vacated.

"Come and sit down again, Rach. Forget the wagging tongues of Tidewater . . . and I'm including Liz and me in that number. Besides, we'll think of something if we're put on the spot, right, Liz? In the meantime," she said in a more sympathetic tone, "tell us about Michael. You can do that, can't you?"

"He's like Jake," Rachel said, sitting down. Her eyes clouded. "Actually, he's more like Jake than . . . than Scotty is. His eyes are the same gray, his hair's the same, he has an identical birthmark . . ." She took a drink, forcing the cold liquid past the knot in her throat.

Suzanne studied her over the rim of her glass. "Then there's no doubt about his paternity?"

Liz was the one who answered. "Although Jake believed him from the beginning, naturally he had me run a check."

Rachel set her glass down. "He's had a hard life," she said, feeling compelled to defend Michael. "Striking out on his own in search of his natural father was a big step for a fourteen-year-old, but he did it. He must have had a few bad moments, but he managed. He's tough. I guess he's had to be." She paused a minute before adding, "Actually, he's a nice kid."

"Where has he been all these years?" Suzanne asked.

"In Iowa, with his grandmother."

"What about his mother?"

"Dead."

For a time, their palpable curiosity hung in the air. Rachel knew they wanted to know about the affair, but she simply wasn't ready to talk about it, even to her sisters. Other people were going to be watching her, too, speculating, gauging her reaction. She knew very well that her reaction could mean the difference between public acceptance or condemnation — Jake's fall from grace. During his years as a public figure, he had been remarkably free of scandal. He was known by his constituents, his friends and his family as rock steady and dependable, a man of integrity and honesty. Surely his reputation was strong enough to weather worse than this, she told herself.

Because until she managed to work through her own tangled emotions, Rachel honestly didn't think she would be much help to him.

CHAPTER SEVEN

The night of the chamber rally came all too soon for Rachel. She went with Jake, of course, and played the role expected of her. If her smile seemed a little fixed, no one noticed. Jake's expression was almost equally strained, but she was probably one of the few people who knew him well enough to see it. As a man who was often in the limelight, he was practiced in masking his feelings. She watched from the door of the ladies' lounge as he chatted with Tidewater's mayor and Jerry Lowe, the president of the chamber, who'd organized the rally. As though sensing her gaze, Jake looked at her over the mayor's balding head. Their eyes met for a second or two before his attention was reclaimed by Jerry.

She made her way through the crowd searching for a friendly — genuinely friendly — face, excluding blood relatives. It was no accident that every member of her family was in attendance. Every one of them was aware that this event would be difficult for her, and they'd been especially attentive, as though she were a child. What was it about her that made people want to run interference for her? she wondered irritably.

A crush of couples headed for the dance floor as the lead singer of the band, a local country-and-western group, launched into "I'm Proud to Be an American." Someone backed blindly into Rachel, then laughingly apologized. One of Jake's deputies asked her to dance. She flashed a bright smile and refused, glancing at her watch to see how soon they could decently leave. Until then, the next best thing was a breath of fresh air and a moment or two of peace and quiet.

She changed direction abruptly, making a beeline for the patio doors. A few others had the same idea, but for the most part the crowd was content to stay inside where the bar was open, the talk friendly and the music loud.

"Rachel!"

Someone caught her just before she managed to slip through the door. She glanced up at Ron Campbell's ready smile and relaxed slightly. "Oh, hi, Ron. I didn't see you earlier. Were you held up at the hospital?"

He gave her arm an intimate squeeze. "I've been right here. It's tough trying to get a word with you, lady. Every time I got close, Jake whisked you away." He grinned engagingly. "When I saw you heading in this direction, I grabbed my chance. Come on, let's get out of this madhouse."

Rachel hesitated briefly, then allowed herself to be drawn outside and across the patio. She did dislike this kind of event, but she hadn't been aware that it showed. As the sounds inside the hall faded, she drew a relieved breath. "At last, peace and quiet."

Ron laughed. "I'm telling you! Another decibel and the chamber'll have to spring for earplugs for that crowd."

"I know what you mean. I always thought of country-and-western music as mellow, laid-back stuff. But tonight it's like a feeding frenzy at the zoo. I was more than ready for a break."

He slid his hand down her arm to her hand and squeezed it. "Then I'm glad I happened along to enjoy it with you."

In the sudden quiet, his tone had an intimate sound. Rachel gently withdrew her fingers. Glancing around, she found that he'd led them to a particularly secluded area of the grounds. With a soft sigh, she sank onto the garden bench, and Ron sat down beside her. For a moment, she hesitated. It had been a long time since she had been alone with a man like this. Probably not since she'd been married. Certainly not since Jake had been sheriff. People were quick to judge, so she was always extremely careful to avoid even the appearance of impropriety. Tonight she felt oddly indifferent to what people might think.

Ron watched her, a small smile playing at his mouth. "You must be used to this kind of thing, being a veteran campaigner."

She plucked a leaf from a gardenia growing close to the bench. "I don't think I'll ever be used to crowds and noise and nosy people." Even as she spoke the words, she couldn't believe she'd said them. As a politician's wife, discretion was as necessary as smiling. What was happening to her?

"Sort of like living in a goldfish bowl, hmm?"

"Sort of. Fortunately the noise and crowds subside somewhat after the election."

"But you're still in the goldfish bowl."

"Unfortunately."

He shifted slightly, lifting his arm and bringing it down to rest on the back of the bench. The maneuver was casual, but Rachel was acutely aware of it. If someone should see them . . .

"We've been friends a long time, Rachel," he said softly. "If you ever need anybody, you know you can talk to me."

"If she needs anybody, she has me."

Jake's voice was like cold steel slicing into the conversation. Startled, Rachel almost jumped to her feet, but caught herself just in time. She wasn't guilty of anything! Ron, however, did rise. As he looked into Jake's face, his expression was wary.

"Hello, Sheriff. Rachel and I were just taking a breather." His laugh sounded a little forced. "A little of that band in there goes a long way."

Jake's features could have been carved from granite. After a long, hard look at Ron, he turned to his wife. "Rachel?"

She stood up. "I'm tired, Jake. Can't we go home now?"

"That's exactly what I had in mind."

He would have ushered her past Ron without another word, but she refused to be hustled away like a naughty child. She pulled her arm free, speaking to Ron as she fell into step beside Jake. "Good night, Ron. I'll see you Monday."

They drove the entire trip home without a word. Jake was furious. The air inside the car vibrated with his rage. Rachel fixed her gaze on the view through the side window of the car, her chin at a defiant angle. She didn't care if he was mad, she told herself. It was nothing new lately. He'd been mad at her ever since she'd accused him of neglecting the search for Scotty. He'd treated her with about as much warmth as he would a stranger in their house. Less, maybe. He would have smiled at a guest. He would have spent a little time with a guest. Besides eating together — which they'd been forced to do because of Michael — he'd made himself scarce. Tonight was the longest he'd spent with her since that night.

He followed her into the bedroom they'd once shared. "What were you trying to prove tonight?"

"I don't want to talk tonight, Jake. I want to go to bed."

"We need to talk whether you feel like it or not. I want an answer, and I want it straight."

"Stop. This is not an interrogation and I'm not one of your suspects." She shot him a sarcastic look. "Besides, you wouldn't want the neighbors to hear, would you? Think of your image."

For a long moment, he stared at her, hard. "Was that it, Rachel? Were you deliberately trying to sabotage me?"

"Don't be ridiculous." She kicked off one shoe then the other. Immediately she regretted it. She was a good six inches shorter than Jake, and without her heels she was too intensely aware of it.

"I want a straight answer, Rachel. Did you go off alone with Campbell just to stir up speculation about us? Do you want me dead in the water before my campaign even gets started?"

"Of course not."

"You know how important appearances are in this business." He released a long breath. "It's tiresome, but it's a fact. After twelve years of campaigning, you know all this as well as I do."

She removed her earrings, then tossed them onto her dresser. "Maybe I'm just fed up with the hypocrisy of it, I don't know."

"Then we're back to square one. If you didn't deliberately mean to start tongues wagging, then why did you put yourself in such a compromising situation?"

"You sound like an outraged guardian, for heaven's sake! This isn't the eighteenth century, Jake. Nobody thinks twice about two adults seeking a peaceful moment at a noisy party."

"It didn't sound like that to me. It

sounded like that . . . Like Ron was coming on to my wife."

Rachel was occupied unfastening the clasp of her watch. She looked up. "He was expressing sympathy for my lifestyle."

Stung, he refused to acknowledge how much that hurt. He resorted to sarcasm. "What's wrong with your lifestyle?" He sent a look around the beautifully furnished bedroom. "From where I stand, your lifestyle doesn't seem too shabby." But even as he said it, he knew where Rachel was coming from. She was in pain, and it was his mistake that had caused it. He might want to deny it, he might wish to forget it, but the truth stood between them like a brick wall.

She tossed her watch on the dresser furiously. "The price for this lifestyle is very high, Jake. We live in a glass house. Our secrets are on display for the whole town to see. Besides, are you sure you want to talk to me about gossip and innuendo? A few quiet moments with my boss won't stir up anything like the fire storm your fourteen-year-old son has inspired."

Suddenly unutterably weary, he plowed a hand through his hair. "That's really what this is all about isn't it, Rachel? It's Michael."

In the act of taking off her skirt, she stopped. "Michael? You think it's about Michael? Well, congratulations! You're so perceptive. Every time I look at Michael, I can't help but be reminded of the night you cheated, Jake. Yet for the sake of appearances I've had to take him in, pretend to those . . . those people that I don't care that my husband was unfaithful, that he took our marriage vows and trampled them into the ground. Even if it was only one night, it was still a vile, dishonorable, rotten thing to do." She looked at him through a sheen of angry tears. "And I have a perfect right to feel this way. So if I agree to attend one of your stupid political rallies and just happen to run into Ron Campbell — or any other person on this planet I feel like talking to, privately or otherwise, that's what I'll do. Your approval means exactly nothing to me."

"So you're going to get back at me by indulging in a flirtation with Ron Campbell?"

She shrugged. "You more than flirted with that woman. Why shouldn't I try it?" It was a ridiculous thing to say, but in the heat of the moment she wasn't pulling any punches.

He was across the room in a heartbeat and caught her by both arms. "So help me, Rachel, if I thought you meant that, I'd personally tear that man limb from limb."

His face was so close to hers that their noses practically touched. She could smell his shaving cologne. Rachel's heart leaped wildly, beating in a crazy rhythm fueled by recklessness and anticipation.

She stared defiantly into his eyes. "Just think what that would do for your precious campaign, Jake."

"Careful, Rachel," he warned in a low, rough tone. "You're pushing."

Rachel knew she was pushing. Her heart was beating so hard she could almost feel the movement against the silk of her blouse. But something beyond her seemed to urge her on.

"What are you going to do, lock me up for the duration?"

A long moment passed. Jake stood unmoving. She felt the quiver of his hands as they fastened around her upper arms.

"I can hardly do that, as you well know. But I can do this."

He pulled her up against him and kissed her. Sealing her mouth with his.

For the first few seconds, Jake was conscious of nothing more than an overwhelming need to express his frustration. Then her warmth flooded his starved senses. It was heaven. Pure heaven. It was everything he'd been missing for weeks. Months. It was deliverance. It stole away his anger and replaced it with tenderness.

As they drew apart Jake saw a longing in his wife's eyes that hadn't been there for a long time.

A shrill sound shattered the moment.

Stunned, their chests rising and falling erratically, they stared at each other. "It's the boat alarm," Jake said, recovering first.

He kept his service revolver loaded and ready. Groping beneath the bed, he found it. Automatically, he checked it with a swift flick of the chamber, then headed for the bedroom door. "Wait here," he told Rachel before slipping silently from the room.

Standing where he'd left her, Rachel felt her heart racing as much from the kiss as from fear of an intruder. Because of Jake's job, they had a fairly sophisticated security system in place, and it wasn't unusual for an animal to trip the signal. And thank goodness for the stray dog, curious raccoon or little possum that had set it off this time! The alarm had kept her from going to bed with Jake. Another minute and it might have been too late.

She was stunned by her response, but now was not the time to examine why she was suddenly interested in her husband again.

Her mouth in a grim line, she pulled on a robe and left the bedroom. Michael's door was ajar, as usual. He never closed it entirely, and he never turned out the light in the aquarium at night. It was odd the noise of the alarm hadn't awakened him. Impulsively, she decided to check on him. She pushed the door fully open and stared in surprise at his empty bed. Where on earth —

The alarm ceased abruptly.

Frowning, she left the room and hurried to the den just in time to see Jake ushering Michael ahead of him through the patio door. Meeting her eyes, Michael looked embarrassed.

"What is it? What happened?" she demanded, transferring her attention to Jake.

"False alarm. It was Mike." He shook his head dismissively. "Everything's under control."

Michael gave her an apologetic look. "I'm sorry, Miss Rachel. I forgot about the security alarm. I left my new headphones in the boat when we docked this afternoon. It was real late when I remembered them and I didn't want to bother you. So since I knew where it was, I figured I wouldn't bother you. I hope you didn't freak out too much when the alarm went off."

"No." She gave a brief shake of her head. "We're used to it, actually. Dogs and cats are always tripping it."

Michael looked relieved. "Yeah. I mean, yes, ma'am. I bet they only do it once. It sure scared me."

"It is loud," she agreed, noting the way he refused to meet her eyes. She wondered how much of their fight he might have overheard. Had he come by their bedroom before he went out?

"But effective," Jake put in.

Michael rubbed his hand over his middle. "Man, when I saw you sprinting for the boathouse like that, I about died." He made a comical face. "I could see you had your gun and I just prayed you'd see it was me before you shot."

"There wasn't much doubt who the intruder was when I heard that yell," Jake drawled, affectionately hooking his arm around Michael's neck.

The boy accepted the rough caress ruefully. "I bet you'd yell, too, if somebody was heading straight at you with a loaded gun."

"You better believe it." Chuckling, Jake released him.

Rachel moved around them and secured the lock on the patio door. "It's late, Michael. You'd better get back to bed."

He gave her an anxious look. "I'm sure sorry about this," he said.

Rachel sensed that he was referring to more than the disturbance over the alarm. But it was Jake who replied. "Forget it, Mike," he said, still smiling. "In my line of work I'm used to being routed out of my house at all hours. Keeps me in practice." He gave the boy a gentle shove. "Good night, son. We'll see you in the morning."

"Okay. G'night." With one final look at Rachel, Michael went.

Jake's smile faded as he went to the wall and punched in the code that reset the security system. Rachel waited until he finished. When he turned, his features had the grim look he'd worn after Scotty disappeared. Until Michael came. She hadn't realized that until just now, and she felt regret and sadness that it had returned.

"He heard us, you know," she said.

"Yes."

"I'm sorry."

He looked at her. "Are you, Rachel?"

"Of course. I'm not so unfeeling that I'd purposely hurt a child."

"Even my illegitimate child?" His tone was bitter.

She picked up a cushion from the couch. "Any child. I was angry . . . *am* angry over this whole situation, and I said some things I sincerely regret he overheard. It goes without saying that Michael is the innocent one in this. I'm sorry he's bound to be hurt because of a mistake you made fifteen years ago. I'll talk to him tomorrow."

After a moment when he didn't answer, she tossed the cushion aside. "It's late and I'm tired."

"Yeah."

She met his look defiantly, thinking of the heated moments they'd just spent. From the expression on Jake's face, she knew he was thinking the same thing.

She pulled the folds of her robe closely around her. "I'm going to my room now."

They both knew that Jake would not be going with her.

Jake glanced at his watch. Nine-thirty. He'd been at his desk for more than two hours without a break. He leaned most of his weight backward in his chair, stretching his cramped muscles. Tipping his head back and then forward, he rotated it a few times. Releasing a deep breath, he straightened up and reached for another file.

The place was quiet. Sundays usually were quiet in Tidewater. Only a skeleton crew was necessary to carry the administrative load. On the street, it was another story. There it was business as usual.

Concentration should have come easy. It was one of his strong points, the ability to focus his mind, to shut out everything but the task at hand. In his line of work, the ability to handle a weapon or subdue a suspect was important, but ninety-eight percent of a man's time was devoted to sheer drudgery, mountainous paperwork, wading through written testimony, analyzing case histories, studying the habits of suspects, looking for vital, often obscure clues that would pull everything together. Jake was good at it. Years ago, in the DEA, where he'd perfected his skills, he'd been known as the best.

Wearily he rubbed a hand over his face. This was the only way he knew to try to unravel the mystery of Scotty's kidnapping. Since it had happened, he'd spent his Sundays scrutinizing cases of known child molesters, analyzing recent arrests all over the United States, following up every lead, no matter how faint. He must have sifted through thousands of photographs of lost and missing kids. Even though he held the top job in Kinard County and could have delegated much of the detail, he didn't dare trust anyone else. Scotty's life was at stake.

His concentration wavered again. He shoved the file aside, but his features relaxed as he caught sight of Michael through the half-glass wall of his office. As usual, Michael was haunting the computer that linked Kinard County with nationwide law-enforcement offices.

Jake stretched in his chair, folding his arms behind his head. Since that first day when he had walked into Jake's domain, Mike had made no secret of the fact that he couldn't wait to be a cop. He had quickly grasped departmental routine and was computer literate within an amazingly short period of time, according to the deputy on Jake's staff who had coached him. At first Jake was amused — along with the rest of his staff. With all the other new experiences in his life, Jake figured Mike would soon find something more interesting than hanging around the sheriff's office, but it hadn't happened. Mike begged to come every chance he got. And whenever Jake could manage it, he allowed it. Sundays it was no problem.

He wished briefly for a cup of coffee, but it was probably so bitter and strong that it would react like battery acid on his stomach. Instead he relaxed a little lower on his spine and put his feet up on his desk. With his hands behind his head, he stared at the ceiling. This morning, for the first time in a long time, he had wanted to stay home. He thought of Rachel as she had looked last night. If that alarm hadn't gone off . . .

He still couldn't believe it. For months Rachel had been locked in some kind of emotional twilight zone where he was excluded, her gentleness and femininity locked away from both of them. They hadn't shared so much as a kiss on the cheek in months.

Raised voices in the outer office brought him upright in his chair. Through the glass, he saw a deputy enter the swinging doors with a handcuffed prisoner in tow. Jake got to his feet, automatically assessing the individual as he went out to the main desk. Young, male, a juvenile, fifteen, sixteen — no more — good clothes, surly expression. Jake drew in a deep breath, heading for the front desk. At least the boy wasn't another runaway.

"What've you got, Dempsey?"

"Morning, Sheriff." Keeping one hand on the youth's shoulder, the deputy tossed a plastic bag on the counter. "Possession and DUI. Stopped him out on Deer Creek near the approach to the interstate. He was all over the road. Lucky he didn't get on I-75.

He coulda killed somebody."

Jake lifted the plastic bag and briefly studied the contents. With a noncommittal grunt, he tossed it to the desk sergeant, who had produced a large brown envelope used to hold evidence. At a look from Jake, the deputy released the boy.

"What's your name, son?"

His head down, the boy mumbled something inaudible.

Deputy Dempsey let out a long sigh. "Speak up when the sheriff asks you a question, boy."

"James."

"James who?" Dempsey said, fast losing patience. "This isn't kindergarten you're visiting, James. You're in trouble, boy. You —"

At a look from Jake, the deputy backed off.

"You live around here, James?" Jake asked, signaling Dempsey to remove the handcuffs.

"Yes, sir." Looking dazed and a little sick, James rubbed at his freed wrists with his fingers. "Fifty-six twenty Brightside. It's in Meadowcrest." He sent Jake an anxious look. "Are you gonna call my dad?"

Meadowcrest was one of Tidewater's better neighborhoods. "It's the law, James. Do your folks know you use?"

164

"I don't think so."

"Well, they will now, kid. Come on, right through these doors." Dempsey grasped his shoulder and nudged him toward the swinging doors. An hour or two in central lockup would probably be more of a deterrent than any lecture. "You know what I hate, boy?" James's reply was indistinct. "Paperwork, that's what. And because of you, I got to do some. I don't like to spend my Sundays doing paperwork, but that's what happens when a kid does something dumb like fooling around with an illegal substance and then acting even dumber by getting behind the wheel of a vehicle. Your daddy's gonna be mad, boy. Let's hope he's a man of patience."

Dempsey's words faded as the doors swung closed with a whoosh. Jake stood a minute, looking troubled as he watched them through the tall, narrow windows in the doors.

"Moody."

Jake glanced at Michael, who was standing at his elbow. "What?"

"His name's James Moody. I've seen him around at school." He looked at Jake. "What'll happen to him, Dad?"

Jake dropped a hand to Michael's shoulder and they walked toward his office. "First of

165

all, he'll be turned over to Jacky Kendall in Juvenile. She'll call his parents, of course. I hope they'll recognize the problem and care enough about their son to want to know what they can do to help. If they listen to our people — the ones whose job it is to deal with this kind of thing — with luck we'll never see James Moody again."

Michael nodded, walking along with his eyes on his feet.

"You say you know James?"

"I don't know him. I just recognize him from school. Anybody would."

"Recognize him, you mean?" When Mike nodded, he went on. "Big name on campus, hmm?"

Mike shrugged. "He's got a hot car and there're always a bunch of people hanging around him."

"Girls, too?"

"Yeah. Yes, sir. Mostly girls."

Jake looked at him, amusement in his eyes. "Amazing what a hot car can do."

"I guess." Michael turned and stared thoughtfully at the swinging doors. "But he didn't look too cool wearing those handcuffs and kinda green around the gills like he was ready to barf all over everything, did he?"

Jake laughed. "No, son, he sure didn't." And simply because he couldn't resist, he clamped an arm around Mike's neck and ruffled his kid's hair. Mike probably thought he was too old for hugging, but if he was going to say things that made his old man proud of him, he'd just have to take it.

"Don't you ever take a day off, Jake?"

Jake looked up and accepted the cup of coffee Jacky Kendall pushed across his desk. Kinard County's petite juvenile officer looked a lot like a juvenile herself in her jeans and T-shirt. Her short red hair was a curly mop that defied any attempts to tame it. Her appearance was deceptive. When the occasion demanded it — and with juveniles, it often did — Jacky could be tough as old boots.

"Thanks." Jake tasted the coffee, then made a face when he realized it was from the pot he'd made when he arrived more than three hours ago. "Am I the only one who knows how to make coffee around here?" he grumbled.

She sat down, curling one of her legs beneath her. "No, you're just the only one who makes it on Sunday."

He grunted, drinking it anyway.

"Here's an idea. Since Michael seems to accompany you every Sunday, maybe he'd be willing to take the coffee detail."

Smiling faintly, Jake looked at Michael in the outer office. He was standing over the fax machine waiting for a photo transmission on a suspect. "I wouldn't count on it. First I'd have to pry him away from the front desk."

Jacky grinned. "I noticed. He monitors every call. If I ever saw a rookie in the making, Michael's it."

"You think so?" Jake said, his eyes still resting fondly on Michael. He felt a rush of fatherly pride.

"I think so," Jacky said, smiling. "He certainly has a super role model. Which is more than I can say for most of the kids I see."

"You here about the Moody kid?"

"James. Yeah. His father's Jay Moody. I just had the pleasure of a twenty-minute interview."

"The Reverend Jay Moody." Jake leaned back deep in his chair. "I didn't make the connection. How'd he take it?"

"Not well. If James hadn't been barfing up his socks in the toilet, I wonder if I could have convinced him."

Jake looked confounded. "Isn't a preacher's kid supposed to be at church on Sunday morning?"

"That's where his dad thought he was,"

she returned dryly. "After he'd cooled down, the reverend admitted James has been cutting Sunday school frequently. They had words over it even though James was sick as a dog."

"They say it's tough being a preacher's kid."

"It's tough being any kind of kid these days," Jacky countered. "But it's still no excuse to get high and then try to drive."

"What did he take?"

"I'm not certain. Dempsey found a couple of capsules in his car. Designer stuff. More than likely that's what brought on the nausea."

Jake got suddenly to his feet. "Where are they getting this stuff! Did you talk to him?"

Jacky shook her head. "It wouldn't have done any good, Jake. Not the shape he was in. He's at Tidewater General right now. We'll handle it as soon as he's able." She stood up. "We might get some repercussions from this. The reverend didn't pull any punches. He claimed it was our responsibility to see that the kids didn't have access to this stuff. He sent you a message."

Jake held her gaze, waiting.

"He said he wasn't going to hesitate to use his pulpit to let people know that unless they see some progress being made to apprehend the people who are dumping this stuff in our town, then maybe we need a new sheriff."

"I want to talk to you, Michael."

"Yes, ma'am."

Here it comes. Michael hitched his gym bag closer to his middle and gave Rachel a quick, wary look. He would probably have the granddaddy of all stomachaches before this ride was over.

He kept his eyes glued straight ahead, nothing on his face giving away his thoughts. As they pulled away from the school, a couple of the guys he'd made friends with waved, but he didn't notice. He'd worried for two days over what he'd overheard Jake and Rachel fighting about, but he hadn't been able to come up with what they might do about it. Only thing he could figure would be to farm him out with a foster family, but somehow he didn't see Jake doing that. Miss Rachel, now . . . She was one tough lady. She just might be that fed up with him. Truth was, he hadn't realized how much of a pain he was to her until he'd overheard her words on Saturday night.

He realized he'd missed some of what she was saying. He pulled himself up to listen.

". . . and sometimes even adults get car-

170

ried away and say things they don't mean."

It was pretty stupid of him not to catch on before now, he decided, staring at a red light. These people really didn't have much reason for wanting him dumped on them. Especially Miss Rachel. Even a dweeb would have caught on before now. The only excuse he had was that he'd been so blinded by the idea of having a real mom and dad. And so dazzled by all the *things* these people had.

"Michael? Are you listening?"

"Yes, ma'am."

Traffic was always heavy when school got out. Rachel kept her eyes on the road. "I thought if you were willing, we'd both just start all over," she said. "Sort of wipe the slate clean and begin again."

"Huh?" He couldn't believe it. Was he going to get to stay?

She gave him a quick look. "I was saying that I regret what you overheard on Saturday night. The argument Jake and I were having wasn't really about you, Michael."

"You said it was."

"I know. I'm sorry I said that. I've had some time to think it over, and I was wrong. I'm angry with Jake. And hurt. You can understand that, can't you? I'm hurt because he turned to another woman, your mother, when we . . . he and I were going through a rocky time in our marriage."

"Are you going to get a divorce?"

She drew in a quick breath. "That's between Jake and me, Michael. It really doesn't concern you."

Michael wondered if she really believed that. If she walked out on Jake, it would be the end of their happy home. It would be the end of his hopes and dreams. Would Jake still care about him if he caused Miss Rachel to walk out?

"Michael?" She stopped at the last red light before their street and looked at him. "Do you think we could begin again? Put the words you overheard behind us and work on being friends again?"

"Yes, ma'am." He nodded, relaxing his hold on his gym bag, and managed a smile. No disaster had happened today. If she wanted to be friends, he guessed he'd have to settle for that. She'd probably freak out if he told her what he really wanted. They pulled into the driveway and he let his gaze linger on the house. He let out a soft sigh. What he really wanted more than almost anything was for Miss Rachel to be his mother.

CHAPTER EIGHT

On Monday morning, Jake had a message waiting for him from Rick Streeter with the DEA in Miami. According to Rick, the rumblings of a major drug connection along the Gulf Coast had materialized into solid evidence. A task force out of Miami was heading for Tidewater, and Jake's department, as well as the city police department, would be expected to cooperate.

"This is all we need," Frank Cordoba grumbled, scanning the notes Jake had taken while listening to Rick. "The county'll be crawling with Feds. If they'd pass this information on to us, we could work up some kind of plan. We know our own territory, they don't."

"We both know that's not the way they do business," Jake said, settling into his chair after helping himself to coffee.

"Yeah, well, if the plan should happen to come together successfully, you can bet they'll take the credit. Us local types will be tossed a token word of thanks, no matter how significant a part we play. You know the drill, Jake. Hell, you used to be one of those guys."

Jake laughed ruefully. "Don't remind me." He gazed thoughtfully beyond Frank to a wall map of the entire county. After a moment, he said, "We're not without a few options ourselves."

Frank looked interested. "Such as?"

"Look here." Jake got up and went to the map. "We know the drugs are getting into the county somehow. So far, they've surfaced mostly in the hands of juveniles . . . here —" he touched the site of Tidewater High School "— and here —" the middle school "— and here." The Burger Barn, popular hangout for teens. "Why is that, Frank? Why haven't we had more incidents with the adult population? Is that just a fluke or is there a reason?" He tossed a folder aside. "I'm assigning a couple of men to keep close watch at the high school and middle school. Call Jacky. Tell her I personally want to question every kid who comes to her if she suspects a drug connection."

He went to his desk. "What about the preacher's kid — Moody?"

"We tried, but I don't think we're going

to get anything from James. He got his stuff from a friend of a friend of a friend. By the time we ran through all his friends there was so much hearsay we couldn't be sure if we were getting truth or fiction. The kids might have been stonewalling, but I don't think so. Whoever's dealing doesn't seem to have much organization."

"Organization or not, he's still putting dangerous stuff in the hands of kids."

Frank finished his coffee. "I hear you."

"If I read Brother Moody right yesterday, we aren't going to get much cooperation there. He's focusing more on calling attention to the shortcomings of my office than he is on helping us."

"Way I see it, there's an up side to that," Frank drawled, getting to his feet.

"Yeah? I'd be interested to hear it."

"Simple. There're two law-enforcement agencies in Tidewater: city and county. As the sheriff, you have to take the heat for the county. But there's a lot more drug trafficking inside the city limits, and that responsibility rests squarely on your challenger's shoulders. So, as much as J. B. Gonzales would like to dump this all on you, Jake, he's not gonna be able to weasel out of it."

After Frank left, Jake stared hard at the map of Kinard County, filled with frustration and tension. It wasn't just the job or his reelection, it wasn't even the creeping influx of drugs into his territory that threatened to defeat him. What ate at him went deeper than that. He could handle the mounting problems in Kinard County a lot better if things were right in his family. If he didn't find Scotty, would he lose Rachel, too?

The ding of a microwave sounded somewhere in the building, followed immediately by the smell of food. It was lunchtime. Although he wasn't particularly hungry, he needed to get out of the office.

In the act of locking away the material on his desk, he glanced at the phone. What he'd really like would be to go home and have lunch with Rachel. That was what he'd really like. In fact . . . Just as he reached for the phone, it rang. Grabbing it, he barked his name into the receiver.

"Jake? You sound busy. Sorry. It's Rachel."

"No. I'm . . ." He sank into his chair and swiveled so that he could see outside. The frown on his face vanished. He could feel his frustration easing. "Hi, honey. I was just thinking about you."

"Oh? Well, I hate to bother you th—"

"You never bother me, Rachel. I always have time for my wife."

"This won't take long. I —"

"How's it going this morning at Tidewater General? Got your finger on the pulse of things?"

"Jake —"

He chuckled. "A little medical humor there, darlin'." He squinted through the window, trying to tell whether it was drizzling rain or just dingy panes. "Have you had lunch yet?"

"No, but —"

"How about having it with me? We could try Santini's. We haven't been there in a long time."

"I don't think so, Jake."

"Campbell does give you time to eat, doesn't he?" Jake turned away from the view. The frown was back.

"Jake . . ."

He heard the exasperation in her voice and cursed himself. Bad-mouthing Campbell was hardly the way to talk her into going anywhere with him. He swallowed the jealousy that made his fingers tighten on the phone and spoke softly. "Sorry, honey. I'm having a downer of a day. However, daydreaming about my beautiful wife keeps me up."

There was a moment's silence, then she chuckled.

Jake closed his eyes, savoring the sound of Rachel's laugh. Idly, he polished his wedding ring along the top of his thigh. "If you can't have lunch with me, then what can I do for you?"

"Michael just called from school. They're out early and he forgot to tell me this morning. I can't get away right now to pick him up, and I thought maybe you could send over a squad car or something. That is, if you can't pick him up yourself."

"No problem." He stood up. "I won't have to eat alone after all. We'll grab something at the Burger Barn and then I'll drop him off at the house."

"Thanks. Tell him I'll be home around three-thirty, as usual."

"Got it."

"Well . . . bye."

He kissed her through the wire. "Bye, sweetheart."

Rachel replaced the receiver, feeling shaky and oddly flustered. She had always reacted to Jake's voice. When he used that deep, quiet tone, it was like a caress.

"Hey, pretty lady."

"Ron! Ah, hello."

Ron gave her a smile that hinted of a familiarity between them that made Rachel slightly wary. He swept a look over her neat desk and tidy work area. "Hmm. It looks as though you have things under control here."

"Don't judge my efficiency by the way things look. You should see my In basket."

He moved around so he stood at her shoulder, crowding her into the L of her work area. "Where is it?"

"Hidden," she said. "I keep it in this drawer." She pulled at a drawer that was blocked by his body so that he had to shift away from her.

"I'm sure you'll handle it with your usual aplomb." With that, he relaxed against the edge of her desk, crossing his ankles. "Helen Falco can't say enough about the way you've settled in here."

"Oh. That's nice to hear." She laughed ruefully. "There were a few times when I wondered if I should have remained a volunteer."

"Don't even think it." He reached over and patted her hand. "It was our lucky day when you decided to take a real job." He stood up briskly. "So, have you had lunch yet?"

"No. I'd planned to work through my lunch hour. I really am swamped, Ron. I brought some yogurt and an apple. I can manage on that."

"We'll just be in the cafeteria. A quick tray won't take much longer." He lifted one eyebrow. "All work and no play . . . as they say."

"I shouldn't . . ." She looked at the stack of insurance forms.

"Actually, you could consider it a working lunch," he said, catching her by the elbow and gently pulling her to her feet. "There's something I wanted to discuss with you."

She reached for her purse. "Well, I suppose a few minutes won't make much difference."

"Hardly." His hand remained at her waist even after they reached the elevator. Feeling decidedly uncomfortable, Rachel stared hard at the call button. Finally, using it as an excuse to free herself, she took a step away from Ron and jiggled it.

"This thing is so slow sometimes."

"You look delicious in that pink outfit."

Delicious? Rachel felt the blush that rose from her neck. Her heart began to pound with a sense of danger, but while she was trying to decide what to do, there was a ping overhead and the elevator door slid open. With his hand once more at the small of her back, Ron ushered her inside.

The cafeteria was packed with the usual lunch-hour crowd. Rachel selected a salad and a hard roll, and after a small skirmish with Ron over who would pay — which he won — she followed him through the tables to the single remaining booth.

"What was it you wanted to discuss, Ron?" she asked as soon as they were seated.

He leaned back, studying her silently for so long that she felt heat bloom in her cheeks again. What was he doing? Suddenly Jake's suspicions didn't seem so farfetched. Her hands not quite steady, she broke the crusty roll in half. Crumbs flew everywhere — into her salad, onto the table, into her lap.

"Look at me," she murmured, brushing at them clumsily. Was this the way affairs began? If so, she would never manage to have one. She was just too . . . too . . .

"I am looking and I like what I see."

Her gaze flew to his. "Ron, I don't think —"

He reached for her hand. "Am I going too fast?" He squeezed her fingers. "Okay. No problem." He reached for his napkin and spread it on his lap. "So, on to business. How do you feel about coming to work as my assistant?"

She looked at him in amazement.

He grinned. "What?"

"I'm just . . . surprised."

"What's so surprising about my wanting to grab you before somebody else does? You're wasted in Emergency. You've organized the paperwork, reduced the drag time between insurance claims dramatically, charmed the housekeeping people into making the place neater and cleaner than it's ever been and acted as resident psychologist for the freaked-out cases who wander in from the streets. Call me selfish, but when I see someone with that kind of talent, I want that person at work where the hospital benefits most."

Rachel stared at her untasted salad. Her heart soared. She'd been working at a real job only a few weeks and here was proof that she could handle it, that she was *good* at it. That she was able to do more than just manage a house and cater to the whims of a husband. An unfaithful husband.

"Well?"

She looked up. "I'm flattered, Ron. Thank you. But I'm not so sure your confidence is warranted. I might not do as well in the business office of the hospital as I do in Emergency."

"Trust me, you'd be great. You'd be perfect. We'd make a dynamite team."

She laughed, shaking her head. "No, what I mean is that I like it in the emergency room. I like the . . . drama, I guess. We never know who's going to come in. We never know what's going to happen." She shrugged.

"I'd pay you big money."

"That's not it." Still smiling, she glanced beyond Ron to the entrance of the cafeteria. The crowd had doubled since they came in, and now the line reached almost to the exit. Her eyes traveled idly over those waiting and her heart gave a little jolt. Jake was standing there watching her. Ignoring the ebb and flow of the crowd, he seemed carved in stone. A few people spoke, but, grim-faced, he acknowledged no one. After another moment or two, he turned on his heel and left.

Rachel worked late. The insurance forms were finished and every patient waiting for treatment processed before she finally called it a day. It wasn't her nature to allow paperwork to pile up, she told herself. So when the woman arrived to relieve her, she'd shifted to another workstation and used the opportunity to catch up.

In the car, she glanced at the time and realized dinner would be late unless she picked up fast food. It took another thirty minutes to do that. The smell of fried chicken made her realize how hungry she was. At lunch, she'd barely swallowed six bites.

Lunch. There was no reason for her to feel guilty, she told herself, pulling into traffic. She had been having lunch with a man, true, but it was business. Jake had over-reacted.

She turned into the driveway of her house a little too fast. The problem with Jake was that he overreacted a lot lately. She had been such a pansy most of their married life that now she was getting a life of her own he was clinging to old habits with a vengeance. She shivered, recalling the look in his eye as he'd stood in the doorway of the cafeteria. Jake had never looked at her quite like that.

She caught up her purse and the box of chicken and opened the car door. Michael appeared instantly from the vicinity of the backyard, a stranger at his heels. Frowning, she closed the door and waited as they headed toward her.

"Hi, Miss Rachel. Sorry about the mix-up in transportation today. Dad picked me up." He glanced at his companion. "Us, I mean. This is Todd Stewart."

"Hi."

Michael and his friend were about the

184

same age and size, but all similarity ended there. Todd Stewart wore a single earring, the proper accessory for his long punk-style hair, she assumed. His sneakers looked ludicrously oversize with his baggy pants. She blinked at the wild print — a dizzying pattern of black, neon orange and green on a white background. Compared with his pants, the black cutoff T-shirt — featuring a picture of Sid Vicious — was hardly out of the ordinary. Rachel tried to hide her dismay as he stuck out his hand.

She took it. "Uh, hi, Todd." His earring was actually a skull and crossbones!

"I showed Todd the boat and everything," Michael volunteered.

"Wow, man. I mean, radical. *It's radical.*"

"Yes." She cleared her throat. "You're at THS, Todd?"

"Yeah. I mean, I've been at a few other schools, but I'm at Tidewater right now."

She glanced quickly at Michael, then back to Todd. "A few other schools?" she echoed faintly.

He shrugged. "State stuff, mostly."

He was a ward of the state. Until her job at the hospital, Rachel had known precious little about Florida's methods of handling disadvantaged children. She looked again at Michael. She supposed his own predica-

185

ment made him sympathetic to boys such as Todd. She was saved from having to make further small talk by the sound of the front door opening.

"Hi, Dad." Michael grinned at Jake, who was standing in the doorway. "We checked out the boat and I secured everything like you said."

"Fine. Why don't you and Todd go heat up the grill? We'll have some barbecued chicken."

"No need," Rachel said, holding up the box. "I stopped and got fried chicken."

"Is it enough for one extra?" Michael wanted to know.

"There's enough for an army. Grab paper plates and we'll set up on the patio outside."

"Hey, all right! C'mon, Todd. I'm starved!"

"Go ahead. Get it off your chest." Rachel set the box of chicken down hard on the counter and tossed her purse in the vicinity of a chair. It missed and landed on the floor, but neither she nor Jake noticed.

His expression tight, Jake looked out the window to the patio where Michael and Todd were setting the table as instructed. "It'll wait."

"I don't think so." Rachel ripped the box

open and dumped the contents into a huge plastic bowl. Turning, she almost bumped into Jake as he reached over her head for glasses. "Were you checking on me today?" she demanded.

He lowered his arm slowly, holding her gaze. "We'll talk later, Rachel," he said, each word evenly spaced.

"I refuse to be treated like a . . . a naughty teenager. How do you think I felt looking up and finding you blocking traffic at the cafeteria door and staring a hole through me like that?"

"I give up, Rachel," he said with heavy sarcasm. "How did you feel? Guilty? Caught in the act?"

"In the act of what? Having lunch?"

"Which you were too busy to have with me!"

"Oh, this is so stupid! Every time —"

The patio door flew open. Michael stuck his head in. "Dad, the table's all set. Where's the chicken?"

"Coming, Mike." Jake yanked open a drawer and began rooting around for something.

"What are you looking for?" Rachel asked through clenched teeth, keeping her voice down.

"Tongs," he snapped, his tone low. Dangerously low.

"Here they are." She thrust them at him. He took them and kept on rooting through the drawer. "Now what?" she said.

"Plastic forks."

"Right here." She shoved them at him.

"Things are never where they're supposed to be around here anymore," he complained.

"Things are exactly where they're supposed to be," she countered instantly. "Besides, how would you know where they're supposed to be? You're hardly handy in the kitchen."

"What's that supposed to mean?"

"Just that you've never bothered to familiarize yourself with the kitchen before."

"Oh, so now I'm a dyed-in-the-wool sexist, right?"

"If the shoe fits . . ."

He glared at her.

"Anyway, we don't need forks. I only bought chicken and corn on the cob."

"I made baked beans."

Her mouth fell open.

"Michael had a guest. His first guest. Since you didn't bother calling, I didn't know whether or not you'd show up at all."

The patio door opened again and Michael yelled, "Hey, can we help? We're about to starve out here."

"We're on our way," Jake told him, his gray eyes locked with Rachel's stormy ones.

Her hands went to her hips. "I have never, *never* neglected my responsibilities around here."

"Which means exactly nothing," he answered angrily. "You're doing a lot of things you've never done before."

"Well, failing to get dinner for my family isn't one of them!"

"I thought maybe you'd skip dinner since lunch was so divine."

"What is that supposed to mean?"

"You couldn't tear yourself away from your job to have lunch with me, but for Campbell suddenly you weren't too busy. What was I supposed to think?"

"I'll tell you what you're supposed to think. You're not supposed to think lunch with my boss is anything except business as usual."

They had reached the door. As Rachel balanced the chicken in one hand and tried to open it, Jake stopped her. "Why not, Rachel? Have you given me any reason lately to think that you still care about our marriage? About me? Until Campbell offered you that job, you seemed only half-alive. How do you think it makes me feel to see you smiling at another man when you never smile at me?"

Rachel stared wordlessly into his eyes. What could she say? A lot of what he said was true. Sometimes she wasn't certain there was anything left between them worth saving.

Movement behind the French door distracted them. Michael again. She sighed. "You're right, Jake. Now is not the time to discuss this. Mike and his friend are starving. We'll talk later."

If Michael and Todd noticed the strained silence between Rachel and Jake, they ignored it. Truthfully, mealtime under less-than-cheery conditions was probably nothing new to Todd. He kept them entertained with a string of vivid recollections of his many foster homes. Rachel was shocked by his treatment at the hands of the state of Florida. From the way he talked, he'd been shunted around like an unwanted puppy. He didn't seem to have a particularly rebellious or incorrigible nature. Surely there could have been a more stable way to manage his case.

She murmured something sympathetic.

"It's nobody's fault, Miss Rachel," he said, addressing her the same way Michael did. He hesitated, finishing up a piece of corn.

"Well, I guess it is somebody's fault. I'm just not sure whose. Every now and then my mother comes back, and when she does, I go live with her. She never stays more than a few months, though."

"Your mother? But where is she now?"

He shrugged and reached for another drumstick. "I don't know. Vegas, I think. She disappeared again about three months ago."

Rachel met Jake's eyes briefly in confusion. "Does she write? Or call you?"

Todd laughed. "Nah. I think she likes to forget about me while she's on her trips." The way he said "trips" did not conjure up scenes of luxury vacations. His mother's neglect was more than shocking. It was criminal. Cruel. Why would a mother throw away a child? Was she an alcoholic or addicted to drugs? Rachel studied Todd's outrageous haircut and bizarre earring and wondered at the psychological statement he was making. What kind of future would he have with so little parental nurturing?

Her eyes strayed to Scotty's swing set in the rear of the yard, standing empty and still in the waning light, and her heart twisted painfully.

What kind of God gives an uncaring woman like that a child and then takes my child away?

Inside the house, the telephone rang.

"I'll get it," Rachel said, glad to escape.

It was Jake's office. She motioned to him through the French doors and went to the sink to make fresh coffee while he talked. She paid little attention until he mentioned the date in February that Scotty had disappeared. Her heart began to beat faster. She turned from the sink, the coffee forgotten.

Jake's questions were short and terse, unrevealing, she realized. Was this something she wasn't supposed to hear?

"Did they fax the picture?" He scribbled something on the scratch pad by the phone.

"Are you sure?" He waited, listening intently.

"What about eye color?" After a second's hesitation, he tossed the pen aside. Pinching the bridge of his nose, he gazed at his feet. "Yeah." Another wait. "Yeah, I know." Another moment. "Right, right."

With a flurry of laughter and talk and good-natured scuffling, the doors opened, and Michael and Todd came inside, each carrying litter from the impromptu meal. "Hey, keep it down," Michael said, realizing Jake was on the phone. "My dad's talking. It's probably police business."

With his gaze fixed on the floor, Jake was

still listening. "Did Phoenix PD have any-thing else?"

Michael, in the act of dumping paper plates in the trash, looked at Jake with an alert expression.

"What's up, man?" Todd asked, sensing the tension in the room. He looked from Jake to Michael to Rachel and back to Michael.

"Nothing. Like I said, police business." Michael gave him a playful shove toward the den. "It's getting late, buddy. Remember curfew? You'd better be hittin' the road."

"Right. I better split." Todd, halfway through the den on his way to the front door, stopped suddenly. "Hey, thanks for the chicken and stuff, Miss Rachel. And nice meetin' you."

"You're welcome. Nice meeting you, too." Rachel smiled and waved distractedly, aware that Jake had lowered his voice so that she could not overhear his conversation. She had a sick feeling in the pit of her stomach. She had heard the word *hospital.* When she reached for a dish towel, her hands were shaking.

With a grim expression, Jake replaced the receiver.

"Was that about Scotty?" Rachel asked.

Deep in thought, he missed her anxiety. "No."

"Then was it about another missing child?"

"I'm sorry, Rachel. I shouldn't have taken the call in here. It's nothing to concern you."

"Stop it! Just don't do that to me."

He finally sensed her agitation. "What? Do what?"

"Don't patronize me, Jake. Don't treat me like a little girl who can't be told the ugly truth. I know that wasn't a routine call. It had something to do with Scotty. I know it did. I want the truth."

He drew in a weary breath. "It wasn't about Scotty. At least, not in the way you imagine. Today we got a missing-child bulletin on the wire from the police department in Phoenix, Arizona. The physical description of the boy matched with Scotty's. I've been waiting to hear from my people whether or not it could possibly be him."

"Dear God," she whispered, sitting down gently.

"Rachel, Rachel . . . I'm sorry, it wasn't Scotty." Jake pulled out a chair and sat in front of her, catching both her hands in his. She was as cold as marble. "He was too old, about eight. It was a parental custody thing.

194

The father had been denied custody and had taken him in California. He was headed east when they were apprehended."

She was shaking her head. "No. I heard something about a hospital. 'Touch and go,' you said. Is the boy hurt?"

He brought her hands to his chest and chafed them gently, trying to infuse some of his warmth into her. "Not hurt, exactly, but he's a diabetic, and apparently the father neglected the boy's medication. He's in a hospital but expected to recover."

"Oh."

"So this is one with a happy ending," Jake said.

Yes. Lucky, lucky mother. Despair, disappointment, renewed grief, all washed through her. She began to cry, silent, soul-deep tears that bathed her cheeks.

Jake watched helplessly, feeling her pain as though it was his own. It *was* his own. In this one thing, the loss of their child, they were united. With a groan, he stood up and, pulling her close, wrapped his arms around her.

With her hands curled in despair against Jake's chest, Rachel sobbed bitterly. She cursed fate and the circumstances that had put Scotty in the path of a madman. With her face buried in his shirtfront, she mourned the little boy she adored, railed against the injustice of having him torn from her.

In her ear, Jake whispered endearments, reassurance, desperately searching for anything that might take away some of her pain. Forgotten by both were the angry words they'd hurled at each other only minutes before. Rachel clung to him, let herself lean on his rock-solid strength. It seemed like forever since she'd felt supported by Jake's warmth and tough-tender masculinity.

"I'm okay now," she said, making no effort to move, her head still nestled beneath his chin.

Jake stroked her back slowly, lazily. "Sure?"

She sniffed and nodded, but still stayed put.

One of his hands found its way into her hair, tangling at her nape. "This feels good, doesn't it? You and me close, the way it ought to be."

It did. It was. Where had they gone astray? She rubbed her cheek against his shirt. He smelled like soap and warm male. "I'm sorry I fell apart. I was just so disappointed. It was the first time we'd even had a hint of a lead and . . ."

He was so still she felt every beat of his

heart. "Jake?"

"Yeah?"

"It *was* the first lead, wasn't it?"

"It wasn't a lead, Rachel. It was a routine bulletin."

She pushed away from him. "It was enough for your office to call you when they knew for certain it wasn't Scotty. You must have left that order. You must have thought it could possibly be important."

He released a long breath. "Rachel —"

"How many other times has this happened, Jake?"

"Never. Nothing has ever surfaced that I considered strong enough to —"

"I don't care how strong a lead you get, Jake!" Her hands curled at her sides. "I want to know the smallest hint of a lead that might affect my son. You have no right to withhold anything from me that pertains to Scotty."

"I'm not withholding anything, Rachel. I just want to protect you from unnecessary pain. Look how upset you became just now."

Neither Jake nor Rachel had noticed Michael's return to the kitchen. "The lead from Phoenix didn't pan out, huh, Dad?"

"No, Mike."

Rachel looked startled. Even Michael knew more than she.

"Was the little kid somebody?"

Jake raked a hand through his hair, looking uncomfortable with Michael's questions. "You mean, was he a missing child?" Michael nodded. "Yeah, he was."

"Was he made by a cop?" Michael asked.

Any other time, Michael's use of police jargon amused Jake, but at the moment, his attention was on Rachel. He sensed her mounting fury. "As a matter of fact, he was," Jake said. "A sharp-eyed rookie ID'd him."

"All right!"

A flicker of amusement softened Jake's features for a second or two. "Hooray for the good guys, right?"

"You bet, Dad."

Jake glanced outside. "Did you and Todd clean up the patio area?"

"Yes, sir."

"All the trash bagged and put away?"

"Yes, sir."

"Good." He sent Rachel a quick look. "My . . . uh, Rachel and I have something we need to discuss, Mike. How about you take a quick hike, okay?"

"Sure thing, Dad. I'll just do some laps in the pool." Although he smiled, he looked anxious, as though picking up on the tension between them. "Don't worry, Miss Rachel. I know Dad's gonna find Scotty."

Rachel nodded, unable to speak.

Michael left, closing the French doors quietly behind him.

CHAPTER NINE

"Even Michael knows more than me," Rachel said coldly. "How could you, Jake?"

"Michael only knows what he picks up at the office," Jake said, shoving his hands deep into his pockets. "He's like a sponge. He loves everything about law enforcement, and he's especially interested in the search for Scotty."

"I'm especially interested in the search for Scotty, too! Why is it okay for Michael to know what's going on, but not me?"

After a quick look at her, Jake turned away, but he could still see her tearstained face and trembling mouth. "Because I love you and I don't want you to have to bear any more!" he whispered fiercely. "Is that so wrong?"

"Yes, it is," she said quietly, without emotion. "It's wrong for you to try to insulate me from the ups and downs of the search for Scotty, and it's wrong for me to allow it." She drew a deep breath. "I want your word that you'll tell me everything from now on, Jake. Everything."

He hesitated, but then said, "All right."

"Your word, Jake."

He slammed his palm on the countertop. "I said I would." His mouth grim, he reached for the notes he'd made from the phone call and stuck them in his shirt pocket. "I've got to get back to the office."

She frowned. "Why? What is it?"

"It's not about Scotty." He gave her a straight look, a look that dared her to challenge him. "Do you think you can bring yourself to believe that?"

She nodded reluctantly. Without another word, he left.

Rachel stood very still, hearing the echo of the front door as Jake slammed it on his way out. He had no right to be angry with her. She was the one who should be angry. And she was. She wasn't making unreasonable demands. What was unreasonable was Jake's chauvinistic need to run interference for her. Silently fuming, she gazed around her perfectly decorated kitchen. What kind of relationship did they have if he continually patronized her? More important, why did he do that? What was it about her that made him believe she was too fragile to bear the harsh realities of life? Without realizing it, had she given off some unspoken message that she needed coddling, needed to be taken care of? He had more confidence in Michael — a fourteen-year-old boy — than in her, his wife of eighteen years! Had she handled the horror of Scotty's disappearance so poorly that Jake felt he could not risk telling her anything that didn't have a silver lining?

She stared at the pattern on the wallpaper, seeing nothing. How he must have quaked in his shoes when Michael showed up. He must have believed that the evidence of his indiscretion in Miami would send her around the bend. But he'd been wrong. She reached up to turn off the light above the sink. It had hurt, yes. It had been crushingly humiliating, but hadn't she borne it with as much grace as could be expected? Yes, she had. What did it take to convince him she didn't forever have to be held by the hand through life's dark moments?

"Miss Rachel?"

She blinked and turned to find Michael watching her anxiously. She had not heard him come inside. He was wet from his swim, his chest heaving with youthful male vitality. Water glistened on his long, lanky limbs. "Yes, Michael. What is it?"

"Are you okay, Miss Rachel?"

"I'm fine. Just fine." She rubbed her temples. Even Michael thought she was a fragile flower.

"Did Dad have to go back to work?"

"Yes. It was something to do with the phone call. Urgent, he said." She gave him a smile, an artificially bright smile. "I think I'll get ready for bed and then read awhile. I picked up a new book today. I'm looking forward to it."

"I think I'll wait up for Dad."

"You do that."

She was still mad the next day. Michael could tell. He'd been worried when he'd gotten out of school and she wasn't waiting for him. Miss Rachel was always on time, the most dependable person he'd ever known. It was one of the things he liked best about her. He liked a lot of things about Rachel, but he didn't think she noticed. She was too busy grieving for little Scotty and making life miserable for his dad.

He wasn't sure why he didn't get mad at Rachel for being that way with Jake, except that he understood misery pretty well himself. She'd lost her little boy and was tormented by not knowing how or why.

That alone was a rotten thing. Then her husband had cheated on her way back when, and the kid — he — had showed up on her doorstep in this small town and she had to be nice to him. She *was* nice, too. Down-deep nice, even though she could have been the original wicked stepmother if she'd wanted to. No, Miss Rachel wasn't the type to be mean to a kid. Even her husband's illegitimate son.

That made him even more worried that she wasn't here to pick him up today. He waited fifteen minutes and then started out jogging to the hospital. Maybe she'd had to work late or something. Maybe she'd forgotten him. Mama Dee had done that sometimes, but she was old and forgetful.

He spotted Rachel at her car as he was cutting through the parking lot. Just before calling out to her, he saw that somebody was with her.

Ron Campbell. That dude she worked for. Michael knew who he was, because after Rachel and Jake had that fight over him, he'd sneaked up to the hospital to get a look at him. He was an all-right-looking guy, but Jake had said it best. Something about Ron Campbell was sort of wimpy. He smiled too much. Michael twisted his mouth into a grimace. Mama Dee had always said never to trust a man who smiled too much.

He moved a little closer, just to check everything out, he told himself. He wasn't spying on Miss Rachel. It was more that he was curious to find out if Campbell was behaving himself around his stepmother. He hadn't forgotten Jake's remark that the man was coming on to Rachel.

"I can't believe I did this, Ron," he heard Rachel saying as he got close. "I've never locked the keys in my car. I feel like such an idiot."

Ron bent slightly, trying to wiggle a slim flexible steel tool between the glass and the door-frame. "Don't worry, we'll have it open before you know it. Fortunately the guard had this tool on hand. Apparently this happens in the parking lot frequently."

Rachel clutched the strap of her purse. "I really appreciate this. I called Jake, but he's not in his office. He has a spare key, but what good is it if I can't reach him?"

"The question's moot because we're going to take care of this little inconvenience in just a second or two," Ron said, beginning to perspire a little as he struggled to jimmy the lock.

Rachel looked on anxiously as another couple of minutes ticked by. "Maybe I should —"

"Wait a minute, wait a minute. I think I've got — Shoot! I felt it start to give, but something happened."

Rachel watched two more failed attempts, then said, "Ron, it's hot out here. Let's forget it. I'll call a locksmith."

At her words, he finally gave up the effort, still smiling amiably when he looked at her. "Well, it's probably best. I might ruin the whole locking system, and instead of thanking me, Jake will charge me with malicious intent."

"Don't be ridiculous."

He braced his arm casually on the roof of the car. "Why don't I just drive you home myself? I was just about to call it a day anyway."

"That's really not necessary. I'm sure —"

"It would be my pleasure. Matter of fact, we could stop at Kelly's and have a drink." He laughed softly, intimately. "After the hassle we went through today putting together the quarterly report, not to mention locking yourself out of your car, you deserve a crisp, frosty margarita. We both do. What do you say?"

"I have to —"

"You said it yourself, Rachel. It's hot." He reached for her purse. "Come on, my car's right over here." With his other hand, he took her arm, then slid his palm all the way down to lace her fingers with his.

That was when Michael made his move. He stepped from the shadow of a souped-up four-wheel drive. "Hi, Miss Rachel."

Campbell dropped Rachel's hand.

"Oh, Michael!" To her own ears, Rachel sounded flustered. Guilty. "How did you get here?"

"I jogged. It's only a few blocks."

She took her purse from Ron. "You haven't met Ron Campbell, have you?"

Michael gave him a look that, coming from an adult male, would have been a declaration of war. "No, ma'am."

"Ron Campbell, Jake's son, Michael."

Ron grinned engagingly. "Hiya, Mike."

Still unsmiling, Michael nodded once, briefly. "Mr. Campbell."

Neither made a move to shake hands. Rachel's agitation increased. "We have a problem, Michael. I've locked the keys in the car, and Jake's not in his office. Mr. Campbell was trying to jimmy the lock with this tool, but we weren't having much luck. It looks like —"

"I've got a key, Miss Rachel."

She paused, staring. "What?"

Michael fished in his pocket and came up with a key ring from which several keys dangled. He wiggled them in the air. "The house, the boat, both cars. Dad gave them to me in case of an emergency." His sudden grin was meant for Rachel and only Rachel. "I guess this is an emergency, huh?"

"Yes," Rachel said faintly. "I guess it is."

Stepping between Rachel and Ron, he inserted the key into the lock and opened the door with a flourish. Ron, standing too close, scrambled hastily out of the way.

"Lucky for us Dad thinks of things like this," Michael said, standing back while she eased into the driver's seat. He waited until she'd started the car before closing the door. Then, pocketing the spare key and standing guard with a protective hand on the door handle, he looked at Rachel's boss.

"I think everything's under control now, Mr. Campbell."

Ron shrugged. His smile, still in place, didn't quite reach his eyes. "Sure, kid. Okay."

Michael waited pointedly while Ron retreated a couple of feet and, unable to catch Rachel's eye, turned reluctantly and headed toward the entrance of the hospital.

For a few more seconds, Michael simply stood and watched. Then, with a careless tap of his hand on the top of the car, he loped around the front end and got in beside Rachel. He was looking straight ahead as they drove off. He didn't say anything, but he appeared satisfied. More than satisfied.

Rachel put the incident of the locked car out of her mind. She wasn't sure how much Michael had overheard, but she knew he'd heard enough to be suspicious of Ron. Oddly enough, it bothered her for Michael to see her in that light. She hadn't encouraged Ron, but a little voice in her head that was excruciatingly honest whispered that she hadn't discouraged him, either. The fact that thought of an affair had even crossed her mind seemed cheap and demeaning when seen through the eyes of a fourteen-year-old boy. Especially if that boy liked and respected you.

The feeling was mutual, Rachel discovered in the weeks that followed. Michael was very appealing. Sometimes she found it hard to remember the house without him in it. At times like that, she was swamped with guilt and confusion. How could she feel that way? Michael had only come to them after Scotty had been lost. But sometimes . . . sometimes when she heard Michael's laughter deep in the house or out on the patio or the pool, she almost lost the sense of pain and deprivation she carried in memory of Scotty.

Even if Scotty and Michael had been the same age, they were so different that comparisons were difficult. Scotty was bright and blond and rambunctious, swaggeringly confident as only a six-year-old child could be. Michael was more hesitant, more introverted and, yes, more sensitive to others' feelings. Kind and nonjudgmental, too. Those friends he brought home . . .

There had been several since Todd Stewart. With the end of the regular school year, Michael had enrolled in summer classes to make up the credits he'd lost when he'd left Des Moines. It seemed there was an unending stream of teenagers underfoot after school, misfit types for the most part, and Michael seemed to want to befriend them all. Not that Rachel had any serious objection to his generosity. It was just that her days seemed so different from the way they used to be. Other summers had been spent chauffeuring Scotty to swim lessons or chaperoning camp outs and trips to the zoo and museums, or any of a dozen other activities dreamed up to entertain the already overindulged children of herself and her friends. Observing the delight Michael's friends took in his upper-middle-class surroundings, Rachel was ashamed to admit how little she'd been aware of the number of needy kids in Tidewater. Until Michael came to live with her and Jake, it seemed she'd gone through her life with blinders on.

Looking out the kitchen window, she swallowed her dismay as Michael offered one of her very best guest bath sheets to a boy who looked as though he'd never seen a swimming pool other than at the YMCA. He was tall with scraggly blond hair, a wispy excuse for a beard and several tattoos. And he was thin to the point of emaciation. Did these kids ever get three square meals a day or did they just look starved? Definitely the misfits of the world, she thought. Whatever their backgrounds, all of Michael's friends had that one thing in common. They were the lost or neglected or simply different kids who didn't quite fit in with Tidewater High's privileged, apple-cheeked, designer-clad offspring of good families.

"How many are we feeding tonight?"

She started at Jake's voice and returned to cleaning vegetables for a salad. "You, me, Michael and Michael's friend."

Leaning around her, Jake looked through the window. "Hmm, looks like that one could use a square meal."

"Among other things."

Jake smiled. "Yeah. Where the heck does he find these kids?"

"Detention hall?" Rachel held a scrubbed carrot on the cutting board and began chopping it. "Where else would there be such a motley collection? Some of these kids look as if they've never seen a house with a real lawn in front and back. One of them — the boy last week whose family were migrant fruit pickers — said that he'd never eaten with utensils that matched." She dropped a handful of sliced radishes into a bowl. "Surely there's a magazine or two in his house."

Jake leaned against the counter, legs crossed at the ankles, watching her fingers fly. "I doubt he has much access to *House Beautiful*. There are lots of indigent families who can barely put food on the table. Magazines are luxuries for those people."

For a second, she stared at her hands. Then, looking at him, she said quietly, "I sound like such a snob, don't I?"

Still smiling, he touched the side of her face gently. "The truth?"

She nodded, knowing what was coming. "You do."

"I don't mean to. It's just that I've never met children like this. I'm ashamed to say that until Michael started bringing them home, I hadn't spent much time thinking about the unfortunate innocents of the world."

"Then that's one good thing to come from having Mike with us, hmm?" With his thumb, he traced the line of her surprisingly firm jaw.

"Yes, it is." She smiled with sudden ruefulness. "Although I could wish he wouldn't be so generous with my expensive bath sheets."

Jake looked again at the boys, each wrapped in a luxurious taupe towel, and laughed. "Generous to a fault, isn't he?"

Rachel studied Jake's expression as he watched Michael. "But you don't really think so, do you?"

"Think he's too generous? No." He moved away from her, settling once more against the counter. "Truth is, I think he's a special kid. I suspect he identifies with the friends he brings here. Like Mike, they've been dealt a hard hand. But he's one of the lucky ones, having been taken in by you and me. I think he enjoys giving them a firsthand look at life as they've always fantasized it. He gets a kick out of letting them swim in a private pool, plying them with whatever you fix for dinner and showing us off as the perfect couple. He's got a sweet nature,

Mike has. I'm proud of him for it. The world needs more people like him."

When she remained silent, he looked slightly uneasy, as though uncertain how she would react to his glowing assessment of Michael.

But all she said was, "We're hardly perfect."

The next day, she had lunch with Suzanne.

"I'm going to have to do something, Suzy. We can't go on like this." With her forefinger, she traced the top of her water glass. "You know what I'm reminded of when I'm at home with Jake?" She pushed the glass aside. "The eye of a hurricane. It's like we walk on eggs with each other, because to say what we really think or feel would open the door to a storm of anger, hurt and pain. So we both keep everything all bottled up. I'm not sure how much longer I can do that."

Suzanne shook her head in bewilderment. "I can't believe this. You and Jake always seemed to have such a solid marriage. You were the perfect wife, mother, homemaker. Can you really just cast all that aside because of a mistake Jake made a hundred years ago?"

"It's not just that, Suzy. I played the role

of perfect wife and mother and homemaker because that's what I thought marriage was all about. You know how much I wanted a child before I finally got pregnant with Scotty. It wasn't only that I wanted to have a child to love and care for — I felt it completed me on some very basic level. As a woman, don't you see? Only when Scotty was gone did I discover that everything I'd cherished had little real substance."

"I just can't accept that, Rachel," Suzy said with quiet intensity, still shaking her head. "You sell yourself short. Lots of women choose homemaking as a career and find it as fulfilling as any job. Even more fulfilling, sometimes."

Rachel hardly heard her. She was caught up in trying to put everything in some kind of understandable perspective. "I don't know, maybe the foundation of our relationship wasn't what it should have been."

"What does that mean? You love Jake, he loves you. How can you get a better foundation than that?"

"If he loved me, why did he sleep with another woman?"

"For heaven's sake, Rachel, what man is perfect?"

"Would you say that if it were Alan?"

Suzy bent her head, rubbing her temple.

"I think we've had this argument before."

"You know something?" When Suzy looked up expectantly, Rachel said, "To tell the truth, I think I was probably a real pain to live with back then. I was such a silly twit, Suzy. I wanted everything to be perfect in my marriage — perfect husband with perfect job, perfect home life, perfect pregnancy. Only I didn't have any of that. I had a good husband, not a perfect one. His job was demanding and dangerous, which was a threat to my perfect home life. To make matters worse, I couldn't get pregnant." She laughed ruefully. "That meant *I* was imperfect."

"Rachel —"

"No." She shook her head. "It's no wonder that Jake strayed, Suzy. The real wonder is that he didn't make a habit of it."

"I'm not saying I agree with that assessment, Rachel, but if you see it that way, then why can't you put it all behind you and get on with your life?"

But Rachel was still knee-deep in self-analysis. "I wouldn't have needed so much perfection or such a guarantee if I'd had more confidence in myself, Suzy. Don't you see? And Jake has to take some of the responsibility for that. He wanted me to be a little girl he could take care of. It was a sort of ego trip, making the important decisions in our lives, being the sole breadwinner, encouraging me to lean on him. Even after we left Miami and that job with the DEA, Jake — like the good caretaker he is — set me up in a lovely house here in Tidewater. Of course, he didn't say all this out loud, but by his actions, he defined the part he wanted me to play. Looking back, I'm not happy that I let myself become relegated to that role."

"Have you really been so unhappy, Rachel?"

"No. That's what I'm saying. Not until I lost Scotty. Then I had to face myself, come to terms with who I really was, and I wasn't anybody, Suzy. I was Mrs. Jake McAdam. Or the sheriff's wife. Or Scotty's mother." She paused as the waiter collected their salad plates. When he left, she said, "Even then we might have rocked along awhile, but Michael came and it seemed that the fabric of our relationship began to unravel. I'm just not sure who I am or what I want anymore."

"Rachel, for God's sake, don't do anything crazy."

Rachel sat quietly studying the single rose centerpiece before looking into Suzanne's eyes. "Ron Campbell is sending me all kinds of signals, Suzy. He wants an affair."

She watched the consternation that clouded her sister's face. Rachel was almost amused. Her family must truly think the stress of the past few months had pushed her around the bend. She knew Suzanne longed to launch into the thousand-and-one reasons that an affair was a stupid, ill-conceived, insane thing to do, not to mention the politically explosive effect such an act would have on Jake's campaign.

Suzanne opened her mouth, but the look on Rachel's face must have told her something. She finally settled for, "Ron Campbell is a notorious womanizer, Rachel. You wouldn't be so naive."

Rachel shrugged. "Apparently the woman Jake slept with wasn't exactly the soul of virtue."

Suzanne leaned forward. "So you're considering this . . . this insanity just to get back at him?" she whispered fiercely.

"Ron is charming and attractive. He sees me as someone who can *do* something, Suzy."

"And I can just imagine what that something is."

"See? See?" Rachel tossed down her napkin. "Even you don't think a man would value me for anything but a bed partner,

Suzanne."

"Hang on, Rachel, that's not what I said!" She leaned forward again. "You're all mixed up. Tell me you don't really mean what you're saying. You are too smart for something like this, I know you are." The waiter interrupted with their coffee. Suzanne waited with impatience while he placed the cups in front of them.

"I'd like a nickel for every time I've fantasized about leaving Alan. But even while I'm thinking it, I know if I had to put my money where my mouth is, I'd choose him all over again every time, warts and all. Jake's a good man, Rachel. And you're just as good a woman. You just need a little more time to work this out. Losing Scotty was horrible. *Is* horrible. An ongoing tragedy. It's knocked you for a loop, understandably. But the two of you can weather it."

"I don't know, Suze. Since Michael came —"

"Michael seems to be the catalyst for all this soul-searching, Rachel, but please don't do anything rash." She reached across the table and squeezed Rachel's hand. "Please. Promise me."

Rachel shrugged and smiled faintly. "What's rash, Suze? I'm not filing for a divorce, at least not today. And I'm not going to sleep with Ron Campbell."

At least not today.

She didn't say the words out loud, but from the look on Suzy's face, she could have.

Suzanne looked at her watch and grimaced. "I have an appointment and I'm already ten minutes late. I've got to go, honey." She stood up. "What's your schedule for the rest of the day?"

"Back to work, of course." Rachel put down the tip and collected her purse and credit card. "The day's only half over."

"You're still happy with your job?"

"Yes . . ."

"But?"

"I think I'd be happier if I could do something where I felt I really made a difference."

"Such as nursing?"

"No, nothing like that. I like my own field, psychology."

"Well, maybe you could try the county. You could do social work there. Is that what you'd like?"

"Maybe." Rachel fell into step beside Suzanne, and they headed for the front door. "I've been thinking about it. There are certainly enough kids out there who need help. I've learned that from working in

Emergency. I've lived long enough with my head buried like an ostrich."

Suzanne stared at her in surprise. "You're really serious about this, aren't you?"

"Yes. About this and other things in my life."

Suzanne nodded, looked thoughtful. "We'll talk more later, okay?"

"Okay." They walked through the door into bright July sunlight. Rachel dug into her purse for her keys. "Say hello to Alan and the kids for me." She reached up and kissed her sister's cheek. "And thanks for listening, Suze."

To everyone's pleasure, there was an uncustomary lull in Emergency after lunch. Monday was usually a very busy day. Patients who'd chosen to avoid a visit to the hospital on the weekend usually lined up early, and the waiting room seldom cleared before nightfall. Why this day should be different, no one could figure out. By the same token, nobody questioned it, and there was an unusual sense of relaxation among the staff, both medical and administrative.

Ron Campbell strolled in about three o'clock.

"Hey, pretty lady." He held up two cups of coffee. "How about a break?"

The coffee was in covered plastic cups and probably lukewarm, but Rachel wasn't feeling particular. She'd spent the past hour discussing the insurance benefits of an elderly patient who'd come in with chest pains. Smiling, she reached to take a cup.

"Uh-uh." Ron backed out of reach, holding the cups. "First rule of slow Mondays — don't waste a coffee break at your desk. Come on, let's go to the waiting lounge, put up our feet and really relax. This has got to be the first Monday in history that it's unoccupied."

She laughed and pushed back from her desk. "Sounds good."

"What? No argument? No excuses? No sweet, shy refusals?" He raised his eyebrows in mock surprise but didn't waste any time falling into step beside her. "Hold all emergencies," he called to Helen Falco, who laughed and shook her head.

"I'm only able to do this because we're having a slow day," Rachel said, entering the lounge. She walked straight to the television and lowered the sound. When she turned, Ron had closed the door.

"My good luck." He sat down on a cushioned sofa and patted the space next to him. After a second's hesitation, Rachel did as he wanted, but she kept a respectable distance between them. Putting the coffee cup in her hand, he sipped from his own then leaned back, fixing her with a teasing look. "I have to grab my moments with you when I can."

"Except for lunch, I'm at my desk eight hours a day, Mr. Campbell," she said primly. One step more and she would be flirting, she realized. Rachel stared into her coffee. Was that what she wanted? Was this how it had started between Jake and that woman in Miami?

"I know, under the watchful eyes of Helen Falco — a dragon when it comes to you — and the entire hospital staff." He reached over and deliberately removed her cup from her hand. "I can't even make a move outside in the parking lot. Your trusty teenage knight, Michael, might be on patrol."

Michael. Rachel swallowed and the coffee almost went down the wrong way. If Michael was standing here, would she be doing this? Ron looked deeply into her eyes. "My proposition is still open."

"Proposition?"

"The job, Rachel. I still want you."

Here it was, time to put her money where her mouth was. He wasn't talking about a job. She knew it, and he knew she knew it. Rachel wondered when her heartbeat would start to accelerate. Shouldn't sexual innuendo from a man other than her husband be exciting? Shouldn't she be feeling something other than this . . . this clinical curiosity? Shouldn't she be thinking that Ron Campbell was a very attractive man — although Jake's chin was better, stronger — rather than noticing that his watch was a fake Rolex? Jake wore a practical no-name with a leather band. She blinked. Why was Jake so vividly present in her mind?

She raised her eyes to Ron's. "My feelings haven't changed about the job, Ron."

"I'm not talking about the job, Rachel, and you know it." He slipped a hand around her waist in a quick, skillful movement. How did he get so close so quickly? she wondered. "I'm talking about this."

Ron seemed unaware of anything except the thrill of kissing her. Whereas her first and overwhelming reaction was refusal. She felt a sense of violation and revulsion. As for sexual excitement, she felt nothing. Not a blessed thing.

What am I doing!

With the thought came the sound of the lounge door opening. Pushing against Ron's arms, Rachel tore away from him, hardly aware of anything except her own stupidity. Dazed with the enormity of what she'd encouraged, or at least failed to discourage, she looked in the direction of the doorway, knowing whoever had opened it would have seen her in Ron Campbell's arms, would have witnessed the kiss. Would assume that she was a willing partner. Worse, would assume, more than likely, that kissing Ron was something she indulged in daily. Hourly. Nightly.

She looked up.

It was Michael.

CHAPTER TEN

"H-hello, Michael." Rachel scrambled to her feet, straightening her blouse even though it really didn't need it. Nothing was disheveled about her, yet she felt like a teenager caught necking in the backseat of a Chevy.

Michael hesitated while his gray eyes darted accusingly from her to Ron Campbell and back again.

"It's . . . I've been taking a break, Michael. What . . ." She cleared her throat and got hold of herself. "What are you doing here? It's early for school to be out."

"Coach Gibson got an emergency call from somebody, and since it was last period, they let us go home. I jogged over yesterday, so I figured I'd do it today, too." He shrugged. "Instead of waiting around school, you know." He gave Ron another scorching look. "I guess my timing wasn't too good, huh?"

Without looking at Ron, Rachel reached for Michael's arm. "It's not what you think, Michael. Come with me to my office and let me get my things, then we can leave. It's almost time for me to go home anyway."

"Look, Miss Rachel, maybe I'd better just jog on home. By myself, okay? I've got a key and all." He looked at Ron, whose glib tongue for once seemed to fail him. "Mr. Campbell here looks like he's got something on his mind."

Michael subtly shifted so that he loosened her hold on his arm.

She felt a pang. He was so disgusted he didn't want to be touched by her.

"He doesn't have anything on his mind, Michael." Feeling exasperated and embarrassed — and guilty! — Rachel looked at Ron. "We'll talk later, Ron." Without waiting for his reply, she fell into step beside Michael, unwilling to let him go on thinking she was unprincipled, promiscuous. "As I said, I'll just get my purse and we'll leave." She took a deep, determined breath. "I can explain this, Michael."

"You don't have to explain anything to me, Miss Rachel."

"Hold on!" She stopped and grabbed him by his shirtsleeve, forcing him to halt. "I'm embarrassed and ashamed at what you think you just saw, Michael. I'm going to try to muddle through an explanation, whether you want to hear it or not."

He looked at a point just beyond her shoulder. "Yes, ma'am."

He looked so much like Jake with his jaw set like that and those gray eyes stormy as a bad day on the Gulf. "It's not what you think."

"You said that already."

"I wasn't —" she cleared her throat awkwardly "— kissing him. Exactly."

"No, ma'am."

"I wasn't!"

"I'll wait for you in the car."

She caught at his sleeve again. "You can't. It's ninety-five degrees in the car."

"I'll stop by the cafeteria and get a cold drink to go."

Tears suddenly filled her eyes. Even though she deserved it, his reaction hurt. She hadn't realized what a good relationship she'd built with Michael. Now, because of her stupidity, because of an asinine, screwed-up need to wound Jake, she'd jeopardized something that she suddenly realized was very valuable to her.

As for Jake, what he would think was too painful to contemplate.

"Okay," she said numbly, giving in. Her

hand clung a moment to his sleeve. With her fingers, she smoothed out a wrinkle, realizing it would probably be a long time before Michael ever trusted her enough to let her touch him again. She tried to smile. "Go ahead to the cafeteria. I won't —"

"Rachel!"

They were both startled. Her hand still on Michael's arm, Rachel turned, alerted by the urgent note in Helen Falco's voice.

"We've got a possible O.D. We need you."

There was a flurry of sound in the vicinity of the first treatment room — raised voices and the crash of an overturned chair. Hearing it, Michael frowned. "Maybe you'd better wait a minute, Miss Rachel. Things sound pretty wild in there."

Rachel was already headed that way, along with two uniformed sheriff's deputies who'd apparently lingered at the admissions desk. Working in Emergency had uncovered an unsuspected ability in Rachel for calming hysterical patients. She was especially skillful in dealing with adolescents. From the look of the youth being restrained by Helen Falco and a single orderly, all her newfound skill would be called to bear with this one.

"I think I can handle it," she told the senior deputy, who reluctantly stood aside while she entered the cubicle. Unnoticed,

Michael followed her.

One look at the youth alarmed her. His expression was glassy-eyed and unfocused and he was sweating profusely. Whatever the drug was, it was powerful and he was completely under its influence. Helen had already sent out the code for the resident on duty.

Everyone was stunned when the boy suddenly screamed and threw up his arms to protect his face as though he were being attacked. He kicked out blindly, just missing Rachel only because Michael managed to drag her out of reach.

"Miss Rachel —"

"It's okay, Michael." Without taking her eyes from the crazed youth, she waved a hand in the general direction of the waiting room. "Wait for me at my desk," she told Michael, walking toward the boy again as he somehow managed to elude both the orderly and Helen.

"Get away from me!" he yelled, backing up against the examining table.

He was trembling all over, his eyes frantic. Rachel's heart went out to him, as she wondered what horrors he was seeing in his mind. "What's his name?" she asked.

"Kevin Nicholson," Michael said.

Rachel blinked, her concentration broken

for an instant. "You know him?"

"No. Yes, ma'am, I guess. I see him around at school."

"Kevin," she began, speaking softly. "My name's Rachel." She managed a smile. "All these people here are friends. We don't want to hurt you. We're here to help you."

"I gotta get outta here!" he cried, giving the waste receptacle a violent shove. It hit the startled orderly and sent him sprawling. Helen let out a distressed sound, but Rachel couldn't afford to look away from Kevin. She put out her hand, palm up. "Kevin, why don't you come over here and just talk to me a few minutes."

Wild-eyed, watching both Rachel and Michael as though they were aliens, he put out both hands to hold them off. "Stay away from me!"

"Okay, Kevin, it's okay. Look." Rachel took a cautious step back. "See? I'll just stand here. Can we talk now?"

Kevin stared blindly, his eyes narrowed in an effort to focus. "They have knives! Jeez, they have knives!"

"No, Kevin. Nobody has knives."

"And guns! Guns and knives!" He threw his arm up. "I don't want to die!"

"Kevin, listen to me. Nobody's going to die. Nobody's going to hurt you. There are no knives, no guns, I promise." Rachel stepped forward instinctively, both hands outstretched.

"You're lying! Everyone always lies." His voice dropped dramatically as his expression changed. "But I'm in charge now. I can hold them all off when they get a load of this!"

Before she had a chance to evade him, he grabbed a handful of her blouse and yanked her almost off her feet, pinning her against his side. She cried out in surprise, vaguely aware that he was fumbling at the small of her back. She thought dazedly of rape, but it was only a fleeting idea, one among a rush of horrifying possibilities that crowded her mind.

Then she realized he was groping for something on his own person. Her eyes flew to Michael's and her terror increased tenfold. Michael should be with the deputies in the safety of the waiting room. Why hadn't he heeded her? Only as she felt the savage nudge of cold steel against her temple did she realize that Kevin had a gun.

Jake closed the door behind Parker Jamison, the editor of the *Tidewater Journal,* and stood for a moment kneading the side of his neck. His muscles were as tight as rawhide.

He thought briefly of phoning Rachel at the hospital. Mike would still be at school. They could talk awhile. He dropped his arm to his side and inhaled wearily. Fat chance.

To distract himself, he focused on Parker Jamison's visit. Parker was a friend as well as a business associate. He'd stopped by to discuss ideas and dates for the political ads that would run in the *Journal* now that the campaign was under way. Liz had been in on the meeting, but she'd left ten minutes before for an appointment with the photographer to view the proofs for a series of photographs that would appear in the *Journal* along with the ads.

He went to his desk and sat down. The campaign was heating up and so was his town. His county. Deep in thought, he scanned the notes he'd made during his conversation with Parker after Liz left. They had nothing and everything to do with his campaign. According to Parker — from sources he'd told Jake he would not divulge — a major drug distribution outfit was operating somewhere along the coastline of Florida and very likely within Jake's jurisdiction in Kinard County. Parker's information dovetailed neatly with DEA intelligence Jake was getting from Rick Streeter.

Jake leaned back and put his feet up. It

wouldn't surprise him if Parker's information was eventually traced to someone at the DEA in Miami. Idly he toyed with the idea of calling Rick and alerting him to the possibility of a leak within his unit. When it came time to execute the operation, a breach of security could mean somebody's life.

Closing his eyes, he rubbed his temple. He'd had another disturbing visit from Joe Crenshaw. Joe was concerned that too many kids were showing up at Tidewater High School high as a kite. He didn't have any evidence, but he told Jake he suspected the source of the drugs was very near the campus. How else were so many kids getting the stuff before the bell rang for first period? He'd come to Jake instead of the local police chief because he worried that J.B. Gonzales might use the information politically. As Jake knew, the problem was county-wide, not confined within the city limits. If he was forewarned, Crenshaw had said, maybe Jake would be able to spike J.B.'s guns before the situation became a political hot potato.

Jake drummed his fingers on his desk. What the hell *was* he going to do?

His phone buzzed. Drawing in a deep breath, he picked it up.

"Line one, Jake."

"Jake? Helen Falco."

"Helen. How are you?"

"Oh . . ." She sounded slightly breathless. "Fine, I'm fine. Jake —"

He tensed at something in her tone and sat up a little. "What is it, Helen?"

"Oh, Jake . . ." Her voice faltered. "Jake, it's Rachel."

He frowned. "What about her?"

"And Michael."

His heart began to pound. He held the receiver with one hand and braced himself against the arm of his chair with the other. "What is it? What's happened?"

"I've already called the police. They're here now."

"Why, Helen? What's going on?"

"We have a boy — about fifteen, I'd say. He's totally out of control, Jake. PCP or something. I'm guessing, of course, but he's hallucinating, he's wild."

"Helen, for God's sake! What does this have to do with Rachel? Or Michael?"

There was a pause. "Oh, Jake, he has them. Both of them."

"He has them?" Jake shook his head blankly. "What —"

"Rachel was trying to calm him. She's so good at that, Jake. Just a few words, usually,

235

and she has them as docile as babies. But this one, Kevin something —"

"What about Rachel?" Jake demanded fiercely.

"He was babbling about guns and knives, extremely agitated . . . paranoid, actually. He thought we were going to hurt him."

"What about my wife!" he shouted. "My son!"

Helen drew in a broken breath. "He has them both, Jake."

"How? How can he have them? You said J.B.'s men were there, didn't you?"

"Yes, but . . . He has them in the supply room, Jake. They're locked in, just Rachel and Michael and the boy."

With a curse, Jake surged up, sending his chair crashing backward.

"Jake —"

"Are they hurt?"

"I don't know. They —"

"I'm on my way. I'll —"

"Jake!"

Something in her tone stopped him. "What?"

"He has a gun, Jake." A sob shuddered from her. "He's in the storeroom with them and he has a gun."

Later, Jake never remembered the trip from

236

headquarters to the hospital. In the course of his career, both as sheriff of Kinard County and in the DEA, he'd lost count of the number of dangerous situations he'd managed successfully. In none of them was there ever anything personal at stake. He squeezed his lower jaw, seeing Rachel's face, Michael's trusting gaze. To a lawman, a hostage situation was the most feared, the most delicate, the most dangerous. He cursed his helplessness. These past few months his whole damn life seemed out of control. Scotty had been snatched from him, his marriage was disintegrating, his town swimming in drugs. Now Rachel and Michael . . . He realized it was possible for a man's blood to freeze while he still functioned.

Rachel, Rachel . . . Michael . . . Please, God, don't let them be hurt.

He pulled to a screeching stop at the hospital in a sea of Tidewater P.D. vehicles, flashing blue lights, squawking radios and general chaos. Before he cleared the front end of his car, J. B. Gonzales met him.

"Jake, I know this is tough, but it's in city jurisdiction and we're handling it. You're gonna have to stand back."

"City jurisdiction?" Jake stared at him in consternation. "J.B., that's my wife and my son in there, and nothing short of an A-bomb will keep me back."

"Jake!" J.B. grabbed at him, but he'd already stepped through the narrow yellow police barrier, snapping the plastic and sending it fluttering crazily to the pavement. Cursing, J.B. stalked along beside him. "We have a hostage situation here, Jake. You can't just go charging in there."

"Watch me." His face grim, Jake took the steps beside the emergency-room ramp two at a time. His hand slammed into the glass door, pushing it open. "Helen told me they're locked in a supply room. Has that changed?"

"Well, no. It appears —"

"Appears?" In the act of assessing the scene, he stopped and looked into Gonzales's indignant face. "Why don't you know? Have you got someone else managing this?"

"Don't mess with me, Jake!" But J.B. was talking to air. Jake had already started across the waiting room. J.B. hurried after him. "Of course, I'm in charge here! I don't have to be inside to take care of things. I'm doing it by radio with the commander of the SWAT team." Finding himself beyond the known secured area for the first time, he looked around warily. "As you see, we've followed procedure here. We've evacuated everyone except the two officers who originally apprehended the suspect."

"Where's the room?"

"Uh . . . well, I'm not sure. Langley!" He beckoned to one of half a dozen men stationed in the hall. All had their weapons drawn, but it was apparent to Jake that, SWAT team or not, everybody seemed stymied as to what to do next.

"Where is my wife, Langley?" Jake asked as the officer approached.

"Sheriff." Langley nodded politely. "There's a small storage room right off the third treatment cubicle. It has a metal door with a tiny window in it at about eye level and a dead bolt lock. Problem is, we can't approach because he . . . Kevin, the boy, is armed and close to panicked."

Jake stared in the direction of the room for a second or two. His lips barely moved as he spoke. "Have you spoken to my wife since he took her?"

"Yes, sir, we have. She called out that we should keep back. She and your boy, Mike, are okay, she said. She wanted a few more minutes with Kevin."

J.B. stepped closer. "Now, Jake —"

Jake ignored him, still focused on Langley. "Do you know what he's on?"

Langley shook his head. "PCP or some-

239

thing like it, according to the orderly and Mrs. Falco."

Jake rubbed at the day's growth of beard on his face and felt his hand tremble. "She's . . . She doesn't know what she's up against," he muttered. "PCP's vicious. He could blow at any minute."

"Begging your pardon, sir," Langley said, looking respectfully determined. "But I think your lady seems remarkably composed, considering. And your boy, too. Just from the time they holed up in there until a few minutes ago, I could tell the difference in the kid, Kevin. He's a lot calmer. At first he was yelling and banging around, knocking stuff over. As you say, just ready to blow. Smith and me —" he nodded in the direction of his cohort, still stationed in the hall "— have been right outside the storeroom, just out of sight. As you can hear for yourself, all's quiet in there right now."

A commotion at the door caught their attention. To Jake's dismay, it was the media. Crowding just outside the entrance was a local news crew complete with minicam. With a sweep of the camera, the electronic eye taped the waiting room, J.B., Jake and the armed policemen for the six o'clock news and posterity.

The red-haired anchorman from Channel

Six spotted Jake. "Sheriff McAdam, is it true your wife and son are the hostages?"

Jake ignored him, turning to the police chief. "Get rid of them, Gonzales," he ordered tersely. "I don't want anything to harm my wife and son. A TV camera might spook the kid into doing something crazy."

J.B. looked annoyed. "This is a free country, Jake. We aren't going to be able to shut out the media."

Jake glowered at J.B. "When in your political life have you ever wanted to shut out the media, J.B.?"

"What does that mean?"

"It means that I know you'll grab any opportunity to get your name on the six o'clock news." He stepped a little closer, lowering his voice to keep the exchange between Gonzales and himself. "You'd better be careful, Chief. As you are so anxious to point out, you're in charge here. If anything, I repeat *anything*, goes down here today except the successful rescue of my family, no amount of media coverage is going to make you look good. And if the people of Tidewater don't string you up, then I promise you I will."

They exchanged a look stripped of all pretense of liking or respect. Jake stared fiercely until J.B. looked away. Then with a sound of disgust, Jake wheeled and strode down the hall.

"Hey, where you going?"

"To see if I can communicate with my wife," Jake snapped, not looking back.

Langley hurried after him. Neither paid any attention to the chief of police, who turned, straightening his tie and smoothing his hair. He cleared his throat, readying himself with a smile for live television.

"Sheriff, I don't know if I'd get too close," Langley warned, matching his stride to Jake's. "That kid doesn't seem inclined to negotiate."

"Is there a phone in that storeroom?"

"Well, no, sir."

"Windows?"

"Not much of one, sir. Just a skinny pane."

"Then how are we going to find out anything if we don't get close enough to talk to him?" Jake demanded.

"Yes, sir."

Approaching the storeroom, Jake flattened himself against the wall. With practiced efficiency, he drew his weapon. The violence inside him was fearsome in its intensity. He motioned the other cop, Smith, aside and leaned forward to see for himself. With a swiftly indrawn breath, he cursed in frustration. The window was draped with something. He curbed an impulse to kick the door down. He needed to see for himself that Rachel and Michael were unhurt.

His gaze traveled around the hall, seeking something, anything, that might get him into the storeroom. There was no air-conditioning duct, no air-intake vent. With his back against the wall, he looked at the door. "Kevin! Kevin, can you hear me in there?"

It was Rachel who answered. "Hello, Sheriff," she said calmly. Jake's throat tightened at the sound. If they'd been passing on the street, she couldn't have sounded more casual.

"We're fine in here, as I told Officer Langley a while ago. Kevin's thinking the situation over. He didn't really intend to cause a stir like this, did you, Kevin?"

Jake heard an indistinct reply and stirred restlessly.

What about Michael?

"Dad . . ." Michael's tone was tentative.

Jake struggled with a renewed surge of emotion. "You okay, Mike?"

"Yes, sir. Fine. Uh, Dad, maybe you and your people should kind of back off for a little while. Miss Rachel's talking to Kevin right now. He's cool."

Jake swallowed with difficulty. He took

heart from the sound of their voices. Surely they couldn't manage that tone if Kevin was ready to blow. He stared at his hands gripping his weapon. Or did they even realize how quickly somebody high on a mind-altering substance could go from calm to crazy?

Suddenly through the door came the muffled sound of a struggle, then Rachel's sharp cry. Jake's heart plunged to his belly. His mouth dry with fear, he tried the door with one hand, but it was locked. Michael shouted. Something fell with a loud crash. Then he heard a single gunshot. The sound galvanized Jake as nothing else could. He forgot procedure. Nothing mattered but getting to Rachel and Michael. He kicked wildly at the base of the heavy door while slamming into it with his shoulder. With a crash, it came open.

He took in the scene frantically, lowering his weapon only when he saw that Kevin lay on the floor and Michael and Rachel seemed unhurt.

"Jake . . ." Her eyes swimming with tears, Rachel looked at him from where she knelt beside Kevin's unconscious form. Michael stood over them holding the gun wrapped in a white hospital washcloth.

"I had to hit him, Dad."

Adrenaline and relief were like a rushing river in Jake's head. He looked at Michael. Blood trickled from a cut on his cheekbone. "What the hell happened?"

"We thought he was calming down when he suddenly stuck the gun up under his chin like he was going to . . ." Michael was suddenly squeamish about actually saying the words.

Langley and Smith shouldered around Jake, taking in the scene. Langley went down on one knee beside Rachel, and Smith held out his hand for the gun, which Michael handed over readily.

Jake managed to holster his weapon a heartbeat before Rachel rose and launched herself at him, choking back sobs. His arms went around her, strong and embracing. He held her tight, his body quaking with relief. With a sigh, he breathed her name, drank in the sound of his own name whispered brokenly. "It's okay, baby," he murmured in her ear, lovingly stroking her hair and the slim, fragile shape of her spine.

Over her head, he focused intently on Michael. The boy was standing tall and taut as though movement might be more than he could manage. Jake's throat closed with a mighty rush of feeling. He didn't say anything. He couldn't. Beneath his hands, he could feel the aftermath of fear still coursing through Rachel. With his eyes, he could see the same vulnerability in Michael. He held out his arm and beckoned. Michael jerked forward and then he was holding them both tight.

His wife.

His son.

Safe. Both of them.

Closing his eyes, he breathed a prayer.

CHAPTER ELEVEN

At first, Rachel thought she could handle the whole thing without collapsing into Jake's arms and allowing him to do and say all the things that would make the horror of the past hour bearable. Over the past few weeks, she'd developed a sense of independence and an even stronger sense of her own identity. In spite of the adversity in her life, her self-esteem had blossomed. But an hour as a hostage had melted her newfound assurance like so much wax in a flame. It felt so good to be held close by Jake. He was so big and solid and *safe*. She'd been so scared.

And Michael. She still went cold at the thought of harm befalling Michael while he was in her care.

With a whimper, she turned her face into Jake's shirtfront. She was trembling almost uncontrollably, now that the danger was past, and Jake's hand felt warm, necessary, as he stroked away her shudders. Would it really matter if she leaned on him for just a minute or two?

When she felt Michael step back, she sighed and started to let go as well.

"Get your things," Jake told her gruffly, leaning back to look into her eyes. Beside them, people worked over Kevin where he lay on the floor.

"I'll need to take care of this," she began, her voice unsteady. Kevin would need to be admitted. There were forms, procedures. She had a job to do.

"Is it bad?" Jake asked, watching a doctor's quick inventory of Kevin's body.

Looking puzzled, the doctor leaned back on his heels. "Doesn't appear to be shot at all. He's unconscious, but it's from the blow he took on the back of his head."

Jake looked at Michael. "Did you hit him with the gun?"

"No, sir. I used that thing." He nodded toward a metal IV pole shoved in the corner.

"What about the shot we heard?"

Rachel shivered with remembered fear. "It went wild, thank God, into that stack of towels, I think. But he meant to k-kill himself." With a shaky hand, she tucked a long strand of hair behind her ear. "If not for Michael, he would have." She looked at him. "You saved his life, Michael."

Michael shrugged, not quite meeting her eyes. "I couldn't just stand by and let him shoot himself, could I? Besides, Miss Rachel kept talking to him, distracting him so that I could sneak over and grab the IV pole. It was the only thing in here other than clean laundry."

Jake reached out and turned Michael's face to the side. His face grew grim as he studied the bloody bruise on his cheek. "How'd this happen?"

Clearly discomfited, Michael averted his eyes. "Kevin was pretty wild when we first got in here, waving the gun and kicking and knocking everything around. I guess he clipped me there."

"With the gun," Rachel said, shivering again. "I think it's going to need stitches."

"Then let's get it done." Jake put a hand on Mike's shoulder, and with his other, he motioned for Rachel. As they approached the turn in the hall, he drew up short. A crowd had gathered in the waiting area. Light from the television mini-cam lent an unusual brightness to the muted mauve-and-blue decor. J.B. was speaking into a microphone, the cadence of his voice rising and falling in tandem with his arms. Beside him, Ron Campbell waited to read a statement.

Spotting Rachel, Helen Falco broke away from the group. She came toward them, her gaze searching and concerned. "Are you okay?" she asked, hugging Rachel tight.

"I'm fine, Helen. But Michael —"

"I know. Officer Langley said he needed stitches. We've got a cubicle set up."

Michael hung back, his eyes on the television crew and the ogling crowd. "Can't we just go home, Dad?"

"Soon as that cut is tended to, son. Helen —"

She took Michael's arm and turned him in the opposite direction. "The doctor's all set up in another wing. We'll just take a little detour and bypass all the commotion in the waiting room."

"Well . . ."

Rachel caught his eyes. "Don't worry, we'll go with you, Michael."

He looked quickly away. "You don't have to."

Rachel winced inwardly. He didn't want her. After what he'd seen between her and Ron Campbell, who could blame him? She managed a smile. "Okay. I need to get to the paperwork anyway."

"Rachel!" Helen gave her an incredulous

look. "You've just been through an ordeal. Someone else will handle the paperwork. Jake needs to take you home."

Jake nodded. "As soon as Mike's fixed up, I'm going to do just that."

With a sigh, Rachel fell into step beside them.

Her house was a welcome sight to Rachel. Her stomach had threatened to rebel with every corner Jake had turned on the way home. Only the knowledge that she had no right to feel ill, that Michael had been the one who was injured, had kept her from giving in to the nausea. She got out of the car on legs that were still wobbly, shamelessly grateful for Jake's steadying hand. Without a word, she headed straight for her bedroom.

That was where Jake found her a few minutes later. She was sitting on the floor with her back against the bed, her knees raised, hugging a pillow. She hadn't turned on a light or removed any of her clothes, not even her shoes.

"Rachel?" His tone was urgent as he bent beside her. "Are you okay, sweetheart?"

She shook her head, her throat clogged with unshed tears. "I'm fine, just —"

"Shook up, I know." He eased an arm

around her and drew her into his embrace. His arms tightened when he heard her choked sob. "You've been through the ringer today. You deserve a good cry."

"Did Michael?"

"Did Michael what?"

"Cry."

He chuckled softly. "No. He stomped around in his room griping because he hadn't managed to protect you from a drugged crazy."

Even Michael. Rachel closed her eyes in defeat. Even now, after she thought she had taken control of her life, men continued to treat her as if she were a little girl. The thought banished the threatening tears with a speed nothing else could have.

"Is he okay?" she asked, wondering why Michael cared if she'd been hurt. She would never forget his expression when he'd opened the door to find Ron kissing her. She felt so guilty . . . So unworthy of Michael's boyish chivalry. Of Jake's husbandly concern.

"Mike's fine." He shifted to see her face, smoothing back strands of her hair. "But I don't think you are. Want to talk about it?"

She tried to control the shudder that swept through her. "I was so scared, Jake."

"I know, baby." He kissed her temple.

"I'm sorry."

"For being scared? Don't be. Even a seasoned cop would be scared facing a situation like that."

"Not for that. For Michael."

"Michael?"

"For placing him in danger. Instead of trying to reason with a strung-out user, I should have made Michael's safety my priority."

He leaned back and frowned at her. "That's crazy talk, Rachel. You had an explosive situation and you handled it far better than many other professionals. As far as Michael's safety is concerned, if there's any finger pointing to be done, you aren't the only person who could have stopped Michael from getting involved. Helen Falco or the two cops who brought Kevin in should have headed him off." She watched his mouth quirk up at one corner in the slow, lazy smile that gave her so much comfort. "So, if you want to beat up on somebody for putting Michael in harm's way, there're plenty of folks around."

She resisted the temptation to snuggle close. Sighing, she was miserably aware that Michael's close call wasn't the only reason for her distress, but she could hardly tell Jake now. She didn't deserve his devotion.

How different he'd be if he knew what had happened just moments before the confrontation with Kevin. What a mess. She longed to crawl into her bed and have Jake right beside her. She longed to feel his arms around her, strong and protective and loving. She longed to close her eyes and sleep and then wake to find the whole tangle of her life just a bad dream.

"Hey . . ." Jake reached out and curled his palm around her nape. "You weren't the only one who was scared. When they told me Kevin had you and Michael and that he was armed, I nearly lost it, Rachel. Everything precious in my life was in the hands of a madman." He pulled her into his arms. With his face close to hers, he murmured, "Danger has a way of putting things into their proper perspective." He waited a moment before saying softly, "Do you know what I'm saying, Rachel?"

She didn't answer. No sound would come from the tight muscles in her throat. She cringed inwardly, thinking of her cold-blooded and half-baked plan to have an affair to spite Jake. She closed her eyes, trying to forget how shameful she felt. Tears suddenly flooded her eyes, spilling over her cheeks.

"Don't cry, sweetheart. We're going to be

okay." He ran his lips over her eyebrows, her lashes, her wet cheeks. He traced the shape of her jaw and chin, stopping at the corner of her mouth. "You taste so good, baby. I've missed you."

He kissed her like a man starving. Rachel responded, giving way to the need that had been locked inside her for so long. She clung to him, wanting to bury the aching pain in her heart that held the ugly little secret of her indiscretion. But she couldn't do this with Jake. Not after what she'd done, almost done . . .

She gasped, trying to pull away. "No . . . wait . . ." She pushed at him, turning away, covering her face with her hands. "I can't."

In the stark silence, Jake's breathing sounded ominous. Rachel held her breath, expecting his temper to explode. Wanting it. She deserved to be yelled at, stormed over.

His voice, when it came, though unsteady, was dangerously soft. "What is going on here, Rachel?"

She didn't get up. With her head still bent, she stared at her hands. Wetting her lips, she whispered, "I need some time."

"Time." He stood above her. Rachel could almost hear his frustration. "How much time, Rachel? I've tiptoed around here like a hired hand for almost six months now.

How much longer?"

Rachel's breath caught with pain and guilt. "I don't know."

"You don't know."

She shook her head mutely.

"You don't know," he repeated, louder.

She wiped both cheeks with her fingers and looked at him. "You probably don't understand, but —"

"Understand?" He scowled at her. "You've got that right, Rachel. I don't understand. In fact, I'm wondering if you yourself understand what's going on." He began pacing, making no effort to keep his voice down. "You can't sit there and tell me you didn't want me just now, Rachel. I ought to know. I've had eighteen years to figure you out."

Reaching the armoire where the dressing area branched off, he turned swiftly and struck the top of it with his fist, making Rachel jump. "So don't talk to me about understanding! I'm thinking maybe I've been too understanding as it is. Maybe that's the problem here. Maybe if I'd been a little less *understanding* and a little more demanding, we wouldn't have limped along for half a year living like brother and sister."

"I'm sorry." It was a whisper.

"That's it? That's all? You're sorry?"

"I . . . It's complicated."

He released a pent-up breath, almost a groan. "Are you trying to drive me crazy, Rachel?" He stared at his hands before raising his eyes. "I don't know what you want."

He waited a moment or two, expecting . . . what? Rachel drew in a deep breath and got slowly to her feet. What was there to say? What kind of defense could she use without revealing what she'd done? Should she confess? Or would a confession relieve her conscience at Jake's expense? She pushed her hair from her face with a shaking hand. She only knew one thing: she couldn't make love with Jake until she'd sorted out the tangled feelings that had driven her to even consider an adulterous liaison.

She got slowly to her feet. How ironic that just when she finally conquered whatever demon had kept her from enjoying sex with her husband, she had entrapped herself in a web of deceit.

"Okay, this is it, Rachel."

Rachel raised her eyes to Jake's. He looked so tired. Her heart turned over. She wanted to touch him, to cradle his strong jaw in her hand, to feel the vulnerability she knew would claim him if she could only just step into his arms and say that she was ready to take up their marriage again.

"I'm not coming to you anymore. It'll have to be you next time, Rachel. You decide when you're ready to be a real wife again." His tone dropped until it was almost a whisper. "That is, if you want to be a wife again. I can't take this anymore."

In his room, Michael closed his eyes and clutched his pillow tight to his belly. He'd been half-asleep when Jake began to yell. He'd heard every word. How could he not? His stomach had gone into a knot like always when things were bad. He'd never thought to hear his dad use that tone with Miss Rachel. He knew Jake loved her more than he loved anything. Or anybody.

Huddled in his bed, he couldn't shut out the low rumble of Jake's voice. He shouldn't be listening to this. These were private things they were saying to each other. Hurtful things. He tossed the pillow aside and grabbed his jeans. Scrambling into them, he slipped from his room, intending to go to the boathouse. He liked it there. It was quiet, peaceful. A person could really think out there.

In the hall, he waited a moment, staring at his feet dejectedly. This was all his fault. They wouldn't be having this trouble if he hadn't come along out of the blue, letting

Miss Rachel find out that Jake had once made a big mistake.

Things were going from bad to worse. That's what really had him worried. Here was Miss Rachel refusing her rightful husband when just that afternoon she'd let that wimpy Ron Campbell slobber all over her. Outrage made Michael's mouth thin and his breath quicken. He shoved his hands deep into his pockets. Good thing it had been him and not Jake who had pushed that door open. For a few heady seconds, he visualized Jake planting a big fist in Campbell's smooth face and a karate-like kick where it hurt the most.

He straightened abruptly as Jake suddenly came out of the bedroom. Jake looked startled but said nothing until he'd closed the door softly. He started down the hall, taking Michael with him.

"I guess you heard some of that, Mike."

"Yes, sir." Michael stretched out his stride to match Jake's. "I didn't mean to be listening to stuff that's none of my business. I was heading for the boathouse."

Jake squeezed his shoulder gently. "I'm sorry you were upset, son, but married couples have their ups and downs. Rachel and I are no exception. It's not the first time and it probably won't be the last."

"Yeah. I mean, yes, sir."

They reached Michael's room, but when the boy didn't enter, Jake leaned back, looking at him. "Cheer up, son. You ought to be feeling good. I couldn't have been prouder of you today. Tomorrow when you get to school, your name will be up, thanks to Channel Six. You're a hero."

"It's hard to feel good when I'm afraid Miss Rachel might leave."

Jake was startled into silence. Then he caught Mike by the shoulder and gently herded him into his room and in the direction of his bed. The boy sat, reaching for his pillow and wrapping his arms around it.

"Listen, Mike. I'd be lying if I said everything was going fine with Rachel and me. It's not. We're . . . She's . . . got some things to work out."

Michael nodded mutely, turning his eyes toward the fish tank. He did understand, sort of. Oh, not the part about dumb Ron Campbell. He for one would never figure out why in blue blazes Miss Rachel would ever look at that jerk when she had Jake McAdam worshiping her. But he was afraid he understood the real problem all too well.

"I don't know how it's going to end, Mike. I love her, I think you know that. But it is really tough for us right now."

She probably could be happy if I hadn't shown up.

The thought settled like lead in Michael's stomach. He hugged the pillow to his middle, knowing what he was going to have to do. He looked at Jake, studying the face of the man who'd fathered him, and knew it was going to be hard. The hardest thing he'd ever done. Harder even than striking out from Des Moines to search for Jake in the first place.

Michael lay back as Jake stood up. Their conversation had cleared up one thing. What he'd overheard had been just the tip of the iceberg. His dad's marriage was in deep trouble. Jake had bent over backward in all the ways that seemed to matter and she was still unhappy. So it had to be him, Michael. He wanted to feel mad at Miss Rachel; he wanted to yell at her and make her see that everything could be good if she'd just love him the way he'd learned to love her. Because he did. He loved her almost as much as he loved his dad. He slid under the covers with a sigh. He knew that that was just a pipe dream. He was going to have to leave.

At the door, Jake turned. "Good night, son. It'll all work out, you'll see."

"Sure, Dad."

After Jake was gone, Michael lay on his side staring into the fish tank. He just wished he'd known his dad a little longer. Jake was the kind of man any kid would thank his lucky stars to be born to. And Miss Rachel would have been the perfect mom. He thought longingly of the plans and dreams he'd made while lying in this bed — his bed — and knew they would never come true. His throat tight, he faced facts. He wouldn't get to go to any Miami Dolphins games with Jake. He wouldn't get to compete on the swim team with Jake on the sidelines looking proud. Leaving now, the way he'd have to, he wouldn't even get to finish summer school and watch his dad's face when he saw those two As and a B plus.

He was too old to cry. Jeez!

Chest aching, bottom lip trembling, he watched the goldfish until they were blurred by his tears.

The jangle of the phone awoke Rachel with a jerk the next morning. She fumbled at the alarm on her clock radio, knocking over a small photo of Scotty before realizing her mistake. By the time she picked up the receiver, Jake was already talking. The call was from his office and she was getting ready to hang up when she heard Scotty's name.

Struggling into an upright position against the headboard, she was suddenly wide awake, the receiver pressed tight to her ear.

Jake was snapping out questions.

"What time did it come through?"

"Just now, Sheriff. Not ten minutes ago. There's something else . . . ."

Rachel recognized the night dispatcher's voice. Lulu Sissons. Holding her breath, she waited.

"He's blond, Jake. About six years old. He's been unconscious since the car crashed, so they don't know much."

Unconscious! Stricken, Rachel held the receiver tighter.

"You say the man he was with has a record?"

"Yes. A known sex offender. His rap sheet's two feet long."

Rachel pressed a hand to her mouth.

"Where's the boy? Which hospital?"

"Doctor's. In Orlando."

"Thanks, Lulu. I'll be there as soon as I can."

Rachel didn't wait for Jake to hang up before she was out of bed and hurrying down the hall to his room. She pushed the door open and her breath caught at the sight of him with his pajama top unbuttoned.

Looking at Jake had always made her

knees weak. He was a beautiful man, tall and powerful. At forty-two he was in better shape than many of his deputies ten years younger.

Rachel's eyes drank in the sight of him, and she felt the warmth of a blush heat her cheeks. The remark she had ready stuck in her throat.

Jake looked up, then, as he shrugged out of his top and tossed it at the hamper.

She fixed her eyes on his face. "I heard Lulu on the phone," she said, her voice husky. "I want to go with you."

"No." He started digging for clothes.

"Yes. I want to go with you, Jake. You can't pat me on the head and dismiss me like a good little girl. Scotty is my son. As his mother, I have as much right as you to go to Orlando."

"It's for your own good that —"

"Stop it!" She put her hands to her ears. "Don't say those words to me again, Jake. For the last time, listen to me. I don't want to be protected. I want to see the boy who's in the hospital. I pray he turns out to be Scotty. If he doesn't . . ."

Jake took a step toward her. "Okay, okay. I'll take you." He would have reached for her, but she wrapped her arms around herself before he could.

"When can we leave?"

"As soon as possible." He glanced at the clock on the bedside table. "Say, thirty minutes?"

"I'll be ready."

Chapter Twelve

Rachel tried not to hope too much that this little boy would be Scotty. Whoever he was, he was sick, sick enough to be in a hospital. Even if his physical injuries weren't serious, there was always the other. His abductor was a known felon with a lengthy rap sheet. Fear was a deep, dark presence held at bay only by the sheer force of her will. What motivated such individuals? She bent her head, rubbing at her temples. What could parents do when there was so much evil in the world?

Jake gave her a concerned look. "Are you okay?"

"I'm fine."

"We can stop for coffee if you'd like a break."

"No." She shook her head. "No, let's just keep going. The sooner we know . . ."

Her life was suddenly so complicated. She'd gone to bed last night determined to straighten it out as much as she could. Starting with Ron Campbell. She wanted the air cleared between them. An explanation would be awkward and difficult, but necessary. He was still her boss, but that was the extent of any relationship she wanted between them. If he was unhappy with her, then so be it. She'd certainly sent out mixed signals. Unconsciously she fingered the wide gold band on her left hand. Not that Ron had needed much encouragement to make a play for her, but with a word or two she could have discouraged him at any time. She felt so embarrassed, so ashamed. She couldn't feel more like a fallen woman if she actually wore a scarlet letter.

And Michael. She desperately wanted to explain to Michael. She'd planned to speak to him on the way to school this morning, but it was going to be next to impossible to explain what he'd seen. She just hoped he was less judgmental than many people would be. She thought briefly of his open-minded acceptance of the people he brought home. Would his liberal attitude extend to a wayward stepmother?

"What are you thinking about?"

She hesitated only a minute. "Michael."

"He'll be all right staying with Jacky

Kendall. Don't worry. As juvenile officer, she's taken in dozens of kids in all kinds of family emergencies. Mike'll do okay with her."

"It isn't that. Some . . . things happened yesterday that we needed to talk about."

"Forget about that ordeal yesterday, Rachel. That kid —"

"Not that. I wasn't thinking of Kevin."

"What, then? You and Michael are tight, closer than I ever dared hope for. Nothing's likely to change that. He likes you and admires you. In fact, I think he fantasizes about having you as his real mother."

Not anymore.

Her eyes flooded with tears and she turned quickly to hide them from Jake. "I like him, too."

Actually, I love him, and I pray I'll have a chance to tell him and that he won't throw it back in my face.

"Can I ask you something, Jake?"

He glanced at her, smiling. "We're going seventy miles an hour. Take your best shot."

"It's a . . . It's something that — that you might not want . . ."

"C'mon, spit it out."

"I'm trying!"

"Does it have anything to do with Ron Campbell?"

Startled, she stared at him. "Ron Campbell? Why would you ask that?"

"I thought maybe you had decided you preferred an Ivy-League type to a jaded small-town sheriff."

"I don't consider that funny, Jake."

"Believe me, I don't joke about some smooth-talker stealing my wife."

"Then why did you say it?"

He shrugged. "You have to admit it hasn't exactly been smooth sailing with you and me lately."

"No."

"So, is this where you ask for a divorce?"

"A divorce? No!"

He met her eyes. "Then what?"

Her gaze fell to her hands as she twisted her wedding ring. "I wanted to ask you about that night."

"What night?"

"That night in Miami. Fifteen years ago . . . when you were . . . with her."

He shifted uncomfortably behind the wheel. "I told you, Rachel. It was nothing. It was all so long ago. It was nothing."

"You're doing it again, Jake."

"Doing what?"

"Keeping me in the dark. Hiding behind a lot of meaningless words. Insisting that what happened was nothing so that the truth can't be examined, even though that night resulted in Michael's birth. *Protecting me again. I hate that! I guess I'm just not strong enough to hear the truth, is that it?"*

"It's not that."

"Then you're protecting yourself."

"No! There's nothing —"

"Then what is it?"

He rubbed a hand over his mouth and jaw. "I don't want to hurt you, Rachel."

"I hurt every time I think of it."

He sent her an anguished look. "I'm ashamed of it."

"Then why did you do it!" Rachel's own pain was in every word.

"It's hard to explain."When she said nothing and the silence stretched too long, he took a slow breath. "I was lonely, that was part of it. You'd gone back to Tidewater, and I knew you were thinking seriously about leaving me for good." He met her gaze and the pain of that time was in her eyes.

"I've never told you this, Rachel, but I never felt . . . sure of you. Even though you said you loved me, I was never sure."

Her mouth fell gently open. "But why —"

"I was a nobody when we got married. I didn't have the social connections or the solid family you did. I didn't have parents,

270

uncles or aunts or cousins, no siblings. I was a rootless, penniless ex-GI, a nobody. But I took one look at you and knew you were the one woman in the world for me."

"I always felt very lucky," she said softly.

"Did you? I never knew that."

"Maybe we should have had this talk a long time ago."

He grunted. Baring his soul would never come easy to Jake. "Did you feel lucky because I loved you or because of the things I gave you?"

She frowned. "Things?"

"A house in the right neighborhood, a high-profile job, above-average income, a baby. Finally."

She looked at him, appalled. "I hope you don't really believe that."

He shrugged. "I believed it that night, all right. Or I feared it, I guess. At the time, we were still living pretty tight. And you had left me," he reminded her.

"I was confused. I needed some time to think!"

"I know that's what you said."

"Every time you left the house to go to work, I was scared to death that you'd be shot and killed."

"You don't leave because you care too much about somebody. You leave because you don't care enough. Your excuses didn't make a lot of sense to me then. I was pretty depressed the night Anne-Marie sat down beside me in that bar. All you ever talked about was getting pregnant or me changing jobs. If I hadn't agreed to leave the DEA and you hadn't eventually gotten pregnant, would we still be together, Rachel?"

"I came back before either one of those things happened, didn't I?"

"Yeah. And I'd vowed to give you what you wanted."

"After you'd sampled Anne-Marie's charms."

"I warned you it was a complicated thing to explain." He looked out the driver's window. "I'd gotten drunk that night. I felt like such a failure. You weren't pregnant, you hated my job, we fought constantly. In some kind of elemental way, everything I valued was threatened. I can't tell you how scared I was that I'd lost you forever, that you'd never come back. Anne-Marie offered . . . sympathy, a sort of mindless understanding with no strings, simple as that. You have to understand my ego was pretty battered. In a kind of stupid, drunken way, it seemed like a good idea at the time."

He looked over and met Rachel's eyes gravely. "That's no excuse. I don't offer it as such. Believe me, I've never regretted anything as deeply as I regret leaving that bar with Anne-Marie D'Angelo."

She could believe that. Now. After coming close to the same kind of folly with Ron Campbell. Rachel leaned her head back and closed her eyes. Something in the way Jake spoke made her think he was still haunted by some of the feelings he had in those days. Had she shortchanged him in the time they'd been married? Had she failed to show him enough love to help him overcome his insecurities? Was that why he'd been so inflexible with her, so afraid to let her seek her own identity? To let her be an individual in her own right as well as his wife?

She gazed out the side window, blind to the wonders of tropical landscape. Was it too late for her and Jake?

The little boy was blond. He had gray eyes. He was six years old. But he wasn't Scotty.

Bitterly disappointed, Rachel gripped the foot of the hospital bed. Cheerful, colorful cartoons painted on the walls mocked her despair. A pediatric nurse watched her, obviously worried that the fragile hold she had on her emotions would crumble any moment. Beside her, Jake was oddly tense, too still. She looked into his face and saw grief and despair to equal her own. She fumbled for his hand and their fingers entwined fiercely. And suddenly, wondrously, her pain was bearable.

Jamey Snowden was thin and pathetically small against the snowy hospital white. His right arm was in a cast and he had a few scratches on his face, but otherwise he was in good shape, according to the nurse. He stirred, fixing Rachel with an anxious look.

"Do you know my mommy?"

"No, love, but she's on her way. You'll see her just as soon as her airplane gets to Orlando."

Although she ached to comfort him, Rachel wasn't certain that he would want to be touched by a stranger. The extent of the abuse he'd suffered hadn't yet been determined, but in the few minutes Jake and Rachel had been in his room, his apprehension about Jake had been painfully obvious.

"Is this town Orlando?"

"Yes, it is."

"I live in Atlanta. I want to go home."

She ventured closer, gently brushing the blond bangs that lay on his forehead. "And you will, Jamey."

"When?"

"Soon."

Jamey was one of the lucky ones. Beneath

the hospital covers, his slight outline blurred in her vision as Rachel squeezed his hand. He had been abducted from a shopping mall in the few moments that his mother had been distracted when his younger brother toddled down another aisle. That had been less than forty-eight hours before. Barely long enough for the system to publicize his vital statistics, which accounted for the confusion over his identity when the accident occurred. By the time Rachel and Jake arrived, he'd been identified and his parents were on their way from an Atlanta suburb.

"What will happen to the man who kidnapped him?" Rachel asked Jake, fumbling in her purse for her sunglasses as they stepped from the cool, dim interior of the hospital into bright Orlando sun.

"He was killed in the accident," Jake said, giving her a long look."

"Oh." With unsteady hands, she put the sunglasses on.

He took her arm and shepherded her gently toward their car. "But if he'd lived, he would have been arrested and tried on a variety of charges."

"But would he have been punished?"

He stopped at the car, realizing that she was trembling all over. "Yes, definitely.

Kidnapping carries a serious penalty. That, on top of his previous record as a pedophile, would have insured the maximum. He would probably have been sentenced to life without parole."

"Good." She stared over the sea of cars to the gently swaying palm trees that dotted the grounds of the hospital. "Good," she repeated.

Jake caught her chin in his hand and tilted her face so he was looking directly into her eyes. "Are we talking about Jamey's kidnapper, Rachel, or someone else?"

"I hate him, Jake," she said in a low, shaking voice. "I despise him. He's scum, too vile to walk this earth with innocent children. I hope he rots. I hope he wakes up every day wondering if today is the day you'll find him and make him pay. I hope he gets run over by a truck. I hope he gets an incurable disease and dies slowly and painfully!"

"Ah, sweetheart, I know. I understand." He pulled her close and for a few minutes stood gently rocking her back and forth, feeling the tremors coursing through her as her pain and anguish and grief flowed out in heart-wrenching sobs. He knew she was talking about Scotty's abductor. Deep in his gut, he echoed her anger and hatred and frustration, even welcomed it. If they'd shared these feelings when Scotty had first disappeared, they both might have been better able to cope with the loss of their son.

"Are you okay?" he asked when her sobs had dwindled to a few soft sniffles.

She nodded, rubbing her cheek against his shirt. Jake caught her face between his hands, and without giving her a chance to object, kissed her once. Then he opened the car door and hustled her into her seat. When he was behind the wheel, he started the car. With a burst of air, the heat inside began to cool.

"Are you hungry?"

She plucked idly at lint on her navy slacks. "Not really." They'd had a light lunch in the hospital cafeteria, which she'd just picked at, but that had been hours ago. "You go ahead. We can stop somewhere before we get on the interstate."

"Tell you what . . ." He shifted to face her, resting his arm on the back of his seat. His fingers toyed with her hair, tangling in the silky curls. "By the time we do that, it'll be dark. Then it's another four-hour drive home. You've had a tough day, and so have I." His tone dropped, became coaxing. "Why don't we have a decent meal, find a motel, get a good night's sleep and then head on home tomorrow morning."

He met Rachel's solemn look squarely. Crying had left her makeup ravaged, her mouth soft and vulnerable. The skin at her nape was as smooth and soft as a baby's to his touch. It had been a long time since Jake had felt free to caress her. He was swamped with a longing so strong that it left him stunned. He removed his hand, turned and looked straight ahead while he waited for her decision.

She studied a distant palm tree. "You'll have to call Michael. He'll be wondering about . . . about the little boy."

"Yeah. I will." Jake reached for the ignition with a hand that wasn't quite steady, then started the car with a roar of horsepower. "Buckle up."

In the bathroom, Rachel stood a long time in front of the mirror. She'd taken a lengthy shower, standing under the warm spray until Jake had knocked on the door wanting to know if she was all right. She wasn't all right. She hadn't been all right since she'd entered the hospital and looked into the eyes of six-year-old Jamey Snowden and seen bewilderment and fear where there should only have been wonder and innocence. She knew she was subconsciously substituting Jamey for Scotty, but it was one thing to recognize an irrational thought and another to banish it.

She was so tired. They'd had wine with dinner. She hoped it would help her sleep. It seemed forever since she had slept a whole night through, deeply and dreamlessly. But there was another way to forget.

She rested a hand on the towel wrapped sarong-like around her as she thought of Jake's warning last night: he would stay away from her until she said the words. The room had two double beds. Unless she said something, they would each take one. She covered her face with her hands. She needed Jake's strength and warmth, she needed to have him beside her tonight.

He tapped on the door. "You okay in there?"

She straightened quickly and gave herself a last look in the mirror, then opened the door. "I'm fine."

"Sure?"

"Uh-huh."

He held out a glass with something pink in it. "Here."

She took it. "What is it?"

"A little more wine."

"Where'd you get it?"

Leaning one shoulder against the doorframe, he gazed at her features lazily. "I went out while you were in the shower."

"Oh." She sipped at it, found it crisp and cool. "It's good."

"I don't know about that. It's not exactly vintage stuff, but I figured it might help you sleep."

She darted a look at the beds.

"I like your outfit," he said, smiling at her over the rim of his glass.

She held in one hand the towel she'd wrapped around herself and reached for his wrist with the other, giving him a penetrating look. "Are you drunk?"

"Only mellow, sweetheart. Just very . . . mellow."

She took another sip of wine. She was suddenly as nervous as a new bride. "Maybe you'd better take your shower now."

"Okay." He pushed away from the doorframe and smiled into her eyes. "Keep my place warm."

As soon as he disappeared into the bathroom and she heard the shower, Rachel stripped off the damp towel and got into one of the beds. She curled herself around the extra pillow and closed her eyes. She wouldn't object if Jake wanted to play the protective male tonight. She was ready to grab at anything to chase away the emptiness, to cushion the pain of yet another disappointment in their search for Scotty. Who understood better than Jake? It seemed the most natural thing in the world to let him take her into his arms. Anything to keep the scenes of what little Jamey Snowden had been subjected to over the past forty-eight hours from turning into pictures of Scotty.

She fixed her gaze on the crack of light under the bathroom door. The monotonous sound of the shower was almost like rain, inducing drowsiness. Her limbs grew heavy. She straightened out a tiny bit, sighing at the feel of the sleek percale sheets against her skin. She probably shouldn't have finished that last glass of wine after all.

Hurry, Jake . . .

Rachel moaned softly, resisting the images flashing through her mind in surrealistic confusion. A dream. A part of her brain knew it, another part responded with a rush of adrenaline to help her escape, but her limbs felt as heavy as lead. She swallowed in an attempt to unclench her jaws. Struggling to breathe, she tried to lift her arms to claw aside the weight of the covers, but she was mired in terror, paralyzed with the nameless horrors in her nightmare. Her eyelids fluttered as she frantically tried to avoid the moment of truth. She screamed silently. She didn't want to see this. But with a fateful, hopeless sense of inevitability, she knew she must.

She heard his beloved voice.

"Scotty, Scotty, I'm coming," she moaned, thrashing her head helplessly on the pillow. A primitive urge for flight made her legs twitch, but they seemed fixed in place, trapped by the same lead weight that rendered the rest of her body impotent.

Tears gathered behind her closed lids, then flowed down her cheeks in hot torrents. Terrified, she watched a black specter hovering over a run-down shack. There was water everywhere and dark, dense vegetation. So much thick, tangled junglelike growth. It was an evil place, and Scotty was there. He was afraid and he was calling for her. She opened her mouth to call him again.

Rachel jerked awake, the sound of her own scream shattering the dark quiet in the room.

"Baby, baby, wake up. You're dreaming." Jake's voice came to her like a lifeline in her terror. She homed in on its promise of safety, deliverance. Trembling, she threw her arms around him, hiding her face in his chest. Over the clamor of her heart, she heard his heartbeat, rock steady, deep and familiar.

"Oh, Jake, Jake, it was Scotty. I heard him. I heard him. He was calling for me."

"No, sweetheart," Jake murmured, stroking her hair. "Shh, shh. You were dreaming."

She shook her head wildly, clutching him with frantic hands. "No, no, it *was* Scotty. He's in a house somewhere. I saw him. I did, Jake. I did."

Holding her by the arms, he gave her an urgent shake. "Wake up, Rachel! You're dreaming. Wake up, sweetheart."

"No!" She fought him off, flailing her arms. "I saw him. I mean it, I saw him. It was Scotty!"

Jake caught her to him, holding her tightly, refusing to let her pull away even as she struggled, whimpering Scotty's name over and over. Against her ear he murmured reassurances, rubbing her back in long, soothing strokes. He sensed the moment she fully awoke. The frantic panting eased and she went still. She lay quiet for several long seconds, then moved a little, making a more comfortable place for herself against his chest.

"I'm sorry," she said, her tone husky and low.

Jake dropped a kiss on her hair. "It was a nightmare, baby. It's okay now."

Her hand moved idly across his chest, tangling gently in the familiar springy curls. "It seemed so real."

He leaned back against the headboard and pulled her close, settling her more fully in his embrace. "Would it help to talk about it?"

She frowned at the shadowy outline of a chair. "I've had a lot of nightmares since Scotty disappeared, but this was different somehow." A small shudder ran through her. "It was all so vivid. So real, Jake. That's the only word to describe it."

As she continued to caress his chest, his hand moved familiarly on her arm. "Real in what way?"

"Well, the location, for one thing. I don't know how my imagination could have conjured up such a place. It was so . . . so awful. I saw a lot of vegetation and trees and water . . . dark, still water."

"Like a swamp."

"Yes, like a swamp. And I've never been in a swamp, Jake."

"But you've seen them in movies and on television."

She sighed. "I suppose so. But what about the shack?" She swallowed, closing her eyes against the onslaught of fresh tears. "He's in that shack, Jake. I know he is."

"Sweetheart, it was a nightmare, the result of your worry and fear and the stress of seeing Jamey Snowden today." He caught her face between his hands and forced her to look at him. "It happens, Rachel. It's upsetting, eerie even, but it happens."

"Has it ever happened to you?"

His expression changed, but he didn't release her. "I've had nightmares over cases before, sure."

"Over Scotty?"

"Yeah, over Scotty."

"Did you ever have one like I just experienced? Did you ever feel like you were getting a message?"

"No."

She nestled against his chest. "You know the weirdest thing?"

"No, what?"

"I'm ashamed of this part."

"Tell me. I can keep a secret." He cupped her neck with his hand and squeezed tenderly. Rachel closed her eyes, feeling reassured and safe. Feeling warm and connected with Jake in the elemental way of a woman with a man.

"Although I've tried to hold on to the thought that Scotty was . . . is . . . still alive

—" her voice caught slightly "— in the past few weeks I've sort of lost hope. I've let myself begin to think that maybe he's . . . gone, you know? Forever. Maybe I'll never see my baby again." She swallowed. "I know you're going to freak out over what I'm getting ready to say, and I understand. I accept it because you see things more practically than I sometimes do. And you're going to say this is something only a woman would come up with. And you're certainly a lot more familiar with the ways of the world, the underworld . . ."

"What exactly are you trying to say, Rachel?" Jake asked indulgently.

"He's alive, Jake."

"Well, of course, that goes without saying, honey. Until we definitely know otherwise, we assume he's alive. When have I ever —"

"No, Jake. I mean he's alive and I know it. We just have to find that place."

"Honey —"

She leaned back to look into his face. "I knew you'd react like that and it's okay. I just wanted to tell you. Believe what you want, but in my heart, I know."

He brushed at a strand of hair that clung to her cheek. "Okay, for the record, you believe with all your heart that our son is alive."

"I do. Just when I was losing hope." She blushed a little at the look in his eyes. "One more thing."

"What?"

"I didn't mean to fall asleep before you got out of the shower."

He chuckled ruefully. "My own fault. I guess the wine worked too well."

She glanced at the other bed. It was smooth, obviously unslept in. But there was a pillow in the chair by the door.

"But not for you."

"I guess not."

"I meant to wait for you, but . . ."

"Why?"

"I didn't want to sleep alone tonight."

He tilted her chin up with his fingers. "If I stay in this bed with you, I'm going to want to do more than sleep, Rachel."

"I know."

"Are you sure?"

Her eyes fell to his chest and she flattened her hand on it. Beneath her touch, his heartbeat was a strong, solid thud. She moved her hand slowly back and forth, savoring a pleasure that she had not known for too long. She impulsively and softly kissed him.

He caught her up in his arms and held her fast, as though to give her one last chance to change her mind.

But her arms went around his waist and she buried her face in his neck. His heart beat beneath her ear. She had one quick look at the hope in his eyes before he ran his fingers into her hair and held her still. "I've waited a long time, Rachel. If you don't want the same thing, now's the time to stop."

Rachel hesitated. Their problems would still be there in the morning. Scotty was still lost. Her indiscretion had happened. There was Michael and the need to mend fences. But nothing seemed important enough to deny the forgetfulness to be found here tonight.

In answer, she lifted her head, offering her lips.

CHAPTER THIRTEEN

Michael worked the combination on his locker with a few deft twists and swung the door open. It was a pain having a locker on the lower level, considering his height, but because he had enrolled late, it was all he could get. When he started summer school, he could have chosen another locker, but he hadn't gotten around to it. He might not have to bother. With Jake and Rachel in Orlando checking out the little kid who might be Scotty, he wasn't sure how much longer he'd be able to hang around.

He sorted through his books looking for his geometry text. Today was the first day since he'd come to Tidewater that he'd felt like holing up at home, but he hadn't asked to cut because Miss Kendall was tough. He guessed it was part of her job description as county juvenile officer. She'd promised Jake that if Michael stayed with her, everything would go on as usual. That nixed skipping school. The only bright spot was that if his dad and Miss Rachel were delayed in Orlando, Miss Kendall would let him hang out at his dad's office, since she worked there, too.

Michael didn't want any delays. He wanted the little kid to be Scotty. The way he saw it, finding Scotty was about the only thing that was going to save his dad's marriage. But he still wasn't holding out a lot of hope. While hanging around the sheriff's office, he'd learned a lot about missing children, and it was all pretty depressing stuff. It would take a miracle for Scotty to be found safe and sound. It seemed to Michael that about the only thing left to do was to pray.

He used to pray a lot. When Mama Dee got so sick, he'd done it every night. When there seemed nowhere else to turn, it was sort of comforting. Although he wasn't sure that prayers were answered. There were a couple of ways to look at it, he'd discovered then. At first he'd prayed that Mama Dee wouldn't die, and sure enough she had lingered for months and months. But his grandmother was old and in a lot of pain. In a way, dying had relieved her pain and suffering. Wasn't that a merciful thing for God to do? So, you could say his prayers were answered, although not in a way that made him happy. On the other hand, if she'd lived, that would have been a straight answer to his prayer. But watching her suffer would have been terrible.

So he had mixed emotions about prayers.

"Hey, Mike! Look out below."

Too late to heed Todd Stewart's warning, Mike grunted as gym shoes balled into a towel struck him on the head. Todd had the locker just above Mike's. It was a running joke how much junk Todd crammed into the thing, and it was also known that you took your life in your hands if you were anywhere near when Todd opened it.

"Jeez, Todd!" Mike straightened, rubbing his head. "When are you gonna throw out some of that crap?"

"Soon, okay? Trust me." Todd's upper torso disappeared into the depths of the locker as he searched for something. "I know it's here somewhere . . ." He emerged waving his math book. "Got it!"

Mike aimed an irate kick at the towel. "Yuck! That thing stinks. Take it home and wash it, for Pete's sake."

Todd gave him a bland look. "Hey, man. Unlike some of us, I don't exactly have a plush setup at home. Thelma Pearson doesn't do laundry for the likes of me."

Mike felt rotten. The Pearsons were Todd's current foster parents, and generous they weren't. He mumbled something apologetic, then kicked his locker door closed.

"So, what's troublin' my man?" Todd wanted to know, glancing into the mirror on the door. A quick check confirmed that the tangerine tuft in his hair was still stiff. He fell into step beside Mike.

"Nothing."

"Tell you what." Todd draped an arm around Mike's shoulders, taking care not to stab him with the spiked studs on his leather bracelet. "Nobody makes double-fudge brownies like Miss Rachel. Whatcha say I drop by your place this afternoon and we do a few laps in the pool, check out those brownies just to see if they're still top of the line and you can tell me what's buggin' you."

"I can't go home this afternoon. My folks are in Orlando."

"Checkin' out Disney World without you?" Todd shook his head dolefully. "Not good, my man. Not good."

"It's business," Mike said. With his eyes on his feet, he completely missed the shy look he received from a petite blonde.

"Yo! Heads up, man. It's Cindy Johns." As she approached, Todd was all eyes even though her gaze was on Mike, who waved distractedly. Dropping his arm, Todd turned all the way around to watch her disappear in the opposite direction.

"Now that is some classy chick," he said.

"Don't call her a chick. She's a nice girl."

Todd stopped abruptly. "Okay, that's it. What's buggin' you? I know Cindy's a nice girl. You know I know Cindy's a nice girl. C'mon, man."

"I've got a lot on my mind, Todd."

"Like what, f'r instance?"

"My folks are in Orlando because a little kid turned up who could be Scotty."

"Wow. No kiddin'?" Todd's face lit up. He knew how much Scotty's return would mean to Mike's folks. He cocked his head, sending his earring swinging. "Hey, radical! Way to go!"

"He might not be Scotty, Todd."

"Well . . . sure, I guess." They started walking again. "Then again, he could be."

Michael kicked a paper ball out of his path. "If it's not Scotty, I might be moving on myself."

Todd sent him a look of disbelief. "Get outta here."

"I mean it."

"Are you losin' it, man? You've got it made with your old man and Miss Rachel."

"No, I don't. Things are . . . not cool. It's for the best, me leaving and all."

"How in hell do you figure that?"

"Nobody can take the place of that little kid, Todd."

"You don't have to take his place, Mike. You've got your own place with them. They like you. Shoot, they love you. Like, I can tell, man. I know real feeling when I see it."

"Miss Rachel doesn't love me."

"She does, man. You're crazy."

"I'm the cause of some bad things around there, Todd. I can't go into it, because it's personal. But that's the way it is. If I don't get out soon, it might be too late."

Todd was shaking his head. "I don't believe this. A great house, with a pool yet, a mom and a dad. You may not believe it, Mike, but I bet when you turn sixteen, he gets you a car."

"Yeah, well, I've thought it over and my mind's made up. If Scotty's not in Orlando, I'm outta here."

"When will you know something?"

Mike shrugged. "Today maybe. Tomorrow for sure. I'm staying with Jacky Kendall out at her place until they get back."

"The juvey lady, huh? She's okay. Tough, but okay."

"I know."

They were silent as they waded through the crowded hall. Todd reached his destination first, but instead of going into class, he stopped at the door, ignoring the students who jostled him trying to get by. "I don't know much about families and stuff, Mike, and I was just kiddin' about the car and all." Looking away for a second, he tugged on the ear that had no ornament, something Michael knew he did when he was troubled. "But I do know this, man — those people really care about you."

Michael, chewing the tender inside of his cheek, said nothing. He'd spent the past twenty-four hours thinking it through. Jake and Miss Rachel did care about him, but having him around was too much of a reminder of bad things. They'd be able to patch everything up better without him. He'd made the right decision. He was sure of it. Almost.

Todd reached over and thumped Mike's geometry book to get his attention. "You hear me, Mike? You'll be making a world-class mistake if you jerk around with the sheriff and his lady. People like that don't show up real often in this world. I'm tellin' it to you straight, man. You better rethink this dumb decision."

Michael managed a tight smile. "And you

better do your laundry." He turned and headed for class. Todd was a good friend. He'd miss him.

When Jake returned to his office, he found Michael waiting for him.

"Ms. Kendall told me the little kid wasn't Scotty," Michael said, watching his dad closely.

Jake shrugged out of the suit coat he'd worn to Orlando and hung it by the collar on a hat rack in the corner of his office. "That's right, son."

"I'm sorry, Dad."

"Thanks." Jake sent him a brief smile. "We'll just have to keep on looking."

He went to his desk and sat down, flexing his shoulders to ease some of the stiffness in his neck. The drive from Orlando had been tense. There had been nothing to cushion Rachel's disappointment. Until the Orlando thing, Jake had checked out all previous leads without her ever even knowing they had surfaced. He still questioned the necessity of subjecting her to unnecessary pain. Every protective instinct he had rebelled at hurting her. If this was the way back into her heart, he was willing to do it, but he didn't have to like it.

He would have spent the rest of the day at

home with her, but even before they'd reached the city limits, he'd sensed her withdrawing. He breathed in, feeling frustration and a niggling unease. Going to bed together should have helped. Maybe it had, but it hadn't solved anything. Though they'd found a few hours of forgetfulness with each other, there was still something missing. It should be so simple. He loved Rachel, and he was certain she still loved him. But he'd lain awake last night long after she'd fallen asleep, wondering if love was going to be enough.

"Is Miss Rachel okay?"

He sorted through a pile of telephone messages. "She's . . . coping, Mike. It's hard on her."

"Is she going to work today?"

"She said it would help to keep busy."

"I wish she worked someplace else."

Jake looked up then, noticing the strain on Mike's face. "Don't worry, son. It may seem dangerous after what happened with Kevin Nicholson, but I don't think anything like that is likely to happen again. They've beefed up their security, especially in Emergency, where they're most vulnerable."

Michael shifted from one leg to the other. "Who told you that?"

"The administrator."

"Oh, yeah, Mr. Campbell."

Jake's gaze narrowed at something in his tone. "You know Campbell?"

"Yes, sir. We've met."

Recognizing antipathy similar to his own, Jake smiled. "Not one of your favorite people, huh?"

"He smiles too much."

Jake had noticed the same thing. It amused him that his son would find crocodile smiles as suspicious as he did. "He's Rachel's boss. I guess we have to tolerate him."

"Yes, sir." Michael made a face, nothing obvious, just a subtle compression of his mouth. Jake chuckled softly. "Better not let Rachel see that look. She seems to like him."

"I gotta go, Dad." Mike turned abruptly, almost tripping over his shoes.

"You mean home?" Jake watched him fumble with the doorknob.

"Uh, I'm . . . I think I left a book at the gym after swim practice. I'll just jog over and pick it up."

"Speaking of which, I guess we're still on with Ocala for the next swim meet, right?"

"Right. Two weeks from Saturday."

"What's the good word?"

"Ocala's not very good. We'll beat them for sure."

Jake grinned and gave him a thumbs-up. "See you at supper."

With his hand on the doorknob, Mike hesitated a second or two, looking over his shoulder at Jake. "Bye, Dad," he said, then closed the door softly behind him.

For a few seconds after Mike left, Jake gazed thoughtfully at the door, a small frown replacing his smile. Something about the conversation with Mike bothered him, but he wasn't able to put his finger on it. He leaned back slowly in his chair. The past couple of days had been hard on Mike, too, he decided. He should have thought of that. Although Mike didn't know Scotty, he was the boy's half brother, and he could hardly live with Jake and Rachel without sharing some of their concern. Jake sat still, considering. Maybe that was it.

Or maybe it had something to do with Rachel and the incident at the hospital. Was it odd that Mike shared Jake's lack of enthusiasm for Rachel's job? He thought of Mike's dislike of Ron Campbell and wondered if he'd somehow communicated his hostility to his son. He was going to have to be more careful in the future. If Rachel was going to work for the . . . for Ron, then —

The phone on his desk buzzed suddenly.

"Something in the McAdam genes, I

guess," he muttered, reaching for the receiver. "Yeah, Mavis."

"Line one for you, Jake. Rick Streeter in Miami."

He thanked her and punched the button. "Rick. How's it going in the big city?"

"Only nine and a half years to retirement."

Jake laughed. "Yeah, well, it's your own fault. I tried to sell you on the joys of small-town life, but you wouldn't listen."

"Uh-huh. And just so you won't feel left out, we of the DEA are bringing big-town excitement to your little corner of the world."

Jake's amusement died. "What's up?"

Rick, too, became serious. "We've got some stuff going down there, Jake. Your county has been pinpointed as the hub for the Ramirez cartel."

"Ramirez? Jaco Ramirez? I thought we put him out of business over a dozen years ago."

"Certain individuals in Jaco's organization survived, and they've rebuilt. Jaco's one shrewd businessman."

Jake made a sound of disgust. "It's amazing."

"Yeah. We hurt them, but we'd have to destroy every sleaze bag who's ever turned up in the past thirty years to put them out of business."

Jake felt the familiar angry frustration that had driven him away from the DEA. "But the man's behind bars, federal bars. Twenty to life, if I remember correctly. How does he manage the cartel from there? Worse, how did he find his way to Kinard County?"

"His first lieutenant is his cousin. A low-life named Luis — also Ramirez. He's as smart as Jaco and ten times meaner."

Rubbing the bridge of his nose, Jake drew in a long breath. "What do you need from me?"

"Actually, not much other than some mutual cooperation. Our sources say there's a major exchange coming up within a day or two. Ramirez's security is tight. We wouldn't have made him except for a fluke when one of our undercovers got involved with one of Luis's women. He uses a lot of women — and kids — as drops and suppliers."

"What about your own security, Rick?"

He sensed Streeter's surprise. "It's tight. You know that absolute security is vital to a project like this. Why? Did you hear something?"

"Nothing you could take to the bank. One of my supporters heard from another nameless source that activity was picking up along the coastal area in the state, and in

Kinard County in particular."

Streeter swore. "When did you get this, Jake?"

"A few days ago. To tell you the truth, I've had a lot of things going, Rick, mostly personal. At the time, I thought about calling you in case there was a security leak in your outfit. I can tell you this — you'll never trace the source from this end. The person who told me is prepared to go to the wall before he'd reveal a source."

Rick swore again. "The press."

"I didn't say that."

"Just what I need, loose lips when I'm two inches from launching a major bust, the biggest to roll down the pike since we put Jaco away."

"Sorry, Rick. I hate to be the one to tell you."

"Forget it," Rick muttered. "I'm just glad to get wind of it. I owe you one, Jake."

"Just round up the sleazes who've invaded my county and we're even."

"You got it."

"Sure you won't need men or units from me?"

"It's possible, of course, but I hope not. We'll just have to play it by ear. I wanted to clue you in. I know how you guys feel when a bunch of *federales* descend on you. I wish we had the day and time. Hell, after what you just told me, I'd rather go fishin'. But I'm stuck, and unfortunately so are you, Jake."

Jake glanced at a stack of bumper stickers that Liz had dropped by his office that morning while he'd been on his way home from Orlando. Lately he'd neglected his campaign. He thought of his challenger. This was exactly the kind of thing J.B. would exploit if given half a chance. Especially if it took place out of the city limits and didn't go well.

"Have you notified Tidewater's finest?" he asked.

"Gonzales? Not yet." Rick also had first-hand experience with the city's chief of police, and none of it was pleasant.

"Don't screw up, Rick. If there's bad publicity, J.B.'ll play this every which way but quiet."

"Which is why I'm keeping him in the dark until I'm forced to do otherwise."

"It's your call, then. Just keep me posted."

"Thanks, Jake. With a little luck, we'll be in and out of Kinard County without alarming your constituents too much."

"I'm going to hold you to that, buddy." Jake straightened in his chair, relieved somewhat that the primary responsibility for the upcoming action was in the hands of the DEA. Unlike Jake's men, Rick's people had the experience. His own were good; he'd seen to that within the limits of his budget and the talent he had to work with. But in a showdown with sophisticated weapons and the sociopathic mercenaries Ramirez hired, loss of life was a definite possibility.

Leaning forward, he hung up the phone.

"Is that you, Michael?"

"No, it's me, honey." Jake paused to glance idly through the mail he'd picked up at the box. Apparently Rachel had forgotten to check it. Right on top was a letter he'd been hoping for from a political group. As he tore it open, Rachel appeared, drying her hands on a dish towel. She looked beyond him toward the front door.

"Michael isn't with you?"

"No, I thought he'd be home by now. He had to go to school and pick up something he'd forgotten." He smiled, scanning the letter. They were going to endorse him.

"Oh."

Still smiling, he looked up. "I guess it's just you and me."

She blinked. "What?"

He tossed the letter onto the table along

with the rest of the mail and pulled her up against him. "I said, I guess it's just you and me." Wrapping her close in a warm, tight embrace, he buried his face in her hair. "Mike's probably taking the long way home," he murmured, nuzzling the side of her neck. "Don't worry about him. He's almost fifteen, the perfect age to get sidetracked by a dozen different things."

"I guess so." It gave her chills when Jake breathed in her ear like that. Still, her gaze went to the windows, where dusk was fast approaching. She hadn't talked to Michael yet and she couldn't rest until she did. "He's always so good about letting me know where he is. It's unusual for him to be even a minute late."

"Mmm, you smell good," he murmured, inhaling the scent of her perfume. He feathered kisses down her neck, stopping at the hollow of her throat.

With her head tilted, Rachel almost gave herself over to Jake's attentions. Through the long midnight hours in Orlando, they had sought and found comfort in each other. But for Rachel, it had been temporary. She could not reach out and claim complete happiness with Jake until all her fences were mended. She'd gone to work today hoping to see Ron Campbell, but he'd

305

been called to Tallahassee for a day or two. And now Michael was nowhere to be found.

It was hard to think with Jake so close. Over Jake's shoulder, she noticed the mail scattered where he'd dropped it. An envelope caught her eye. Her name was printed across the front in large, childishly plain letters. Unstamped, wrinkled, unaddressed — obviously hand-delivered — it looked different from the rest.

"Jake!" She pushed urgently against his arms.

"We're okay, sweetheart," he whispered, breathing into her ear.

He thought she was worried about Michael walking in. Rachel arched her neck, pulling away. Her eyes were still on the envelope. "Jake, look at that."

"What?"

Her heart was thumping. Maybe it was about Scotty. She'd fantasized about receiving anonymous notes, phone calls, messages over the radio, television, through the sheriff's department. Could somebody actually have slipped something into her mailbox in broad daylight?

She snatched it up. On the point of tearing it open, she came to her senses. If it was about Scotty, it might contain valuable evidence, fingerprints. Her hands shaking, she showed it to Jake. "I just noticed this on the table. Was it in the mail when you picked it up?"

He took it, frowning. "I don't know. I didn't get through everything."

Her hand at her throat, she whispered, "Open it, Jake."

Holding it gingerly, touching only the edges, he picked up the letter opener that lay on the hall table and quickly slit the end open. He'd scanned only the first few lines when his face went slack.

"It's from Michael," he said.

"Michael?"

His hands shook slightly as he finished reading. "It's not to me, it's to you."

"I know, but . . ." She took it, frowning, not noticing the grim look on his face.

"There's another one for me."

Rachel glanced at the mail spread over the table as Jake reached for an envelope identical to the one addressed to her. Without the care he'd used in opening hers, he ripped the end off his own.

"He's gone."

"Gone?" She looked at the letter, noticing vaguely that it was printed on a sheet of notebook paper, the kind students used. Her note was forgotten in her hand. A few nights before, she'd helped Michael with an essay. He'd written it on paper just like that. "Where did he go?"

"Back on the road," Jake said, looking as though his face were carved in granite. "He says it's the best thing to do, that his presence has caused problems between you and me."

"Problems?" Rachel raised the note she held and began to read it. After the first two lines, her face paled. Her heart beating like a wild thing, she sank into the small antique straight chair that sat in the foyer. It took a second to steady the paper enough to read it. She blinked rapidly, trying to bring Michael's words into focus.

Dear Miss Rachel,
I wrote a letter to Dad explaining why I'm gone. Please don't worry. I'll be okay. I'm sending you this confidential note to beg you to tell Mr. Campbell to take a hike. He isn't half the man my dad is. I know you wouldn't even look at him twice if things hadn't been rough for you because of me and the circumstances that brought me to Tidewater. I know you think of my dad's mistake every time you look at me. If you aren't reminded every time you turn around

and find me underfoot, I know you will love him again and overcome the problems you two have been having lately.

Thank you for letting me stay with you while I was in Tidewater. I know it was hard for you, but I hope you will remember me best from the things we did together that were fun. I liked our rides to and from school, did I ever tell you that? I even liked shopping. I will always think of you when I eat kiwifruit or papayas. I never even saw that stuff in Iowa.

I will pray every night that my little brother will be found.

Your friend always,
Michael McAdam

Rachel closed her fingers on the single sheet, crumpling it into a shapeless wad. Holding it tight against her chest, she looked at Jake. "It's my fault."

He snatched the paper out of her hand. "What is he talking about? What's been going on with you and Campbell?" He lowered his voice, but his eyes were murderous. "If you've done anything to make my son take to the streets, I swear you'll answer for it, Rachel."

"No, no, I didn't," she whispered. "He

misunderstood. He — we . . ."

"Who misunderstood? Mike?"

Rachel bobbed her head. "Yes. It —"

"Misunderstood what?" He rattled the note from Michael under her nose. "What is this about Campbell?"

Still sitting, she gazed at him, her eyes swimming with unshed tears, making no effort to hide the misery and guilt that had haunted her since those stupid, wicked few minutes with Ron Campbell. "Oh, Jake."

"Tell me!"

She could hardly form the words. "He saw us together."

"Who? You and Campbell?"

"Yes."

He backed away as though to distance himself from what he might hear. "What did he see?"

"It was nothing, Jake. It didn't mean anything. I wanted to explain to Michael. I tried to explain at the time, but that was when Kevin . . ." Her voice caught on a sob. She gulped. "Kevin — Ah, the thing with Kevin and the gun."

"Forget Kevin!" he roared, making her jump. His voice lowered menacingly. "What did Michael see?"

"Oh, Jake . . ." She buried her face in her hands. "I'm so sorry. It was a stupid mistake. I knew it when he —"

"Who! When he what?"

She raised her head and looked at him then. "Ron. He kissed me."

He swung away, plowing his fingers through his hair. Realizing he held Michael's note to Rachel, Jake threw it down as though it burned his fingers. With his back to her, he asked, "What else did he see?"

"Nothing." Pulling herself together, she stood up. Seeing the dish towel she'd brought from the kitchen, she picked it up and wiped her eyes and her nose. "There was nothing else to see."

"Meaning you sent Michael away, or that that was the extent of Campbell's seduction of my wife?"

"Neither. I mean, both. Oh, I don't —"

She stared at her hands holding the towel. "It wasn't really Ron's fault, Jake." She took a deep breath, knowing she might be sounding the death knell of her marriage. "It was mine. I . . . I didn't discourage him as I should have."

"I knew he had eyes for you! I should have decked him when I had the chance at the fundraiser. He wouldn't have had the guts to try anything after that."

"Jake!" She gave him a hard look. "Are

311

you listening to me? It wasn't Ron's fault. It was mine!" With her forefinger, she poked herself in the chest and repeated quietly, "Mine."

They looked into each other's eyes in silence until Jake finally spoke. "Why?"

She shook her head helplessly. "I was so angry. And hurt. For weeks I was so mad at you I could barely breathe. I had this stupid notion that since you'd had an affair then I should have one, too. Tit for tat." She shrugged, a weary, dispirited gesture. "Ron Campbell just happened along at the right time."

"And that justifies it?"

She looked at him. "No more than your words justified that night in Miami."

He turned, unwilling to acknowledge that she'd scored a hit. "What's the matter?" he demanded, falling back on sarcasm. "Life in the fast lane's not all it's hyped up to be?"

"It was a silly, immature thing to do. I knew it the minute it happened. The worst thing is that I dishonored myself. I betrayed the vows I took eighteen years ago and I destroyed something valuable and precious I had with Michael." She bravely met his eyes again. "I hope I didn't destroy something else equally valuable and precious to me."

For a long moment, the two of them stood frozen in time. The silence thrummed with the things they didn't say. Both seemed aware that the moment was fraught with danger — for their relationship, for the two of them personally and for the future, if they wanted to spend it together.

Jake moved first. "We'd better find him," he warned in a level tone. "He's my son as much as Scotty is whether you like it or not. If I have to comb every inch of this state, I mean to bring him back."

"I know." Rachel wanted to find Michael every bit as much as Jake did, but she doubted Jake would believe her if she said so now. All this time Michael had been reaching out to her and she'd been locked in the cold prison of her grief over Scotty and her bitterness over Jake's betrayal. Still, he'd somehow slipped through her defenses anyway, right into her heart.

"What are we going to do?" she whispered.

"Find him," Jake said, clipping the words. "From the sound of his letter to you, it appears the two of you were closer than I realized. So you tell me, Rachel, where would my son run to?"

"I don't know." Rachel's eyes flooded with fresh tears. She bent over and picked up Michael's letter. He was her son, too, she realized suddenly, tenderly smoothing it out. Had she waited too long to admit that?

CHAPTER FOURTEEN

The bar was noisy and smelled of mildew and stale cigarette smoke. A few months before, when Tidewater had received seven inches of rain within a three-hour period, the bar, along with a lot of businesses located on the same ugly strip of Highway 6, had flooded. In Lou's Bar, long after the mud and water were mopped up, the stench lingered.

Just inside the door, Jake hesitated, squinting a little to see in the dimly lit interior. The crowd was almost exclusively working-class males. A burst of laughter and coarse profanity rose momentarily above the twang of Willie Nelson's guitar emanating from the jukebox. Jake didn't expect to learn much. Lou's patrons played as hard as they worked and stayed healthy by minding their own business. Looking at the rough, hard-bitten clientele, he wondered again how it was that Michael had stopped here. With his thumb, he pushed his hat back a little and made his way across the floor to the bartender.

"Sheriff."

"Lou."

Wiping his hands on his filthy apron, Lou Frank eyed the lawman warily. Until three days ago, in the eighteen months he'd owned the bar, Lou had never seen Sheriff Jake McAdam. His deputies always showed up when trouble broke out, but never the sheriff. Not even at election time.

"What'll you have, Sheriff?"

"Beer."

Lou filled a mug and set it down in front of Jake. "There you go, ice cold," he said heartily. "On the house."

As though he hadn't heard, Jake peeled two dollar bills from his clip and tossed them on the bar. Settling on the stool, he pulled the beer toward him, cupping it with both hands but leaving it untasted. Reflected in the mirror behind the bar were several tables, all occupied, and the pool table. He studied the two men playing, pegging them as the owners of a couple of the motorcycles parked outside. No one within his line of vision looked familiar. Turning his head, he surveyed the rest of them. A barmaid, a table of bikers, some construction types, a lone drunk, two decent-looking business-men. All strangers.

"Heard anything about your boy?" Lou asked.

Jake turned and stared directly into Lou's eyes. "Have you?"

Lou wiped both hands on his filthy apron. "I told you when you come in here a coupla days ago that I ain't seen him. I thought he might have turned up."

"I wouldn't be in here if he had."

"Yeah, well —"

"He hasn't turned up, and this pigsty is the only lead I've got, Lou." The door to the toilet slammed, and Jake glanced at the man who emerged, still adjusting the fly on his jeans. Seeing Jake, he looked quickly away and headed for a rear booth, where a woman waited.

Lou wiped off a sweat ring on the bar next to Jake. "Whaddaya want me to say, Sheriff? I run my business legal. I buy my license and I keep my nose clean. I don't have no hankerin' to make you mad, but I don't know nothin' about your boy."

"He disappeared three days ago," Jake said, keeping his tone low and his eye on Frank. "The only information we have is from a beer distributor who was using the pay phone in your parking lot. He said he saw Michael go into this bar. He was on foot carrying his duffel bag. It was three o'clock in the afternoon — the same time it is right now. Somebody in this place had to have seen him. I want to talk to whoever that is." He placed his hands flat on the bar and leaned slightly forward, pinning Lou with his gaze as surely as if he held a handful of his shirtfront. "Now. Are we communicating, Lou?"

Lou swallowed thickly. "I swear, Sheriff —"

"Just talk!" Jake slammed his fist down, sloshing foam from his beer over his knuckles.

"I'm tellin' the truth, Sheriff. If that boy come in here, I don't know nothin' about it. I didn't see him, honest."

"How could a boy, fourteen years old, unaccompanied, *clean,* come into this establishment, Lou, and not be noticed?"

Lou shrugged, sweating. "It purely beats me, Sheriff."

"Yeah, well, it beats me, too," Jake said, sliding from the stool and standing up. "It is so puzzling that I'm not giving up until I'm satisfied that I've had the truth from you."

"I know it sounds crazy, but that *is* the truth, Sheriff." Miserably, Lou looked from

318

Jake to his clientele. The jukebox was playing another cheating song. Three overhead fans stirred the stale air, squeaking rhythmically. It wasn't much of a business, but it was all he had. His customers were hard-ass, hard-drinking types. Many of them couldn't afford to fall under the scrutiny of the sheriff. None would put up with a hassle from the law. There were plenty of other places to hang out and drink. If Jake cared to, he could ruin Lou's business. They both knew it.

"I'm coming back tomorrow, Lou." Jake squared his hat, still looking straight into the bartender's eyes. "I want to talk with the individual who saw my son."

"Hey, Lou! We need some service over here."

Lou wiped his hands on the front of his apron. "Keep your shirt on, I'm comin'!" He gave Jake a sickly smile. "I'll see what I can do, Sheriff."

"You do that." Turning, Jake glanced around the bar again. In the rear, the man who'd been in the toilet was just rising to leave the booth. Catching Jake's eye, he sat down. Jake frowned, realizing where he'd seen him. He was the ex-con with the pickup at the accident scene on the highway several months ago. A name hovered just out of reach. He made his way to the door still trying to recall it.

Outside, he breathed deeply, needing some air. Of all the bars and dives in the county, Lou Frank's place ranked at the bottom. He took little pleasure in pushing the owner, but Lou's and its patrons were his only link to Michael's movements the day he'd left. He stood for a minute, considering. The facts were confounding. Except for the two notes, Michael had left no clue as to his intentions. Without a car, he would have been forced to rely on public transportation or friends, but nothing had turned up after an exhaustive search. It did not appear that he'd hitchhiked. On his trip from Iowa, he'd relied exclusively on truckers, yet no one appeared to have seen him at any of the truck stops within a thousand miles. Jake stared at the motley collection of motorcycles, pickups and ragtag cars. Why in hell had he stopped at this bar? Fighting discouragement and defeat, he started across the shelled parking lot. He couldn't face losing Mike as well as Scotty. There had to be something he could do.

But what?

Already he'd tried everything humanly possible to trace him, beginning with an immediate APB and unabashed exploitation of the whole law-enforcement network. He'd leaned heavily on personal contacts from Miami to Atlanta and New Orleans to New York. In Florida and the neighboring states, Mike's name and physical description were as familiar to the residents as the face of their favorite newscaster.

And still nothing — except for the sighting at Lou's Bar.

He made his way slowly to his car. Notwithstanding the cloudy circumstances, Michael's disappearance, like Scotty's, was producing a flurry of publicity. Ironically, most of it was favorable to Jake, valuable from the standpoint of his candidacy for sheriff of Kinard County, as Liz had pointed out pragmatically. Jake remarked bitterly to Rachel that until he had his sons safe in his house, he couldn't care less about politics.

Rachel. She had been beside him the first thirty-six hours as he'd combed the county searching for Mike. It had surprised Jake how well she knew Mike and his friends and habits. They'd gotten close in the months Mike had been with them. She was devastated that Mike had assumed their marriage could be mended by the simple act of his leaving. She wore her guilt and remorse like a curse. Her nights were sleepless, leaving her with a bruised look. She seemed as fragile as she'd been during the early days when Scotty had disappeared. If he'd doubted Rachel's feelings before, he no longer did. Repressing a sigh, Jake opened the car door and got inside. He could probably relieve a lot of her guilt, he supposed, but every time he was tempted, he got a clear picture of her kissing Ron Campbell. Campbell's hands on her.

He swore as a flood tide of jealousy and pure masculine outrage welled up in him. The thought of any man but him touching Rachel was enough to drive him over the edge. Fumbling in his shirt pocket, he found his sunglasses and shoved them on his face. As always, when his emotions threatened to take hold of him, Jake shut down. He was backing out when his radio squawked. Picking it up, he barked his code into the transmitter.

"Sheriff, we've got a situation here at the station. What's your ETA?"

"I'm headed back right now. Give me eight minutes." Jake accelerated. Grabbing the portable bubble, he clapped it on the top of his car. "Situation" could mean anything, but the fact that Mavis had not defined it meant it wasn't something to be aired on the radio. Hope spiraled. First and foremost, he was a father, not a lawman. "Is it Mike?" he said.

He knew when he heard Mavis hesitate. "Uh, sorry, Jake. No."

He nodded, his eyes bleak. "Six minutes." He signed off.

Rachel was in Michael's room, standing in front of the aquarium, when she heard Jake's car in the driveway. Hastily she wiped her cheeks with the heels of her hands. Glancing in the mirror, she saw that she looked reasonably together. Not that it mattered. Jake had not looked at her, really looked at her, since Michael ran away.

She reached for the can of fish food and with a shaky hand sprinkled some of it in the water. She was usually calmed by the fish and the soft, gurgling sounds of the water, but when Michael disappeared, most of her peace of mind went with him. At least here, in Mike's room, she didn't climb the walls in her guilt and pain and loneliness. In here, she felt close to him. When he came home again — she fiercely refused to think otherwise — she had so much to tell him. It would be difficult to explain to a fourteen-year-old why she had focused so deeply on her resentment and the circumstances of his birth, but Michael was mature beyond his years. He possessed a sensitivity to other people that was rare in a teenage boy. She was counting on his forgiveness and understanding. She wanted to be his mother. He'd started creeping into her heart that first night, the moment he'd looked at her with Jake's gray eyes and apologized for causing her pain. She blinked rapidly as tears stung her eyes. She *was* his mother. In every way imaginable, she was Michael's mother and she wanted to tell him so.

"Hi."

Rachel jumped at the sound of Jake's voice. She hadn't expected him to look for her in the house. Surreptitiously, she wiped her eyes again, glad that it was late. Except for the dim glow of the aquarium, the room was dark.

"Hello." She searched his face anxiously. "What is it? Have you heard something?"

He shook his head as he came toward her. He stopped at the aquarium, and for a minute, like her, watched the gentle undulations of a fantail weaving among the leaves of artificial ivy. "How was your day?"

"Sort of empty. I still haven't gone back to work," she said, her gaze on the fish. "In case he calls . . ."

"He knows your number at the hospital, Rachel. He knows my number at work. You don't have to do this."

"I want to."

Jake studied her profile a moment. "Are you crying?"

She shrugged mutely, unable to reply. "A little," she said finally.

He picked up the fish food and stared at it before placing it on the table. Then, inhaling deeply, he looked around the room. "I see this room, his bed, his chest, his desk, and I can hardly tell he lived here."

"That's because he took everything."

"What?"

"It's the only thing that comforts me." She waved a hand at the furniture with its cleared surfaces, the desk without a scrap of paper or a single pencil, the naked walls stripped of the posters Mike had tacked up within a few days of moving in. "He ran away, but he took everything from his life with you and me that wasn't nailed down. So I know he was happy here," she said fiercely. "Wherever he is, he's carrying those reminders of us. I'm counting on him missing you so much, he'll come home no matter what he thinks of me."

Jake touched her shoulder, just one gentle brush of his fingers. "He loves you, Rachel. That's part of his reason for running. He understood the problems we had a lot better than most kids would have. I suppose his decision to leave us might even make sense to an idealistic teenage boy."

"Oh, Jake." She closed her eyes, and the tension that held her together seemed to disintegrate. She wilted like a sunbaked flower on a stem. "I'm so sorry."

With his thumb, he stroked her trembling lips. "Don't be. Maybe we both should have paid more attention. We could have set him straight if we had been aware he was contemplating something so drastic."

Without thinking, she leaned into him, slipping her arms around his waist. "I miss him so much, Jake."

Drawing her close, his hands met at the small of her back. "Yeah, me, too." His eyes fell on the aquarium and he chuckled softly. "He probably would have taken the fish tank if he could have figured a way."

She made a small, distressed sound.

"I'll find him, sweetheart. I'll find him and bring him home."

With her cheek against his chest and the strong beat of his heart in her ear, Rachel sighed. She was forgiven. She felt it in the warmth of his embrace, in the wordless sound he made as his lips touched her temple.

"I love you, Jake."

"Ah, Rachel . . ."

326

She felt foolish, almost light-headed, her relief was so great. Oh, how the forgiveness of one person could mean the difference between living and dying. Her hands clenched on the material of his shirt at his waist. "I thought . . . I wondered if I'd ever get to tell you again."

"Hush." He kissed her ear and the soft underside of her jaw. Rachel's breath caught. He was so dear, their love so special and precious.

"Jake . . ."

He lifted his head to gaze questioningly into her eyes.

Holding on to him, she wondered if she could make him understand. The night in Orlando they'd both needed comfort; trouble shared was trouble halved. But when she'd awakened the next morning, there had been no sense of peace, no feeling that their problems had been resolved. She didn't want that again. She didn't think she could bear that again.

"I need to know how you feel, Jake."

He inhaled, then with a rush of breath, gave a short laugh. Pulling her tight against him, he asked, "How do you think I feel, baby? What does this tell you about how I feel?"

"To tell the truth, not very much."

"I want to go to bed, Rachel. I want to make love to you. That's what I feel, Rachel."

"And then what?"

For a few seconds he just looked at her. Rachel felt a brief pang of sympathy for his confusion. In all the years they'd been married, she'd never asked to know his feelings. It had been enough to know he loved her and showed her often. In a way, it was a testimony to the depth of their devotion to each other that their marriage had endured as long — and as well — as it had, considering that neither of them had been very skillful in communicating the really important things. Now, left with only each other and a somewhat tattered relationship, they needed more than a union of bodies. They needed to share their minds and hearts and souls.

Rachel wondered wryly how the idea would strike Jake. She sensed he was waiting for her to speak. But when she remained stubbornly silent, he drew in a deep breath.

"Okay. Okay. There's something important going down here, but I'm not sure I know what it is. Help me out, sweetheart."

Rachel prayed for the right words. "We made love in that motel in Orlando, but we didn't . . . it didn't . . ."

"Fix everything? We didn't come home

and live happily ever after?"

Sagging a little with relief, she rested her forehead against his chest. "See? You felt it, too."

He closed his eyes and after a moment, he said, "I know what you mean. I didn't want to admit it. I figured we could work it out. We'd restored that part of our relationship. And if Mike hadn't disappeared . . ."

And my stupidity over Ron Campbell hadn't come out . . . She finished the thought for him with an inward flinch.

Jake rested his chin on her head. "I guess one night wasn't enough to fix everything."

She nodded, moving her palm across his chest in a slow caress. "There was a lot to fix, Jake."

"Yeah."

"Scotty, my emptiness, then Michael, what he saw with Ron, the Miami thing, your . . ."

Affair. One-night stand. Betrayal. Yet how could she judge him now? Her guilt and torment washed over her anew.

"We hadn't worked it all out then, Jake." She looked at him intently. "Have we now?"

He studied her with equal intensity. "We still haven't found Scotty."

"We haven't found Michael."

"But we will."

"Yes, we will," she told him softly, leaning into him. Then she smiled, just a tiny fleeting flutter of her mouth. "Remember my dream?"

"Yeah." With his hand cradling her face, he said, "Are you okay now with the Miami thing?"

She looked away for a long moment before nodding. "I think so. It hurt, but it was a long time ago, and we have Michael." She took a little breath. "Are you okay with Ron Campbell?" she asked, watching him carefully.

"I will be after I kill him."

"Jake!"

"I'm okay, I'm okay. But let's just put it this way: wouldn't you like to work someplace else?"

Shaking her head, smiling, she kissed his palm, thinking that only temporary insanity could have made her consider jeopardizing her place in this man's heart. Whatever his faults, he was simply the only man she'd ever loved.

"So . . ." Jake's arms tightened fractionally, prodding her. "Can we go to bed now, sweetheart?"

"Make love," she corrected gently, touching her mouth to his. There were other things, but they could be dealt with another

330

time. She wanted to be a full partner, a complete woman. She wanted to be all that she could be, and she wanted it with this man. It was enough for tonight that they seize this moment.

"Jake."

"Mmm."

"I've been thinking . . ."

He groaned, then grunted in protest when she gently yanked a few of his curly hairs. "Don't go to sleep yet."

He squeezed her sleepily. "I'm all ears, baby."

"I'm giving notice tomorrow."

Shifting, he pulled back a little so that he could see her face. "You're quitting your job? Honey, I was just kidding when I said that about —"

"I know. I'm not quitting because you think it's the thing to do. I'm quitting because it's what I want to do. I'm going back to school."

When he didn't say anything straightaway, Rachel said, "Well?"

"Well, what? I know better than to open my mouth on these career announcements. Any opinions I have on this subject are going to stay locked in, buttoned up."

"That is not communication, Jake. That's pique."

He gave a short laugh. "Pique?"

"Annoyance, irritation," she said.

"I know what it means, sugar."

"I'm resigning because I want to do something more worthwhile than admitting people to the emergency room."

"What about Campbell's offer? Assistant to the administrator has more prestige than a clerk in Emergency."

"Prestige isn't what I want, Jake. Besides, do you realize how patronizing that sounds? I'm not working for a lark. I want to make a difference. Is that so hard to understand? I already have a degree in psychology. I want to take some more courses, subjects that will help me get a job as a counselor at a school. Or I might consider casework for the county. From some of the things I've seen in the foster-care system, there's plenty of opportunity. Or maybe something like Jacky Kendall does."

"Jacky Kendall is a qualified police officer, Rachel. She's been to the academy. I don't want you to —" He stopped, then drew in a deep breath. "Tell me you don't want to be a police officer, baby. Please."

She chuckled softly. "I don't want to be a police officer, Jake. I just meant I like the way Jacky works with troubled kids. I think I might like to do that, but not necessarily in a law-enforcement setting."

"Then the foster-care thing might be your best bet."

She looked at him in surprise. "You mean you think it's a good idea? You don't have a problem with it?"

He reached for her, then leaned back against the pillows, bringing her with him. "I want you to be happy, sweetheart. If you want it, as they say — go for it."

Smiling, she settled against him and stared at the lazily revolving ceiling fan, gathering her thoughts. "I'm almost happy tonight, Jake."

"Well, thanks, I think."

"No, seriously. I feel as if I've spent the past few months battling demons and I didn't even know their names."

"You've had to bear the cruelest tragedy imaginable, Rachel. Losing a child can take down the strongest person. It's natural for something like that to have serious repercussions."

"It isn't only Scotty. I always believed there were certain things in life that I had to have in order to be happy and satisfied, and the funny thing is, I don't have any of them now, Jake." She glanced at him before nuzzling her cheek against him. "Except you."

"What things don't you have?"

"Well, the things were never a big house and a BMW and membership in a country club. At least I was wise enough to know that all along. But having a child, rearing him in a way other people approved of, running my home flawlessly, playing the role of the perfect wife for you and your constituents . . . Those were the things. My identity always hinged on something, or someone, else." She studied the fan with a frown. "I'm amazed that I wasted so many years feeling that way. Now Scotty is gone, Michael has run away, scandal has touched my perfect world, my brief stab at a career has turned sour. In fact —"

"You make it sound as if your life is in ashes at your feet."

"Well, in some ways it is." It took a second before she picked up on the wary note in his tone. He didn't like hearing her voice dissatisfaction with her life. She realized with a flash of insight that he felt threatened. Had she given him so little assurance that she would love him through thick and thin? If so, was it any wonder he felt he must always fix everything for her? What a crushing responsibility, even for a man of Jake's strength.

"What I mean is that I finally discovered that I can be fulfilled and at peace with myself without many of the things I once thought necessary."

"Has it been so awful being Mrs. Jake McAdam?"

This time she definitely heard the hurt in his voice.

"No, it's just that I've been a fair-weather wife to you, Jake, and you deserved better. I've been little girl instead of a partner. You sheltered me from the harsh realities of the search for Scotty because you've always taken care of me."

Jake's hand on hers was a little too tight. "It's natural for a man to want to protect his wife," he said gruffly.

"Yes, but not to the extent I demanded or allowed. I wound up being somebody I didn't like."

"Rachel, you didn't demand any such thing. We did what we wanted."

"Okay, we'll share the blame."

He dropped his head back against the headboard. "How come that doesn't sound as if I won this debate?"

"This is not a debate, Jake. It's —"

"Communication," he finished, saying the

word as though it left a bad taste in his mouth.

"You can see the pattern all the way back to the beginning, in Miami," she said, pausing thoughtfully. "The miscarriages were hard for me. I wanted a baby so much. But for the wrong reasons, I know now. To complete me." She glanced at him. "That was hard for you, it must have been. A few times you've hinted at feeling short-changed. . . ."

Jake made a move as though to protest, but she shushed him with a quick shake of her head. "And you were right. But I did love you then, Jake. I was just so mixed up, so insecure. Your job didn't help, either. Working for the DEA was dangerous. It was hard for me to cope with that."

"It must have scared you to death when I actually got shot."

"It truly did. But oddly enough, it took something that drastic to make me realize how much I loved you and that with or without a baby, I wanted to be your wife. I had gone home to Tidewater that week to think it out." She rubbed her cheek idly against his arm. "If you hadn't left the DEA, I might have grown up faster. But you did leave Miami, which subdued most of my fears, and life in Tidewater was safe from the harsh things in the world. There has certainly been less stress here. But looking back I can see where I missed opportunities to focus on a personal goal, a career or some worthy cause, that would have boosted my self-esteem. Being here made it easier to continue along until at last the miracle happened. I got pregnant."

"I wanted a child as much as you, Rachel."

She rubbed against him affectionately. "Not quite, but it's sweet of you to say so."

One of his eyebrows rose. "Taking care of you again, am I?"

"It's okay to do it a little." She angled her head so that she could see his profile. "I've always envied your . . . steadfastness, did I ever tell you that? You were always so sure, so confident, whereas I've always dithered over things, been blown around by every little wayward wind. Awful as it is, I feel as though losing Scotty forced me to grow up. Does that make any sense?"

He was silent so long that Rachel pushed back to see him fully. "Jake?"

"I'm just wondering how you could have been so deep in all this soul-searching without my knowing it."

"Communication isn't something we've been very good at," she told him softly. "But

337

don't feel bad. I've always internalized things. You haven't been aware of my thoughts because I haven't been sharing them."

"I guess it's a good thing you've grown up, then, because you would have been in trouble depending on me lately."

His remark derailed her thoughts for a second. She frowned in the dimness. "What do you mean by that?"

"You're not the only one fighting a few demons, Rachel."

It was so rare for Jake to express any personal doubt or to admit to any shortcomings that she paused, uncertain what to say. Had talking out her own tangled thoughts made it easier for him to let down his guard? "It has been a bad time all around, for everyone," she said cautiously. "I —"

She stopped at the sound of his harsh, mirthless laugh. " 'Bad' is an understatement, wouldn't you say?"

"Are we talking about Michael's disappearance? Or Scotty's? Or what?"

Both, she realized suddenly as he threw the sheet aside and got out of bed. All of the above. It was dark in the bedroom, but he didn't touch the lights. He went to the window and swept the drapes aside. Light from the street outlined Jake in sharp, stark silhouette.

"He seems to have just vanished, Rachel."

He meant Michael, although he could just as easily have been referring to Scotty. For the first time, Rachel glimpsed the immense depth of Jake's pain. He was a man dedicated to his family, his town, his county, to keeping them all safe. How bitterly frustrating it must feel to have failed in that mission. He would see it as failure, she knew with sudden insight. And, to her shame, she had done so little to ease his burden.

"I know you're doing everything you can."

"For what it's worth!" he said bitterly.

Rachel slipped out of bed and reached for a nightshirt. "I can't believe that in this whole town no one noticed a lone teenage boy carrying a duffel bag. He'd have had to seek transportation of some kind." She pulled the nightshirt over her head. "What about that bar?"

"I went again today. I didn't get a thing out of Lou Frank, but he knows something. I can feel it."

Rachel went over to him, wanting to see his face. "If he does, why keep it from you?"

"Good question." With a grim look at the empty street, he said, "And I plan to get some answers. I'm going back tomorrow.

One way or another, Lou's going to talk to me."

She put out a hand and touched him. "Jake, be careful. The people at that bar are rough."

He looked at her. "Is that right?"

"Yes!" Her fingers tightened as she gave him a little shake. "In the emergency room, we were always patching up Lou's customers. Knives, guns . . ." She shuddered. "You name it."

"I don't care how rough Lou's place is, Rachel. Like I said, I'm going back tomorrow, and I'm going to find out what my son was doing there." The words came vehemently, unleashing the frustration and fear he'd kept locked inside. "I'm not failing here, too!"

"Fail —" The look in his eyes shook Rachel. "Jake, what's the matter? What is it?"

Turning from her, he clasped the back of his neck. "It's — it's nothing." He paused momentarily. "But don't you worry. I've got everything and everybody going flat-out to find them both, Rachel. Believe me, I —"

"Jake." Before he could say another word, she reached up and put her fingers over his mouth. "Don't do that anymore, Jake. You promised."

"Sorry, baby. I forget." Shaking his head,

he laughed harshly. "No protecting my woman anymore. No pulling my punches at home. No more pretending to take care of everything." His mouth twisted bitterly. "There shouldn't be any problem there. Up to now, I sure haven't taken care of much. My whole world is falling down around my ears and I'm helpless to do a thing about it."

Her heart aching for him, Rachel searched for something to say to comfort him. She noticed for the first time the weary look about him. He usually seemed so tireless, so confident, but tonight there were lines of strain and worry etched on his face.

"The fact is, Rachel —" he hesitated, meeting her eyes bleakly "— I'm thinking of dropping out of the race."

"Jake, you don't mean that!"

"Yeah, I do."

"But you can't!"

"Why not?"

"Because . . . Well, because law enforcement is what you do. It's what you love. You're the best sheriff Kinard County has ever had. You're the best man —"

"The best man?" He walked away from the window and stopped at his dresser. On the top was his badge. He picked it up. "That's a laugh. That's rich." With a snort, he dropped it and looked at her. "Open your eyes, Rach. Take a look at my county. Drugs are everywhere, the town is poised to become a major distribution center, my six-year-old has been snatched practically out of my own yard, my other son vanished — I know something bad happened there. Mike wouldn't just take a hike like that."

Some of his rage seemed to fizzle. "What kind of lawman am I if I can't keep my own sons safe? What about keeping other kids safe on the streets? How can you possibly say I'm the best man to hold the office of sheriff?" He shook his head. "Wake up and smell the coffee, baby."

"But you are, Jake," she said softly, as though he had said nothing of significance. "You are the best man."

He raised his gaze to the ceiling and kept it there. "Why? Give me one reason."

"I know you."

"I know me, too," he said with disgust.

"Okay. I know your integrity, your deep sense of responsibility, your basic goodness. I know how you hate injustice and I know you're not afraid to lay your life on the line for all your principles." In her earnestness, she put both her hands on his arm. "Where else can the citizens of Kinard County find a man like that?"

He studied her in silence. The clock she'd given him for his birthday chimed the half hour. Next door, the dog barked. Somewhere in the night sky, distant thunder rumbled.

"You really believe all that?"

"With all my heart."

After a minute, Jake sighed. "Well, J. B. Gonzales certainly isn't the answer."

"Right!"

With a deep sigh, he put his arm around her. "What if I don't find them, Rach?"

She remembered her dream, how vivid it was.

How certain she'd been that it had meaning. Clinging to that belief now, she rubbed her cheek against Jake's arm. "We'll find them."

CHAPTER FIFTEEN

Rachel stood at the kitchen counter and poured coffee into two cups. From the bedroom, she heard the familiar sounds of Jake's morning routine. The slam of the shower door meant he'd finished showering and would begin shaving at the sink on the right side of the double vanity. His side. Hers was on the left. Carrying the coffee, she left the kitchen and headed down the hall. It was the first time since she'd banished him that Jake had showered and shaved in the master bedroom. She didn't plan for him to use the guest bathroom ever again.

"Ready for coffee?" she asked, placing the cup near him on the marble top.

"Morning, sweetheart." Freshly shaved, he was sleek and masculine. Specks of foam still clung here and there, but he ignored them and leaned over and kissed her sweetly. "Mmm, you taste cool and tart."

"Orange juice," she murmured. "You like it?"

"Uh-huh."

When he stepped back and began wiping the foamy residue off his face, she leaned against the vanity to watch him. She'd always enjoyed their time together before he left to go to work. During their months of estrangement, these moments of intimacy had been missing. She'd tried hard to tell herself she hadn't felt the loss. But she had. Oh, she had.

"Still planning to resign today?" he asked.

"I've got the letter all typed and signed. Anything special on your agenda today?"

"Lou Frank," he said succinctly, pulling on a pair of white briefs.

"You will be careful."

"I will be careful, baby." As he reached into the closet for a shirt, he looked at her over his shoulder.

"I may be late getting home," Jake said a few minutes later, securing the belt on his pants. "Rick Streeter's in town."

"From the DEA? That Rick Streeter?"

"Yeah. They've got this whole area of the coastline under close surveillance, and Kinard County in particular. Something major's in the works." He looked up, sliding his wallet into his hip pocket. "Don't worry.

It's DEA all the way. We'll have to stand by, that's to be expected. But they won't want us locals mixing it up with the bad guys any more than I want us to get involved in it."

She stared thoughtfully at a spot beyond him. "That would explain the epidemic of drug activity here in Tidewater, wouldn't it?"

"It might." He was completely dressed, but he didn't make any move to leave the bedroom. Instead, he paused for a moment, studying her with an odd look on his face.

"What is it?" she said.

"Is that all you've got to say?"

"About the DEA thing?"

"Yeah."

"You mean where's the tearful lecture on the danger of anything connected with Rick Streeter? And, oh, the checklist of dos and don'ts if Rick should just happen to need you and your people?" She shrugged, smiling. "I'm trying not to nag so much."

Cramming his keys into his pocket, he reached out and pulled her against him. "A little nagging makes a man feel loved," he said, rubbing her nose with his.

"I have other ways to make you feel loved." She planted a kiss on his neck, just under his ear.

He was reaching for his tie when the

phone rang.

He jerked up the receiver. "Yeah?"

Frank Cordoba said, "Sorry, Jake, but we need you here."

"What's up?"

"The DEA thing. Streeter's arrived."

"Loaded for bear?"

"Loaded for bear."

"Give me ten minutes." He hung up, fishing for his keys with his other hand.

"Complications?" Rachel asked, knowing the signs.

"Looks like it. I'll call you when I get a chance."

She put her arm around his waist and walked with him to the door. When he pulled it open, he drew her forward and kissed her.

She smiled against his mouth.

"I love you, baby."

"I love you, too."

She was already dressed to go to work and was standing in front of the aquarium feeding the goldfish when the doorbell rang. Her heart jumped and she ran from the room, hope springing to life as she hurried toward the door. Every time she looked at those dumb goldfish it was as though Michael stood right at her shoulder. She was almost at the door when she realized it couldn't be Michael. Why would he need to ring the doorbell?

It was Todd Stewart.

"Todd!" In spite of herself, she looked hopefully beyond him, but there was no one there.

" 'Lo, Miss Rachel." He grinned with a winning mix of diffidence and brass.

"Hello, Todd." Her smile came spontaneously. She realized, with some surprise, that she was glad to see him. Very glad to see him. His hair, as usual, was stiff with gel and colorful dye. The last time Michael had brought him home, the left side had been bright purple. Today it was tangerine. The earring, she noted, was different. Instead of the macabre skull and crossbones, a pewter circle with the word *peace* inside it dangled from his left earlobe. His parents must have been activists in the sixties, Rachel thought. But then she remembered the absolute dearth of parental influence in Todd's life, and her own loss rose in her like an unexpected thorn in a bouquet.

"Can I come in for a minute, Miss Rachel?"

"Oh, Todd, of course." She stepped back, opening the door wide. "I'm sorry. I was just —" She managed a smile. "When I saw you, I thought of Michael and it . . . he . . ."

"I know. He split."

"I've been trying to find you for two days," she said.

"My mom made one of her pit stops," he explained, shrugging as though a visit from his mother was insignificant.

"I know." She'd learned that much from his caseworker. "Is she staying?"

"Nah, she's already gone, headin' for Atlanta this time. At least, that's the plan. She's travelin' with her agent. They said they'd try to send for me if this gig works out. She's a singer, did you know that?"

"Not really," Rachel murmured, struck again by the hardships some children suffered. How could Todd's mother bear to leave him to the care of the state?

"Todd, I wanted to ask you about Michael. I've talked to most of his other friends, trying to get some clue as to where he might have gone."

"He told me he might have to do something like this."

"Have to?"

"His thinking was a bit messed up, Miss Rachel. And I told him so. But he was not in a listenin' mood, if you get my drift." He looked beyond her to the den and the doors that led to the patio and pool and shook his

349

head wonderingly. "I could tell he was wrestlin' in his mind with a lot of heavy stuff. He said it was mostly personal, but it had to do with you and the sheriff. That day the two of you went to Orlando and the little kid didn't turn out to be — what was his name? Sammy?"

"Scotty," she whispered, her hand resting at her throat.

"Well, that day he was down, man, really down."

"Todd, did he tell you anything?" She caught his arm eagerly and began to urge him toward the den.

"Well, that's what I've been wonderin' about." He sank down on the couch, obviously thinking back on his conversation with Mike. "When I heard he'd split, I got to thinkin' about what we said, goin' over and over it in my head. Mostly I was mad at him for even thinkin' about tossin' all this away." He looked again at the pool, where late-afternoon sun shone like Fourth-of-July sparklers on the blue water. "I told him he was dumb to think you didn't love him."

Rachel pressed her fingers to her mouth, stung by guilt and a sense of remorse. "I do love him, Todd, but I'm so ashamed that he had to run away before I realized just how much. Before I could tell him. If only —"

"I'm not sure he ran away, Miss Rachel."

"Why?"

He drew in a breath and stared at his hands. "This is gonna sound crazy." He laughed shortly. "But hey, my kinfolk are crazy. At least, most of them, from what I've seen."

"Todd, you're not making sense. What does your family have to do with Michael leaving?"

He leaned back, giving her a sideways glance. "I've got some relations living out in the boonies, Miss Rachel. Cross Corners. You ever heard of it?" When she nodded, he hunched one shoulder. "Man, it's like a swamp out there. Anyway, they're . . . Well, let's just say they're not your kind of people."

"And —" she prompted. This was not the time to dwell on her past snobbery. She'd make it up to Todd later. To Michael.

"I was talkin' to Mike about them the other day. I never go out there if I can help it because . . ." He shrugged. "Face it, they're mean types. Really low-down, you know?"

He looked at her and continued. "Nah, I can see you don't know. Well, anyway, the last time I was there, they had this little kid. He just sort of hung around, didn't say much. They said he was a cousin or something."

Rachel sat down simply because her legs wouldn't hold her another moment.

"Y'see, up to the time I met Mike, I'd never noticed those pictures of your little boy. Scotty? Even when I did, it still didn't click, y'know? But once me and Mike got to be friendly, I couldn't help but think about Scotty. Man, Mike was always, *always* dreamin' up schemes to find him. He was gonna flush out the porn people in case they were the ones who took him. Or he was hitchin' to Miami because they have the most street people. . . ." He shook his head. "Like he was gonna spot one little six-year-old in a place with a coupla million people."

"Todd, please —"

"Oh, yeah, well . . . The more I thought about that little kid out at Cross Corners, the more it seemed to me he looked like the kid in the pictures."

For a second, Rachel thought she would not be able to breathe. Hope and fear were a painful tangle in the place where her heart was beating madly. "Oh, Todd."

Todd looked directly into her eyes. "I told Mike about him that day."

"You think Michael went out to . . . to Cross Corners?"

"I don't know nothin' for sure, but it could be."

"You think the little boy could be . . . Scotty?"

"Oh, now, ma'am, I don't want to get your hopes up. I —"

"And if he is, and if Michael just showed up . . ." She stopped, frowning. "How would he have found the place? That swamp is huge. People get lost in there."

"I got a cousin hangs out at a bar on Highway 6," Todd told her. "He lives out at Cross —"

"Lou's Bar?"

Todd gave her a surprised look. "Yeah, Lou's. You talk about mean . . . Those dudes are the worst. They like to mix it up with knives and whips and —"

"Jake." Rachel came to her feet abruptly. "We've got to call Jake. No, we've got to go and *see* Jake." She wheeled toward the bar, where her car keys were. "Todd, do you know where these people live?"

Todd stood up. "Yes, ma'am, but we can't just head out there blind. They might be my kinfolk, but they're still mean people, Miss Rachel."

She put a hand to her throat, resisting the thought of what Scotty might have been

353

forced to endure for six months. "In what way?"

"Just mean," Todd said darkly, as though that explained everything. "It may be Scotty or it may not be, the little kid out there. But I've been thinkin' about Mike. If he did go out there, where is he now? How is it he just disappeared?" He pulled at his T-shirt. "To tell the truth, Miss Rachel, I'm real worried."

Jake was standing with Rick Streeter in front of a map of the county when he heard the commotion outside his office door. When he recognized Rachel with Todd Stewart, his breath caught in his chest. Michael! They'd found Michael!

Seeing Jake's expression, Rick stopped mid-sentence, his gaze following Jake's to the woman hovering in the doorway. A teenage boy with tangerine hair stood behind her.

"Jake!" Rachel's tone was enough to make Jake move involuntarily toward her, his arms opening. She flew to him and let herself be enfolded and held close for a fervent moment before pushing back and looking up at him. "I'm sorry to barge in like this, but you have to hear what Todd . . ." She swallowed and began again. "Todd thinks —

Todd told me . . ."

"Is it Michael?" Jake asked, giving her a little shake.

She nodded frantically. "And Scotty! Both of them!"

He sent a quick look at Todd, who shuffled his overlarge feet self-consciously but held his gaze. "Todd?"

"I'm not sure, Sheriff. I told Miss Rachel it might not be Scotty." He shrugged. "But he sure looks like those pictures."

With his hand on Rachel's arm, he reached for Todd's shoulder and ushered them both into his office.

"How are you, Rachel?"

Jake had forgotten Rick. At his greeting, Rachel gave him a quick, distracted smile and introduced Todd. Jake plowed his hand through his hair. "Rick, how about a break here? There should be fresh coffee." He glanced at the clock on the wall, even though the last thing on his mind was a coffee break.

"Sounds good," Rick said, moving obligingly to the door. "Nice seeing you, Rachel. Todd. Take your time, Jake. I'm going to brief my team and try to work out some logistical snags. The terrain out there is rugged. We have to keep in mind that they're in their natural habitat and we're not."

Nobody sat after he left. As soon as the door closed, Rachel and Todd spoke simultaneously.

"Jake, you have to —"

"Sheriff, I could be —"

Jake raised a hand. "Wait. I can't listen to you both at once. Rachel, you tell me what's going on."

Looking at him, she pressed her fingers to her lips, trying to gather herself together, but she couldn't prevent her hand from trembling. "Jake, this is . . . You're not going to believe this."

"Just tell me and let me decide that," he said, hanging on to his patience by a thread.

"Todd has seen a child who looks like Scotty, living with some of his relatives."

Jake shot a quick look at Todd. "Why didn't you say something before now, boy?"

"It wasn't intentional," Rachel said quickly, wanting to protect Todd. Jake could be intimidating if riled. "He only put it together today."

"Put what together?" Jake demanded, his attention centered again on Rachel. "And what does this have to do with Michael?"

"Todd never thought much about this little boy suddenly coming to live with his relatives until he met Michael at school and they became friends. According to Todd,

356

Michael was concerned about Scotty. Since his picture is all over town, when he and Todd were together, Michael talked about it frequently."

"All the time, man," Todd put in.

"Todd gradually became aware of the resemblance between the pictures of Scotty and the little boy in Cross Corners. He —"

"Where?" Jake whipped out the word.

"Cross Corners," Rachel repeated. "But that's not all, Jake. You —"

Stunned, Jake leaned against the edge of his desk.

"What is it?"

He rubbed his temples, realizing he couldn't say more. He couldn't tell Rachel that Cross Corners was the suspected center of operations for the drug cartel and that the DEA team was moving in tonight. The amount of heavy artillery Rick had assembled for the raid had shocked even Jake. In the decade he'd been out of the business, things had gone downhill.

"What is it, Jake?" Rachel demanded again.

"Cross Corners is not Disney World," he said. "There are some bad types out there, Rachel."

"I told her that already," Todd said.

Jake fixed his attention on Todd. "What

makes you think Michael might be out there, Todd?"

"We talked at school a couple of days ago, then that afternoon Mike disappeared. I don't know if he's out there, but he was so bent on finding Scotty that I don't think he'd pass up a chance to at least check it out."

"How would he find the place?" Jake asked. "The logical thing would be for you to take him."

Todd looked wary, suspecting criticism. Rachel spoke up quickly. "Todd spent the past two days with his mother. She came home to Tidewater unexpectedly."

Jake nodded. "Then how did Mike get out there? How did he locate your relatives?"

"That's the amazing thing," Rachel said, touching his arm. Her eyes were alight with excitement. "His cousin is sort of an unsavory type, according to Todd, and he often hangs out at —"

"Lou's Bar," Jake finished for her.

"Yes!" Her smile was both wobbly and triumphant.

"What's your cousin's name, Todd?"

"Willard Biggs."

"Bingo," Jake said softly.

"What?" Rachel's smile wavered.

Jake stood up and began to pace. "I saw

358

him yesterday. At Lou's. He ducked when he noticed me, then headed toward the back where the booths are."

"Why would he take Scotty, Jake?"

He covered her hand where it lay on his arm and squeezed it reassuringly. "I don't know, baby, but I'm going to find out."

"Sheriff —"

Both Jake and Rachel looked at Todd.

"If Mike showed up askin' questions and my cousin did take him to Cross Corners and Scotty is there . . ."

It wasn't necessary for Todd to go any further. All three were aware that Michael had placed himself in jeopardy when he approached Willard Biggs.

Rachel's stomach was in a knot. She'd spent six months imagining the horrors her little boy might have endured. But always she had clung to one belief, and it was that he had endured. He was alive. Both her sons were alive. They had to be.

With a blinding flash of lightning and a mighty boom that rattled the walls of the shed, the rain came. It poured down in sheets so heavy that Michael thought the galvanized roof would collapse under the strain. *I wish,* he thought dejectedly. He'd explored every crack and crevice of the smokehouse a thousand times, and it was built to last. It would take more than a thunderstorm to destroy it.

"I'm scared, Mike."

He wrapped his arm around Scotty's skinny shoulders and hugged his little brother closer. "Don't be scared, Scotty. A little rain never hurt anybody. It could be worse."

Scotty turned wide eyes up to his big brother's. "How could it be worse?"

Mike grinned at him. "Hey, it could be snowing!"

"I've never seen snow."

"Well, I have, and trust me, rain's better."

Accepting that, Scotty relaxed a little. When the next fierce boom exploded, he barely cringed. "Tell me about how we're gonna escape again," he said.

"Well, first we've got to figure a way to get out of this shed, and I'm working on that. It'll have to be at night, because they won't be able to track us down at night."

As he had every time Mike reached this point in their escape plans, Scotty interrupted him. "Are you afraid of the dark, Mike?"

"Nah. Heck, it's the same as daytime, only better for escaping."

"Then me, neither."

"Awright." Mike squeezed the small shoulders.

Scotty settled back again. "And then what?"

"We'll stick to the road, but we'll be real careful. We hear anything, we'll hit the dirt. I figure it's about five miles to the fork that leads to Highway 6. Can you handle five miles?"

"I can if you can."

"Then we're home free, buddy, 'cause once we get on Highway 6, we'll catch a hitch from a big rig, and they'll drop us right at our front door."

"It'll be easy, because you hitched all the way from Iowa."

"That's right."

Scotty's eyes were drooping. They didn't get enough to eat most days and his stamina flagged early. "My mom'll sure be glad to see me, I bet," he said sleepily.

"She sure will," Mike agreed softly, swallowing hard. He shifted so that Scotty could straighten out a little. He might sleep longer that way. It meant Michael would have to sleep with one leg bent, but it was the only way. With the two of them tethered by the chain, he never slept much anyway.

CHAPTER SIXTEEN

Rick Streeter stared in disbelief. "You can't be serious, Jake! The DEA's got nearly two years invested in this operation. We're ready to take Ramirez and his whole organization down and you say cancel it?"

The fear that had tied Jake's stomach in a knot suddenly exploded in fury. "I don't care about Ramirez or his organization, Rick. Both my sons are hostages to those sleazes out there in the swamp, and I'm going after them. You know as well as I do that there's going to be enough firepower to start another war when you come down on Ramirez. I don't want my sons caught in it."

"I sympathize with your position, Jake, but —"

"No offense, Rick, but your sympathy doesn't mean much when it comes to my sons' lives. Now you can work with me on this if you want to, but this is my county, and the people in it take precedence over any scum that might be hiding in the swamps."

"I don't want to pull rank on you, Jake."

"Then don't, Rick. I'm speaking as the ranking law-enforcement officer in Kinard County with a mandate from the public to uphold order, to protect and serve as I see fit. I know the agency has a lot invested in this bust. I don't want to see it scrapped any more than you do, but you'll have to let me get my sons out of Cross Corners before you go in there. That's just the way it is."

Rick grimaced. "Jake . . ."

Jake knew he'd won. He drew in an unsteady breath. It had been close for a minute. No telling how many DEA dollars were tied up in the Cross Corners bust. He felt for Rick. As a former agency man himself, he understood too well what it would mean if Ramirez was tipped off.

Thank goodness Rick Streeter was his friend.

"I'm coming with you."

In the act of strapping on his service revolver, Jake paused to stare at the ceiling. "Rachel, this is not the time for one of your lectures on chauvinism. Cross Corners is no place for you. These people are vicious. They have no respect for the law or law-

363

men, and even less for civilians. Once they realize the threat to their organization, they'll open up with all the firepower they've got. And they've got plenty."

"I didn't mean that I wanted to storm the grounds with you, Jake," Rachel said patiently. "But I don't want to sit at home and wait, either." She knew no one was willing to allow her within miles of Cross Corners; Jake because he feared for her safety, and Rick Streeter because any civilian added a complication he didn't need.

"Please, Jake." At her whispered plea, he reluctantly faced her.

"Be reasonable, Rachel. Rick is already sticking his neck out by holding off long enough for me to find out if the boys are anywhere near Ramirez's compound. This is the only way."

"Uh, Sheriff . . ."

"What is it, Todd?"

"You don't have any idea where Mike and Scotty are, do you?"

"No. I'm going in to try to locate them." His mouth was a thin line as he clamped his hat on his head. "If they're there, I'll find them. And when I find them, I'll bring them out."

Todd shifted awkwardly from one foot to the other. "Well, I was just thinkin' . . ."

"What?" Jake eyed him sharply.

"I know my way around the Biggs place pretty good. Maybe I could go in ahead of you and sorta check it out."

Jake gave him a quick smile. "Thanks, Todd, but it's just too risky."

"I know where you're comin' from, Sheriff, but if they should see me, they probably wouldn't make a big deal over it. They know me. I don't think they'd freak over a surprise visit from me like they would if they spotted you." He shrugged as though apologizing for his relatives. " 'Scuse me, sir, but they don't exactly cotton to strangers, especially the law. If they spot you, you're gonna be in big trouble."

"Jake —" Rachel gave him a distressed look.

"It'll be all right, Rachel. I hope it hasn't come to the point where I have to resort to using a teenage boy to do my job." His words were almost lost in a loud crack of thunder. He swept up a rain poncho and urged them both ahead of him through his office door.

Spotting him, Frank Cordoba left the front desk with a cup of coffee in his hand. "Weather looks rotten, Jake."

Jake grunted, shrugging into the poncho. The storm might be an advantage. Heavy rain made visibility a problem, but it worked two ways. Biggs couldn't see well, either. "Where's Rick?"

"I was just about to come into your office and —"

"They didn't leave, did they?"

"Uh-uh." Frank finished his coffee and, ignoring the glare of the sergeant on duty, set the mug on the counter. "They're out back with their vehicles set on ready. You know these Fed types. After twenty months of planning, they're smelling blood. I just hope Rick doesn't let the thought of that promotion prod him into doing something big and bad before we can get to your boys."

"We?" Jake raised an eyebrow.

Frank shrugged. "You don't think you're going into that garbage dump without me, do you, boss?"

Jake opened his mouth, but Rachel spoke before he could. "Thanks, Frank."

Frank sent Rachel a quick grin. "But just in case," he said to Jake, "I've assigned a cruiser to keep Streeter and his crew under surveillance until we go in. Once we give the all clear, they can do whatever their eager little government-issue hearts desire."

Shaking his head, Jake ushered them all toward the doors ahead of him. Frank's distrust of the Miami task force was as strong as ever. Still, to be on the safe side, Jake had no desire to pull the cruiser assigned to keep tabs on Rick's group. If they jumped the gun before he had his hands on his sons, it could spell disaster. Stepping out into the rain, he waited for Rachel to put up her umbrella. Then, hunching his shoulders, he hurried his wife and Todd toward Rachel's car. There was no room in his life for any more disaster.

Following behind Jake, Rachel slowed and signaled for a left turn at the first intersection. As she watched, the red taillights on his car drew rapidly away, finally disappearing down the boulevard in the rainy twilight.

"I can't thank you enough for coming forward like this, Todd. Jake and I will never forget it."

Beside her, Todd ducked his head. "It's okay. I just wish I'da put it all together before now."

She gave him a smile. "Let's just be thankful you did at all. Your help just might save them both."

Realizing she'd embarrassed him, she kept the rest of her thoughts to herself. After Scotty and Michael were found — and they would be, she told herself fiercely — there would be time enough to explore the events that had led to this night. If Michael hadn't come, if he hadn't been who he was, if he hadn't befriended Todd and if he hadn't felt compelled to leave . . . So many ifs. So many fateful happenings. It was enough to humble her, to make her swear never to lose sight of what was really important — people, family, children, love, simple human kindness.

For a few minutes, the swish of the wiper blades was the only sound in the car. Rachel was vaguely aware of Todd's restlessness. He jiggled one knee nervously. His hands rubbed the tops of his thighs. Shifting position, he looked out the side window of the car as though weighing something he wanted to say.

"Is something on your mind, Todd?"

"Ah, you know that road that leads out to my cousin's place, Miss Rachel?"

She took her eyes off the road and shot him a quick look. "It's the only access, isn't it?"

"Not exactly. There's another way. It's pretty bad, potholes and stuff. It's a shell road, and no one uses it much since they resurfaced the spur off Highway 6. I was just thinkin' . . ."

"We'd better not take any chances like that, Todd. As Jake pointed out, these are dangerous people. If they've kidnapped

Scotty and are holding Michael, who knows what they might do if they feel they don't have much more to lose."

"I guess you're right. It was a dumb idea."

"No, not a dumb idea, Todd. It's just that we should leave this up to people who are trained to deal with these situations. Law-enforcement types."

"I guess."

There was more silence. The rain slackened and Rachel turned the wipers to intermittent. "Where exactly is this road, Todd?"

He gave her a quick grin. "Take a left at the next stop sign."

Jake guessed that Rick Streeter was probably cursing the weather. Four inches of rain had fallen in as many hours. It was just past dark and the rain had finally stopped. Water level in the swamp was rising. As Jake and Frank lifted the small pirogue off the top of the car, Jake could see the dark shallows lapping right up to the edge of the road. He waited while Frank Cordoba climbed into the small boat, a design originally used by Louisiana Creoles to navigate shallow swamp waters. The pirogue had it all over the motorized swamp buggies and flat-bottomed rigs Streeter's men would be using. The task force numbered a couple of dozen, and bigger craft were necessary. Luckily, one little pirogue would take Jake and Frank right up to Biggs's doorstep quickly and silently.

"Okay, climb in."

From about ten feet away, Frank's low-pitched voice barely reached him. Stepping into water that reached his knees, Jake disregarded the mud and wet and whatever life-forms lurked beneath the swamp waters and got in the pirogue. Both he and Frank Cordoba had fished and hunted in the swamp. Both knew the folly of underestimating it. The still waters and ancient cypress sentinels knew secrets that were the stuff of legends.

Using the oar, Jake pushed hard away from the marshy edge of the road. All his thoughts were fixed on his sons and the problems he might encounter. He swallowed a primitive surge of father love mixed with grim resolution as they slipped silently through water black as the moonless sky. He was close. At last, he was close. Looking around at the dark, eerie landscape, he thought of Rachel's dream. But instead of being fearful or uneasy, he felt confident.

Hold on, boys. I'm coming.

They sensed Ramirez's compound before

they saw it. Hoping to locate the main base, Jake had chosen to veer in a northerly direction from the access road, assuming that Ramirez was not fool enough to construct a holding area for millions of dollars' worth of drugs where anybody might drive up. Situating it where the only access was by boat made more sense. A few more strokes propelled them through a maze of cypress knees and thick, low-growing vegetation. Then, sure enough, there it was.

There was little light. Another reasonable precaution, Jake noted. Air surveillance would have quickly revealed a well-lit, newly fenced warehouse compound in the middle of the swamp.

At another time, both he and Frank might have felt keen interest in the holdings of a world-class drug cartel, but not tonight. Signaling to Frank, Jake indicated that they should move on. According to Todd, Willard Biggs lived somewhere nearby.

Knowing how sound carried on water, Jake and Frank were silent as they steered the pirogue through the rain-soaked marsh, always careful to keep to the left of the vicinity of the compound.

Five minutes later, they heard country music. Nodding to Frank, Jake propelled the pirogue in that direction. Suddenly, through a stand of cypress trees, they saw the lighted windows of a house. Stopping, both studied the run-down dwelling and outbuildings. The house itself was constructed on stilts rising a good eight feet off the ground. The music blared from a room that was obviously the kitchen. Several people moved around inside.

"Kids," Frank growled softly. The presence of children was a complication neither lawman liked. If it came to the point where they'd have to use their guns, they didn't want to hurt a child.

Jake's heart was pounding. He studied everybody he could see through the windows. After a minute, he decided there were probably only two children. One was a little girl with yellow hair, no older than Scotty. The other was a dark-haired boy who looked to be about ten. There was no sign of Michael or Scotty.

"Couple of outbuildings," Frank observed, keeping his tone almost inaudible. "We ought to check them out first. They'll be easier than the house."

Jake nodded. With half a dozen people in the house, they were going to have their work cut out trying to check every room without being spotted. Seeing inside the raised house was even more of a problem.

He didn't want to think about the consequences if his sons were in the house and closely watched. With any luck, the boys would be in a shed outside or confined somewhere in a bedroom.

A distant flicker of lightning illuminated two sheds at the rear of the main dwelling. Both were too close for comfort, Jake thought with a swift look at the house. Through the curtainless windows, he easily recognized Willard Biggs sitting at a table with four other men. All were studying cards held in their hands. Beer cans, ashtrays and junk food littered the tabletop.

"Poker," Jake muttered.

Frank grunted in reply.

They propelled the pirogue into the cover of a stand of trees and silently climbed out. From where they stood, they heard the mix of conversation and an occasional burst of laughter, but it was impossible to hear anything clearly. As they watched, the men tossed their cards down and Biggs hauled in the pot. Another immediately began shuffling for a new hand.

Jake touched Frank, motioning toward the first shed to be inspected.

Frank nodded. "Let's do it."

They started with the shed farthest from the house. It had no windows, but the wood planks used for walls had sizable cracks. Peering through, they could see nothing but the outline of tools and machinery. Jake had a small penlight with him, but he was afraid to use it. The shed appeared to be used for storage. To make sure, he tried the door. It opened at a touch, but he froze when the rusty hinges squeaked.

"Relax," Frank breathed. "They can't hear thunder above that music."

After a tense ten seconds, Jake agreed. The radio was sitting in the open window with the volume so loud that it muffled anything short of an explosion. Still, not willing to chance another squeak, Jake pushed a shovel handle against the door to hold it where it stood, after making sure the shed was empty.

The other shed was even closer to the house and appeared to be in better shape. It also had no windows, and the boards were tight. Not even driving rain could penetrate the walls.

"Smokehouse," Frank ventured softly.

Jake agreed, recognizing the smoky, charcoal smell. Biggs probably hunted and smoked the game he killed in the shed. He stood for a moment in silent frustration. The door faced the back of the house, and the light from the window in the kitchen fell directly on it, so he couldn't try it. How in hell was he going to get a look inside? He couldn't call out or knock on the walls.

"We're going to have to pry a board loose in the back," he told Frank. "I saw a crowbar in the other shed."

"Yeah. I'll get it." Moving with surprising stealth for his size, Frank melted into the darkness.

Left alone, Jake stood for a moment, his head bent and his hand against the wall of the shed. That was when he felt it. Movement of some kind. Then he heard a dull clink. With his heart pounding in his chest, he frowned, trying to place the sound.

Frank materialized by his side and extended the crowbar. In his other hand, he held an iron rod of some kind. Between the two, they should be able to pry a board loose.

"Something or someone's inside," he told Frank, barely moving his lips. It was all he could do not to call out to his sons. Was it Michael? Or Scotty? Or both? Maybe it was a chained dog. Biggs was the type to chain an animal in a dark shed. But if it were an animal of some kind, wouldn't it raise an alarm?

Using his fingers, he found a space between two boards just big enough to wedge in the flat side of the crowbar. He put his weight on the lever and easily pried the board away from the two-by-four framing.

He and Frank exchanged a triumphant look. Inside, the shed was pitch black. Nothing for it but to use the penlight, if only for a second or two. Luckily they were on the back side of the shed, completely blocked from the view of the poker players.

He pulled the small light out and flashed it. One fraction of a second was all it took to see both his sons huddled against the wall of the filthy smokehouse.

"Keep quiet, boys," he said quickly, softly, closing his mind against the rush of emotion that threatened to knock him to his knees. Joy and relief and pain and outrage all swirled together as Jake took in the sight of his sons. Michael blinked in confusion and reached instinctively for the smaller, sleepy Scotty, who burrowed into his older brother's shirtfront with a whimper.

Jake heard the dull clink again, but in the dark he missed its significance. He flashed the penlight again, and what he saw sent rage, white-hot and fierce, roaring through him with the force of a freight train.

His sons were chained like animals.

"Take it easy, Jake." Frank's voice cut through the red tide of fury inside Jake's head. With his bare fingers, Jake fumbled blindly at a second board. Frank moved in close, working the iron bar between the planks. "Here, let me get in position and then you use the crowbar."

"They're alive!" Jake muttered, needing to affirm the miracle, to keep the rest of the horror at bay.

There still wasn't enough space for Jake to wedge his hundred and eighty pounds through. He was nearly wild to touch his sons, to sweep them up and hold them so tight that nothing would ever threaten them again. Tossing the crowbar aside, he ripped away the third board with his bare hands.

At that exact moment, the music ceased. The sound of the nails pulling through the wood was like a shriek in the night. From the house, there was a second or two of charged silence, then a door opened and a dog began barking. Willard Biggs walked out onto the porch and looked into the yard. "Who's out there?"

Rachel's hands were tight on the steering wheel to keep Todd from seeing how scared she was. It was her dream all over again. The swamp, endless dark water, trees draped with Spanish moss looking like ancient gray ghosts. Long ago swamp vegetation had threatened to swallow up the miserable excuse for a road. She could well believe that no one used it anymore.

"Todd, are you sure you know where the house is from here?"

"Yes, ma'am. I know it doesn't look it, but it's no more than a few hundred feet around that curve. We can't drive the car. They're sure to hear it."

They'd doused the headlights two miles back. If the road hadn't once been overlaid with crushed white shells, it would have been impossible to drive without going off into the marsh. As it was, Rachel had worried every inch of the way. Now she had to force herself to press onward. She wasn't sure what she could do if things didn't go well for Jake and Frank, but with the lives of her sons at stake, she simply had to be there.

She took a deep breath and looked at Todd. "You can't go any farther, you know that, don't you, Todd?"

"I know."

She was surprised. She'd expected him to want to stay with her all the way. "Okay, then, I'm out of here," she said, borrowing a phrase she'd heard from Mike. She reached for the door handle, hoping she wouldn't step on a snake.

The moment she stepped out of the car, a heavy splash sounded not thirty feet away. She swallowed a scream and closed her eyes, trying to calm her heartbeat. A hopeless endeavor. She'd already had one miracle today. Expecting no wildlife in a swamp would constitute two in one day.

She leaned down and focused on Todd's shape in the pitch blackness. "Don't leave the car for anything, Todd. I'll be back as soon as I can."

"No sweat," he said, sounding no more concerned by the prospect of being abandoned in the middle of a swamp than at being dropped off at the movies.

Two steps away from the car and Rachel knew that traveling the dark trail alone in the swamp would forever rank as the most harrowing experience of her life. She was suffocatingly aware of every sound, every hoot and call, every splash and plunk. If slithering had a sound, she was convinced she heard it. She was not brave and fearless like her sisters. She was only a mother going to her sons. And only her love for Scotty and Michael gave her the courage to keep moving ahead into the very jaws of her nightmare.

She stopped, trembling, and listened. From somewhere, she heard country music.

She had to be close. Rounding the bend finally, she nearly cried out with relief as she spotted the outline of a house.

At the same moment, she caught the brief flash of Jake's penlight behind a shed situated close — too close! — to the house. Frank was with him. Keeping well back, Rachel watched, holding her breath as they worked to loosen the boards of the building. Her heart leaped as she sensed their haste. Was Scotty inside? Michael? Was their search almost over?

A burst of male laughter drew her gaze toward the house. From her vantage point it was difficult to tell who was inside or how many, but it seemed that most were men. Then she spotted two children. Her hand went to her throat. *Please, please, don't let anything go wrong.* Fear and anxiety made her teeth chatter as she stood watching like a spectator at a horror show. Her mouth dry, she glanced from the house to the shed, where Jake's movements had taken on a frantic urgency. She chewed her lip, debating whether to let them know she was there. And then she froze with terror when she heard a sound behind her.

"Don't yell, it's just me."

She almost fainted as Todd materialized out of the swamp. Because she was afraid to make a sound, she gave him a fierce look in lieu of a sound thrashing. Recognizing it, he grinned and shrugged with the charm that he would probably use with devastating success when he got a little older.

When a dog barked, they both turned. To Rachel's horror, a man opened the door and stepped onto the porch. She heard him call out.

"It's Willard," Todd murmured. "He heard them. Shoot! He's goin' out there."

Rachel's eyes flew to Jake and Frank, who stood frozen in the dark shadow of the shed. She reached out helplessly to touch Todd, but she only brushed his arm. He was already half a dozen steps in front of her when she realized what he intended. With a sense of impending doom, she watched Todd step boldly from the haven of the shadows and begin jogging straight toward Willard Biggs.

Flattened against the shed, both Jake and Frank were motionless. Biggs was striding across the porch. Beside him, the dog barked eagerly. Jake searched the outlying yard frantically for something, anything, that might distract Biggs. He just needed a few more minutes to free the boys. Without a tool, that chain was a problem. He didn't want to confront Biggs and his cohorts if he could avoid it. Rick Streeter wouldn't appreciate any complications that threatened the success of his coup. As he weighed his options — all of them poor — he heard another voice.

"Hey, Will! It's me, Todd."

Jake felt a moment of blank shock. Todd Stewart. What was Todd doing here? As though echoing Jake's thought, he heard Biggs demand, "What the hell are you doing out here, kid?"

Easing to the edge of the smokehouse, Jake watched the dog dart ahead past Biggs, making a beeline for the shed. His body went taut, but Todd darted sideways in a deceptively casual move and caught the animal by the collar.

"It's Hazel's kid!" Biggs yelled loud enough to carry inside. To Todd, he said, "You better have a good excuse to be out here, kid."

"I'm just bummin' around," Todd told Biggs. Then, holding the dog firmly by the collar, he went forward to meet him.

Beside Jake, Frank Cordoba released a pent-up breath as Todd jogged up the steps, obviously bent on keeping Biggs on the porch. Both were now too far away for much of their conversation to be heard.

"Jeez," Frank said with feeling, his admiration for Todd's spunk plain.

"Yeah." Jake turned and slipped through the space they'd cleared in the shed wall. "Let's free Mike and Scotty. After that —"

"After that, I'll take care of Todd," Frank said in a tone that told Jake an argument would get him nowhere.

"How'll you get him out if I'm gone in the car?"

"You let me worry about that."

"Daddy —"

Jake drew in a shaky breath and bent down and pulled Scotty into his arms. "Shh, I'm here, son. Everything's going to be fine, now. We're going home." Even as he embraced Scotty, he reached for Mike, who threw his arms around Jake with a choked sob.

"Jake —"

Jake looked up at Frank's urgent whisper and nodded. The real danger still lay in front of them: getting the boys — and that included Todd — safely away. Still holding Scotty, whose arms were locked around Jake's neck, Jake stood still while Frank examined the chain anchored to the wall.

"Any ideas?"

Frank leaned back on his heels and spoke softly. "We could place the crowbar just right, and using the steel rod as a hammer, one solid hit to that bolt would do the job, I think."

"I think you're right. Now, if they'll only turn the radio back on."

"Dad . . ."

Both men looked at Michael.

"Scotty's chained to me. We can't run until the chain's cut."

"I see that, son." Shifting Scotty slightly, Jake lifted the little boy's foot and grimly examined the shackles.

"They used regular handcuffs on Scotty because his ankles were small," Mike stated, keeping his voice down but unable to disguise the tremor. "Then they chained me to him, wrapping the chains around both of us. I couldn't jimmy the cuffs open, Dad, no matter how hard I tried." He cast a desperate look around the dark shed, giving both men a glimpse of the torture he'd undergone. "There wasn't anything in here to use. I'm sorry, Dad."

"There's nothing to be sorry about, son." Jake's throat threatened to close with the power of the emotion that rose inside him. "Just hold still for another minute or two and we'll have you free. Then we'll slip out of here as slick as you please."

Scotty stirred, obviously wanting to speak. Jake touched his finger to the little boy's mouth. "Shh, hush, son. Soon as we get back to the car, I promise you can tell me everything."

Scotty nodded solemnly, his eyes fixed on Jake's. Then he mouthed the words, "Mike's my big brother, did you know?"

Clamping his jaw, Jake nodded.

Still whispering, Scotty added, "He came to get me."

"I know."

"Even if we have to go into the swamp, we aren't scared."

Jake hugged him wordlessly, sending Mike a look that made the older boy squirm and duck his head.

"Jake, we've gotta get out of here," Frank reminded him.

Jake set Scotty on his feet and stood up. Taking the crowbar from Frank, he felt around the bolt, looking for the best place to set it for the blow. Right on cue, someone turned the radio on in the middle of a loud used-car commercial.

"Perfect," Jake muttered as Frank struck once, hard, with the steel rod. The chain fell away from the wall.

"Now for the easy part," Jake murmured. Reaching into his pocket, he withdrew a key and quickly slipped it into the handcuffs. One touch and they fell away, freeing Scotty's ankles.

The links binding the boys took a little more time, but with Jake and Frank working together, both were soon rid of the steel that had shackled them to the wall for three days. Jake didn't ask, but he wondered whether the boys were hungry and how they'd been forced to relieve themselves. He sent a cold look toward Biggs's house, wondering how much time over the past six months Scotty had spent alone in the shed.

He swallowed the violence simmering in his chest, knowing the first priority was getting the boys out of there. But nothing would prevent him from personally seeing that Biggs paid for the agony his family had suffered.

They were slipping through the boards to head back to Jake's car when they heard the shots.

"What the —"

A frenzy of shouts and commotion came from the cabin, and light suddenly flooded the grounds. Men spilled out of the door and down the steps, pulling on shirts and stumbling in drunken confusion. No one spared a glance for the shed or the two boys supposedly chained inside for the night. A footpath, unnoticed by Jake earlier, led away from the house on the opposite side. Within moments, the men had disappeared in that direction, and all sound was soon swallowed up in the dense growth. Only the dog, barking wildly, went in a different direction. Cheated of his quarry earlier, he headed directly for the rear of the shed.

Jake stepped protectively in front of his sons, his revolver drawn, and braced himself. Rounding the corner, the dog stopped, confused when Mike and Scotty both lunged for him.

"I'll chain him up!" Mike said.

Nodding, Jake holstered his weapon and swept Scotty up in his arms. Obviously the dog recognized the boys.

"Don't forget Todd."

Everyone turned, gaping as Rachel stepped out of the shadows into the light.

"Rachel —"

"Mommy!"

"Wow, it's Miss Rachel."

Frank grinned. "I'll go rescue Todd. By my reckoning, he's the only one left in the house except the two kids."

"Bring them, too, just to be safe," Rachel told him, then holding out her arms, she burst into tears as Jake handed Scotty over. Crushing him to her, whispering his name over and over, she buried her face in his grubby, precious little neck.

CHAPTER SEVENTEEN

Rachel was not sleeping. She lay quietly on her side, snuggled against Jake in their bed as the clock solemnly chimed the hour, and watched the intermittent flicker of lightning outside.

Three o'clock.

A second storm front had followed on the heels of the first, and now more rain and wind lashed at the windows. Strong gusts whipped the palms just outside, sending leaves and loose debris flying. She squirmed a little, fitting her back to Jake's front, smiling at the warm bulk of him. He groaned sleepily, tightening his arms around her, then relaxed again almost immediately.

How could he sleep? she wondered. Her thoughts were chasing around in her brain like the wind-tossed debris outside. Her children were home!

Scotty. She closed her eyes in fervent thanksgiving.

Michael. Her throat tightened.

Thank you, God.

The facts surrounding Scotty's kidnapping were still murky, but Michael had given them a pretty good idea of what happened. It had been so uncomplicated. On the day of his disappearance, there had been a moving van in the next block. In the original investigation, Jake had questioned the driver, but there seemed nothing to connect him to the kidnapping. There was nothing irregular about the job, nothing to arouse his suspicion. The company was a large national one, the driver bonded and reputable, the laborers local. That was the connection. Willard Biggs was one of the laborers.

For a long time Biggs had nursed a grudge against the law in Kinard County, where he'd served time for a crime he still claimed he didn't commit. When Biggs realized one of the children watching the van loading up that day was the son of Sheriff Jake McAdam, he had seized his chance to retaliate against the whole system and the sheriff in particular. He had hidden Scotty, bound and gagged, in the back of the eighteen-wheeler without the driver's knowledge, then taken him to his property in the swamp, where he'd turned him loose to survive as best he could with his own neglected children. It was an act of meanness and sheer spite. If he'd been older, Scotty might have had a chance to get away, but he'd been intimidated by the swampy surroundings and Biggs's frequent threats. In six months, Scotty had not traveled more than twenty yards from Biggs's back porch.

Suddenly needing to see him, to touch him, Rachel slipped quietly from the bed, trying not to disturb Jake. She still trembled thinking of everything that could have gone wrong in the rescue. When the shooting started, her heart had stopped. Biggs and his cohorts as well as Ramirez's men had scattered in the chaos that followed. Jake and Frank had not wasted the opportunity. Jake had swept up his family, using Rachel's car to get away. Frank had returned to rescue Todd and the two Biggs children. Both were now in Jacky Kendall's custody at Juvenile Hall. Frank took Todd home with him. Jake had been startled when Rachel suggested that Frank Cordoba would be an excellent foster parent for Todd. She still thought it was a great idea. Frank was already half-convinced. He had bragged to everyone who would listen about Todd's role in the rescue.

She donned a robe quickly, then left the

bedroom. The hall was lit with a dim glow, probably Scotty's night-light. He'd been a little anxious when she'd finally settled him in his bed, and she would have taken him in with her and Jake, but he refused when he found out Mike wasn't going. He already had a world-class case of hero worship for his big brother.

She went into his room and stopped short. It was empty. Her heart thumping, she started to tell Jake when she noticed the greenish glow from the door of Michael's room. The aquarium, of course. Looking inside, she relaxed against the doorframe. Scotty lay curled up beside Michael.

Moving silently, she went to the bed. Both boys were sleeping, lulled by the bubble and gurgle of the fish tank. With a faint smile, she saw that Michael had given up his cherished spot closest to the aquarium to make room for Scotty. Her eyes stinging, Rachel bent and gently moved his small out-flung leg and sat down. Already the covers were kicked away. She smoothed the tangled sheet, touched him on his cheek, brushed his bangs aside. He'd have to have a haircut, she thought, rejoicing quietly that she had that small motherly task to handle once again. He stirred and mumbled something. She bent closer and with a catch in her chest made out the words.

"Mike . . . Go home . . ."

His new big brother dominated even his dreams, she thought with a soft smile. Then, sifting the silky blond hair through her fingers, she wondered about his dreams. Were they about his captivity? Michael's arrival to save him? The chaotic rescue? Would he be tormented forever by his ordeal? According to Michael, Scotty had been hungry and cold sometimes. A few times, he'd been callously shut in the shed, but only when Michael appeared had he been chained. Leaning close, she kissed his baby-soft cheek, thankful that he hadn't suffered other abuse, the kind that might have destroyed his life or left him with deep-seated problems he could never overcome.

Stroking the small hand thrown innocently above his head, she vowed that, as a family, they'd overcome the nightmare that had nearly destroyed them. She was so thankful her family was whole again. She felt a new faith in herself, in her marriage, a new joy in her life. With one last caress of Scotty's silky blond head, she stood up. Then she tiptoed to the other side of the bed and sat down.

Michael wore the T-shirt Jake had given him that first night. Unable to resist, she touched his dark hair. Studying him in the shadowy glow, she realized she no longer thought of Michael's resemblance to Jake. The likeness was still there, but now he was just . . . Michael.

He stirred and she realized he was awake.

"Hi, Miss Rachel." His voice was soft and sleep-husky.

"I'm sorry, Michael. I didn't mean to wake you."

"That's okay. I guess you were worried about Scotty."

"Only until I found him."

"He was still a little scared. The swamp and all. He'll get over it in a little while — you'll see."

She smiled. "You're probably right. In the meantime, do you mind?"

"Nah. He's fine. He was out like a light once he started watching the fish."

She laughed softly. "We certainly understand that, don't we?"

"Yes, ma'am."

She touched his jaw, cradling it in her palm. "You should be asleep, too, you know."

At her touch, his eyes fell. "I guess all the excitement and everything . . . ." Without seeming aware of it, he lifted his shoulder as though to capture her caress and hold it.

She reached for his hand, and when their fingers met, both squeezed tight.

"I'm so glad to have you back home, Michael," she whispered.

He didn't say anything, just looked at her with wide, serious eyes. His hand stayed intertwined with hers.

"I don't ever want you to leave again. No matter what happens. No matter what you see or think you see. We're a family, Michael. You, me, Jake and Scotty. Nobody can just take off." Her voice blended with the soft gurgle of the water. "Because when someone you love is missing, nothing can fill that hole in your heart."

He looked away quickly, but not before she saw the glint of his tears.

"Promise me, Michael."

"Okay." It came out a croak.

She brought their clasped hands to the V of her shoulder and neck and squeezed. "Thank you for going to Scotty. Thank you for protecting him, for being there and helping him handle his fears. But even if you hadn't found him, Michael, I would still want you as my son."

Manfully, he tried to blink back his tears, but they spilled over anyway. Rachel smiled through tears of her own. "Now, are you too old or can I please have a hug?"

He went into the haven of her arms as though it were the most natural thing in the world to do. And it was.

Trying not to make a sound, Rachel eased back into bed beside Jake. With a sleepy grunt, he pulled her close until they fit like spoons. She relaxed, loving the feel of him. His breath stirred the hair at her nape and she felt safe and happy. She thought he'd fallen back to sleep when he spoke softly.

"Where have you been?"

"Checking on our children."

"Mmm. They okay?"

"Uh-huh."

His hand caressed her shoulder. "How about you?"

She didn't reply right away. After a moment, she turned onto her back and rested her head on his arm. "I guess I've got to be the luckiest woman in the world tonight, Jake."

"Counting your blessings, hmm?"

"Miracles, Jake. It's been a day of miracles."

"I know, sweetheart."

"So many things could have gone wrong."

"But they didn't."

"I thought I would die when Biggs came out on the porch and that dog with him.

Thank heaven Todd was there."

"Yeah." Jake shifted so he could look at her. "I've been meaning to talk to you about that. Do you realize what a crazy stunt it was following us out to Biggs's place like that? And bringing Todd with you." He shook his head. "He could have been hurt, Rachel. Both of you could have been hurt."

"I thought he was going to wait for me in the car," she said lamely, knowing he had every right to scold. Not because she'd felt compelled to help in the rescue of her children, but for endangering Todd. "As for myself, I felt I had to be there. And it's a good thing I was. Don't forget we used my car to get everyone out of there safely. If you had tried to get back to yours, someone might have been shot."

He grunted. "Speaking of which, Rick Streeter was really ticked off when the shooting started."

"What happened? I thought it was understood you needed time to get Scotty and Michael out before they began the bust."

"He's got a leak somewhere. And because of it, the bust wasn't as successful as it would have been. They confiscated a substantial amount of cocaine and marijuana, and they destroyed a laboratory where Ramirez was manufacturing designer drugs, but unfortunately Ramirez had time to organize his men. As soon as his lookouts spotted the Feds, they began shooting and managed to salvage some of his inventory."

"But how?"

"They hauled it out in pirogues, the same type of boat Frank and I used. Silent and quick. Impossible to trace." He lifted a strand of her hair and tucked it behind her ear. "They probably made a connection somewhere deep in the swamp and are airborne to St. Louis by now. Or Detroit. Or New York."

She sighed. "So it goes on."

Jake settled back again, pulling her close and entwining her legs with his. "I'm afraid so. Not in Kinard County, but the cartel will simply find someplace else. As long as there is a demand for illegal drugs, there will be people like Ramirez to supply them. But at least we've destroyed the pipeline into our town and our schools. That's something."

"Why did he do it, Jake?"

"Who, Ramirez?"

"No, Biggs. Why would he take a little boy away from his parents? How was he able to watch Scotty's bewilderment and fear and do nothing? He must have been so scared,

Jake. What would make a man so . . . so vile?"

"I don't know, sweetheart, but he'll have a long, long time to think about it."

Rachel shivered. "Jail seems almost too kind for a person like that. He won't ever be hungry or cold or ch-chained like . . ."

His arms tightened around her. "No, he won't."

Both lay silent, struggling to banish the ugly pictures that would probably be with them forever. But it was a small price to pay to have Scotty safe at last and home where he belonged.

"Aren't you proud of Michael?" she asked, wanting to ease Jake's tension.

"Yeah." She didn't see it, but she felt him smile.

"Me, too."

He stroked her jaw with his thumb. "I sorta sensed that."

"I guess his vocation is pretty much a sure thing."

Jake's hand stilled. "Did you hear what he said about 'deep cover'? I didn't even know he knew what deep cover meant."

Rachel giggled. "You're going to have to cut the hours he spends at the department, Jake. You really are. He has to finish high school and college before becoming a cop."

She sobered then. "But between you and me, I was pretty impressed by what he discovered while he was supposedly Biggs's prisoner."

"Yeah, but Biggs's stupidity is the really amazing thing. The man was running a whole network of kids from middle school to Tidewater High. Naturally, Mike recognized a bunch of them."

"James Moody, the preacher's kid, for one."

"It was monumentally stupid to conduct business right in front of Mike."

"The sheriff's son, no less," Rachel said, stroking the sheriff's chest. "And in case there was any doubt before, I think it's a sure thing you will continue to be the sheriff as long as you want it."

Jake chuckled softly, bringing her hand to his mouth. "Such confidence."

"You bet."

"But about Mike . . . I don't think even my most seasoned undercover man could have done a better job than he did while he was kidnapped."

Rachel curled into his warmth. "Must be something in the genes."

Soft male laughter rumbled from his chest.

Suddenly serious again, Jake looked into her eyes. "I love you, Rachel."

"I love you, Jake."

Smiling, she wrapped her arms around him tightly, holding on, feeling pure joy and pleasure. Celebration. Commitment. Renewal. She felt it all. And gloried in it.

Outside, the storm had quieted to soft rain. Thunder still rumbled, but it was distant and moving farther and farther away.

No one noticed.

ABOUT THE AUTHOR

Karen Young didn't choose writing as a career; it chose her. After numerous long-distance moves necessitated by her husband's career, she realized she would never be in one place long enough to climb the corporate ladder. So after the tenth move, in sheer desperation, she decided to try writing a book. When a major publisher bought it, she knew she'd found a career! Or, rather, it had found her.

The employees of Thorndike Press hope you have enjoyed this Large Print book. All our Thorndike, Wheeler, and Kennebec Large Print titles are designed for easy reading, and all our books are made to last. Other Thorndike Press Large Print books are available at your library, through selected bookstores, or directly from us.

For information about titles, please call:
(800) 223-1244

or visit our Web site at:
http://gale.cengage.com/thorndike

To share your comments, please write:
Publisher
Thorndike Press
10 Water St., Suite 310
Waterville, ME 04901